The space lanes as man knew them were in the constricting grasp of Earth's giant corporations, deathless economic mechanisms which exploited the wealth of a hundred planets. The only law on the planets was corporate law, and dreamed-of Utopias had become penal colonies. The comparatively small number of independent pioneers seemed to have no hope of breaking the bonds of these leviathans, for Earth's government and the Solspace Merchant Fleet controlled every ship in space.

Then, suddenly, they controlled every ship but *one*. A single man, Dublin Gallagher, had set himself against the corporate giants with a ship carved from an interstellar glacier.

Were one ship, one man, and a handful of allies enough to defeat the powers that had held hegemony so long? Gallagher and his renegades could not know, but they were willing to die trying!

GALLAGHER'S GLACIER

WALT and LEIGH RICHMOND

AN ACE BOOK

Ace Publishing Corporation
1120 Avenue of the Americas
New York, N. Y. 10036

GALLAGHER'S GLACIER

Cover art by Kelly Freas.

To Nancy

. . . who chose between

static and dynamic stability

POSITIVE CHARGE

Printed in U.S.A.

I

It's hard to tell whether men make history or history makes men.

One example is Gallagher and his glacier. One might say that he changed history, or one might figure that history would have changed anyway and that he just happened to be in the right spot at the time. I wouldn't know. But he was a colorful character; history needs its Paul Bunyans.

When men first went into space, mortality was high, but the corporations survived. When men die as independents, that's that; but when they're representatives of a corporation, the corporation can replace them with more men, and the corporation stays alive.

People begin to think that only corporations belong in space and act accordingly. Soon space is tied up in blue corporate ribbons, and it's no longer a pioneering venture. Then a man doesn't stand so tall, and the colonies learn to obey corporate rules.

That was the way things were going. But the corporations had one drawback: they tended to employ bright young technicians, like me, with much education and very little know-how. In space, what one really needs, experience has taught me, is what some people call horse sense. One needs the ability to translate what is in a book into what makes sense in the concrete situation.

That kind of man, though, isn't the kind the corporations can hire, even when they want to. That kind of man is almost always an independent.

From this, frictions arose.

One might think that space is big enough so that the bright young men of the corporations, with their seemingly endless replacements, and the independents that managed to survive after all would not be at odds. But, though space is big, the meeting places are common to both groups, and the frictions are real.

The independents that survived had the horse sense, or know-how, which was a needed thing on the planets. The corporations could send in all the bright young men they liked to control their colonies, but it was the surviving independents that controlled the colonies that paid off.

The corporations controlled the ships, and they were push-button ships in those days. One didn't need horse sense. It took a great deal of cash to buy a ship and a great deal of equipment to build one. As far as anyone could see, it would be a cold year in hell before the independents could master their own fleets and break the hold of the corporations. So maybe it *was* Gallagher and his glacier that changed the times, and not the times that fitted Gallagher.

A pioneer goes out into the unknown and solves problems as he meets them. In that respect Gallagher was a pioneer. He had all the degrees of an engineer, but also an incurable wanderlust. His name was black in the company books, for he'd jump a ship or stow away out of a colony as soon as sign the papers.

Just before I met him, he sat, mostly in Joe's Bar, waiting for a ship to berth that was setting a course the way he wanted to go. How he was planning to sign on, with his record, he would not say.

But when my ship orbited, heading for Altura, there was a series of incidents that left my engineer in the hospital. At the same time I got the news of the "incidents," Gallagher presented himself with a piece of paper.

"Your next port is Altura, Captain Harald Dundee," he said. His name was N. N. Gallagher, and they called him Dublin; it was a pun and a reference to his origin. He was more than six feet tall, his red hair nearly brushing the roof of my cabin, and making me feel small and insignificant despite my fine uniform, for I clear the ceiling by a good four inches. "And," he said, "it's toward Altura I'm headin'. Now, seeing as it's not rightly your fault you're minus an engineer for the course, I'll take on the job without much cost to you. There's a glacier," he said, "that's moving towards Altura. You can compute to intersect her within three hours of your port. I'll take on your engineer's post that far and charge you nothing, if you'll put me aboard the glacier with my equipment. Your assistant engineer can take the ship from there."

I was a young man then, and it was my first command. I went by the book, and I didn't like the proposition. I didn't even really believe it, though there wasn't anything about it to disbelieve. I had heard that, though Gallagher might be footloose and black in the books, he could engineer a ship like the angel of machines.

I turned him down with a coldness that would have been an insult, if he'd been looking for one. I told him curtly that I would have no part of horsetrading engineering for passage.

He turned on his heel and left with a half smile. Within two hours I knew what that half smile meant. There wouldn't be another engineer available in that port. I soon found I could knuckle under, or wait until the next ship through brought me an engineer and forget the tight company schedule on which I was operating.

I swallowed my pride and started to send a messenger to get the man back. Then I thought twice and put on my best uniform, to make my way into the port town. If he refused the messenger, I would have to go to him or run late with the company; he knew a young man with his first commission could not afford to run late.

I also went unaccompanied, though the custom was for not less than three to go ashore together in any space port. I headed for Joe's Bar, and though I could spy his red hair from the entrance, I pretended not to see him and sat down three stools away.

I drank the first two drinks slowly and saw from the corner of my eye that Gallagher paced me drink for drink. Then I spoke aloud to the bartender, and I called him Joe, though it was not his name.

"Joe," I said, stumbling over the words just a bit to show I'd been consuming, "my ship's out there with the sweetest motors that all the technical brains of Earth could put into her. These guys they call engineers are just racketeers," I said loudly. "There's not a thing they can do to a motor to make it purr more sweetly than the designer intended. They just figure to go along for the ride; it don't take a man to push the buttons."

By the time I'd finished, red hair was standing on end and there was no pretense as to whether Gallagher was listening. He gulped a couple of times and bit his tongue. When he finally spoke, it was in a soft brogue, and he had his temper where he wanted it, pushing from beneath but not pulling ahead.

"Mister," said Gallagher, "or perhaps I should say Captain—though button pushers never seemed to me to rate that title—you show me the drive that I can't tune, and I'll pay you the privilege of shipping me as engineer for three times five ports and not jump your ship. There's not a drive operating in a company ship since the corporations took over the shipping lanes that couldn't stand the touch of Gallagher and fly so much sweeter because of that touch that even her imbecile master would be forced to admit it, though it cost him his pride, if he had honor to boot."

No man impugns my honor, and I was on my feet looking up into his grinning Irish face with my fists doubled.

"Sit down, Captain," he said quietly. "Let's talk this over, for it was a good ploy, and it's got me aboard the *Starfire*, me *and* my equipment."

When I found out what Gallagher meant by *equipment*, I nearly reneged. The holds would take it, but we'd be shipping heavy.

"You'll only be heavy as long as I'm aboard, and I'll have your drive talking so pretty she'll use less mass than if you were running light with anybody else to engineer her," Gallagher said. "Your assistant will only have to take in a light ship, and the motors already purring."

The equipment included one of the old Antolaric drives that used to power the ships they sent out when man first entered space, and it was as massive as the old ships had been. There were also supplies to last a man for months, but those weren't much, and equipment enough to stock a small machine shop.

I was stuck with it, but that didn't make me like it. I liked it even less when he demanded—he didn't ask he demanded, but I ignored the manner of his request—twenty-four hours to work on the drive before we lifted.

When we lifted I didn't begrudge a minute of that twenty-four hours. The *Starfire* acted like a thing alive, tuned to my every motion. I changed from worrying over what he'd been doing in those twenty-four hours to worrying whether the changes in the engineering set-up could be justified to a port inspection engineer, even though the results were such as captains dream of. Port inspection engineers are the brightest of the bright young men, and I knew my breed and its shortcomings. The drive wasn't tuned by the book; it wouldn't pass.

I didn't understand Gallagher, but I knew him for a

breed that caught at my heart, for we were both from the "old sod" and we were both out in the new spaceways, though he was an independent and I was a corporation man.

I understood the man even less when we matched courses with his glacier and I had him and his equipment drifted over to it. It couldn't have been more than a mile the long way and a quarter mile through, an ungainly hunk of ice idling through space. What the man could want with it was more than I could see. There were plenty of steel meteors that size, if Gallagher wanted to make himself a meteor ship, and I admit that seeing his old drive was the first inkling I'd gotten of such a use. Then I realized that a steel meteor wouldn't have given him reaction mass for his fusion chamber, but the ice contained ample hydrogen, and that would be his mass.

We blasted on for Altura. There I spent my best wiles and the finest whiskey I could buy on the port inspection engineer, but to little avail. That ship had to be retuned before we blasted again, and he wouldn't even test it with me so I could let him handle a ship when it was tuned the way the *Starfire* was. He had a few cutting things to say about what would be in my records for letting a man like Gallagher manhandle my drive.

I spent the first planet-bound days wandering the company town and sitting in the port bar. By the end of the first day I was so furious with Gallagher that I was making up conversations with him, telling him off. Also, I was curious. I couldn't figure how he was going to manage the job alone; I had to see.

By midnight I'd rationalized myself into good reasons: the man was daft, he was alone on an iceberg, drifting helplessly in space, and by now he'd have realized how helplessly. I told myself that the least I could do, now that his senses had had a chance to reorganize, was to offer him an oiler's job to get him out of the mess he'd talked himself into. I wouldn't leave a dog alone out there, I told myself. I owed him a chance to get off honorably.

I rented a small interplanet scout and headed for Gallagher's glacier.

What I expected to find I'm not sure. What I found was the glacier, lonely and sparkling cold. I could make out Gallagher's vac-suited figure working on its surface as I matched orbit two kilometers off.

Since he was on the surface and in a vac suit, I hailed him over the ship's suit comm, but he failed to answer. I maneuvered the scout closer, seeking a place to tie up. That's when I got an answer.

"Sheer off, you lunkhead," came his voice. "I'll not have you upsetting my balances here."

I was readying a tart reply when he went on. "Anyhow, this is already claimed."

"Okay, Dublin," I said. "If you're too proud to let your former captain see the mess you've got into, I'll be heading back to port. I was just being sociable anyhow."

The figure stood and waved, and Gallagher's tones, hardly less gruff than before, came back over the suit comm. "Neighborly of you, Captain. Take her around on the far side and hitch up to a mooring line, but gently, mind you. I'll still not have you upsetting my balances."

I could not see what he had in mind about balances, but I eased the scout around to the far side. That's when I got my first good look at what Gallagher had been doing.

There was a bubble dome anchored firmly to one of the smoother parts of the big ice chunk and a half-dozen standard Bourdon mooring tubes, long, snaky pipes of plastic inflated with gas, that extended out from the surface and to which various "dumps" had been attached. The bubble dome was normal equipment for airless planetary living and the mooring tubes were normal, *if* they were attached securely to the iceberg.

I hesitated before mooring to a vacant tube. I decided to moor and keep an eye on the scout. If it pulled the line loose and started to drift, I could catch it in the first few minutes with the rockets on my suit.

I nudged up to the tube and was rewarded with the hollow clink of a magna lock. The line was a good kilometer long, but I could see a tiny shuttlebug start its whirring way up the mooring line, so I'd have fast travel going in. The response was fully automatic, keyed to the impulse of the magna lock. Gallagher, I decided, was doing better than might have been expected.

While I waited, I looked over the cargo dumps attached to the other tubes; there was nothing but the things we had left, of course. The Antolaric drive was not moored to a tube, but carefully stanchioned directly at the far end of the berg itself, lined up with the balance point of the berg, as though it were nudging the glacier from behind. I asked myself sarcastically, *Is he planning to push the damned berg to the nearest planet?* It won't work that way, I assured myself; a drive is internal to a ship. But I had a haunting feeling that maybe I was missing something; the memory of the *Starfire*'s tuning was fresh upon me.

The shuttlebug arrived and I reached out to grasp the awkward thing. I gave the trigger a nudge and got the giddy sensation of being thrown forward at nearly half a gee as the tiny electric motor whined along the semi-geared tracks. The acceleration was brief, and I seemed more to be floating than actually riding a conveyance as I descended towards the glacier.

The glacier below me was a panorama, nearing rapidly. As I neared, I could make out curious black spots, huge black spots. They were probably radiator surfaces, but I wondered how Gallagher had spread radiators directly on an ice surface and how he had handled a standard radiator surface by himself at all.

I postponed my curiosity. I'd have at least an hour or so to inspect what had been done while Gallagher made his way around the glacier, and I did not intend to waste the time.

But as the shuttlebug threw me into deceleration for the landing, I saw a suited figure emerge from the bubble dome near the terminus and wave to me.

"Welcome aboard, Captain." The voice over the intercom was Gallagher's. Most voices one can't recognize over an intercom, but Gallagher's is different; no intercom can cover his particular tonal quality. How he'd gotten there so quickly I didn't know. One couldn't have walked that distance on the skin of a metal ship, much less on the surface of a glacier with whatever cramp-ons or ice locks he'd dreamed up to keep him from drifting off the berg.

"Hi," I said weakly. "About ready to give up this foolishness?" It was too late to change my rationale now, though it did sound silly, considering the efficiency with which he'd got his equipment secured and gotten ready to go to work.

"I rather thought you'd come because you were ready to give up *your* foolishness," he replied. "Have they got the *Starfire* back to its sluggish norm yet? Independent Spaceways, namely me, can use a good navigator. Glad you're volunteering."

I could feel myself getting red. I was glad I was in a vac suit and he couldn't see it. I kept my voice calm and merely said, "You seem to be handling the initial stages okay. But maybe you've had some second thoughts."

I dropped from the shuttlebug and, as my feet touched the ice, I was surprised to find that the electret shoes of my suit gripped it quite satisfactorily. I hadn't expected the electrostatic field to work on ice, even though I could see Gallagher had no gripping problem.

He laughed and led me to the bubble dome, and, as we unhelmeted in the air lock, I put my foot in my mouth again. "Who's working on the far side of your berg?" I asked. "I saw somebody in a vac suit there as I came in. I thought you were alone."

He didn't answer at once, but just opened the inner door. There, leading from the far side of the dome was a yawning shaft going straight down into the ice, with a shuttlebug hanging in its mouth as though it was just as logical to use one inside a ship as out.

"Just me and my bugs, Captain," he said grinning.

"Bugs?" I glanced sidewise at Gallagher and then back at the hole. "Shuttlebugs I understand, but tunnels like *that?* Why, it would take a man a month to dig a tunnel like that through a berg like this."

He nodded solemnly. "Aye, you're right, Captain. But I didn't mean just shuttlebugs. Most of the cargo you landed me here with was bugs of one kind and another." He pointed to an odd-looking, circular, metallic device lying against a wall of the dome. "There's one of the bigger ones there."

I walked over and looked at the thing. It had a rim which I judged would just fit inside the tunnel; in the center of the rim was a rotating nose with a screw thread on it. It made about one turn every two centimeters, I decided. I looked more closely at the rim and saw that there were ridges so that if it were passing through ice it could slide easily forward, but could not readily turn. The rim itself seemed to be of two different materials, with a leading edge of metal and a ten-centimeter trailing section of plastic that matched the shape, including the grooves.

"Quite a fancy gadget," I said, "but how can a thing like this drill through ice? That nose with the screw thread on it doesn't look very sharp, and certainly there aren't any teeth here." I pointed to the surface between the protruding screw nose and the rim.

"Careful, it's hot," Gallagher said. The idea of the machine clicked into my mind as an operating device. The surface was sensibly hot. The screw would be heated too; and, if you turned it nose-first against a piece of ice and gave it a shove, it could probably melt its way rapidly in and then get hold and keep going. A sievelike mesh that formed the metallic surface between the rim and the spinner screw would take in water, I realized.

"Clever," I said. "Is it self-programming?"

"Pretty much so. It's got maybe the brains of a mouse. That's what I call it, an ice mouse."

"What does it do with the water?" I asked.

"Just kicks it out the back into the tunnel. I have to pump it from there. I've smaller ones as well, and they make nice little water pipes for wherever I want to program them to go, so the pumping's not that much of a problem."

"And you pump the water out of those radiator surfaces for refreezing?" I asked. "How did you manage to move radiators like that around anyhow? For that matter, where did you get them? I don't recall having landed anything as heavy as a radiator here."

"Well, now, which question first? The radiators were part of the equipment you landed, believe it or not. But they're not heavy. They're very light plastic and high-temperature stuff at that. It's amazing how much more heat you can reject at four or five hundred degrees than you can from a low-temperature surface.

Since it's the difference you're working with, it makes good sense to have high-temperature radiators where the only energy dumped is by black box radiation.

"To answer the first question last, though," Gallagher went on, "the water is *not* pumped directly into the radiators. If it were, that's where it would freeze up. Actually, the refrigeration system is a little more complicated than that. But you're right that the water is refrozen—after it's pumped where I want it. I scoop it out here and freeze it on there, and in a few weeks I'll have this berg balanced, hollowed and set up just the way I want it."

I shivered as obviously as possible as I said, "It would seem that you've picked a pretty well air-conditioned environment, but aren't you afraid that the constant cold will get to you?"

Gallagher grinned and motioned me to the tunnel leading down. "Come on in," he said. "This dome *is* sort of chilly. It's acting as my air lock right now, but I'll probably replace it with a more conventional air lock sooner or later."

Taking a shuttlebug through a tunnel where I could have reached both walls by simply outstretching my arms was a weird sensation. The smooth, glistening ridges that had been left behind by Gallagher's ice mouse were as regularly milled and precise as the machine that had made them. It seemed to me that we'd not gone halfway through when the shuttlebug paused and I swung myself off into a short corridor at right angles.

This one wasn't milled; it wasn't ice, for that matter. There was proper decking for the soles of my shoes. Of course, there was no gravity, but I assumed that Gallagher would take care of that, and in the not-too-distant future, at the rate he was going.

"Your hot-headed ice mice," I asked, "can they be suitably programmed for making the necessary spin and balance tubing for a spin-grav system?"

"Sure. Ought to have that operating now," Gallagher said, glancing at his wristwatch, "in another four or five hours. The mice are much busier than I am."

"But with water rushing around in ice tubes, won't you have some tendency for the tubes to melt and distort?"

"Melt? Sure they will, except that the water will be brine, and a bit colder than the melting point of ice, so they won't melt very fast. Distort? Well, maybe. Under some conditions of acceleration the tubes will probably distort a bit, but since the fluid in the spin tubes goes in one direction and the ship goes in the other, the net friction and thrust is radial to the spin. There shouldn't be much distortion. The tubes will simply gradually work themselves towards the surface. But long before that happens, I'll make a new tube inside. Anything a mouse can do once, he can do all over again. Like I said, they're going to be busier than I am."

"But won't each spin tube leave a hollow place behind it?" I asked.

"Nope. You see, right above each spin tube there's a much smaller, much colder tube. The tubes will plate back on the top what they lose on the bottom."

I paused for a minute and thought about it. *Up*, of course, was towards the center of the ship, since we were talking about spin gravity. *Down* would be towards the outside of the ship.

"Wait a minute, though. Will the tube on top move out along with the other, larger tube? Or for that matter, why couldn't you put the cold tube underneath the spin tube to prevent the spin tube from wearing out?"

"One at a time." Gallagher waved me through the bulkhead and into a comfortable cabin. "No matter how cold I made the ice, it would have a tendency to melt under pressure. Obviously, the spin tubes will be under pressure. They would gradually melt, even if they were kept much colder than would be efficient. Actually, it's much simpler to allow the tube to melt and move itself out, say, three times the distance of its own diameter, and then simply make a new tube in the part it started from. It'll probably be more complicated than that, though. There'll be one tube being made and another being filled while a third, somewhere between them, is operating to keep the spin going."

I could follow that much, but I had a feeling that if I let Gallagher go on there would be more and more complications added. I could even visualize part of it.

"Okay, but just one more point," I said. "This cabin is nice and warm and insulated no doubt. But it *does* have mass, and it *will* walk, just like a spin tube. What do you plan to do about that?"

"Now you're getting the picture, Harald!" Gallagher broke into a huge grin. "There's no such thing as static stability in a malleable ship, and ice is one of the most malleable mediums you could ask to work with. Actually, this cabin is built with a hot head something like that the mice use. If you turned everything off and let it sink, it would sink right through the ice and get spun off into space, once we got spin gravity going. But its rate of sinking won't be very fast, when you consider the square area of floor and the actual mass involved. As a matter of fact, it will float and have a tendency to go towards the inside. But we can do something about it whether it floats or sinks. It's merely a matter of melting a little bit of the ice around the room and then repositioning it by hydrostatic pressure. If I want to move a cabin to the other side of the ship, I can do it in two or three days and scarcely disturb a thing in the process."

I shook my head in awe. The idea of floating cabins

around in a ship to make new layouts at will was a bit much for me.

"You see," he said, in a voice that wasn't even sarcastic, "you're used to thinking in terms of static stability, forms that keep their shape by being rigid, forms that can't change because any major change destroys them.

"My glacier," he went on, "she can change, adapt, grow and evolve. She has dynamic stability, and that's quite a different thing!" With that, Gallagher had pointed out the difference between what we represented as well.

I cursed the day I'd met him, as I orbited back to Altura in my spick-and-span ship with all its proper gadgets and technological advances added as they were developed. I'd never own my own ship, I told myself, but I captained a good one!

Gallagher seemed to be mocking me, with an old Antolaric drive and probably the finest engineering talent on the starlanes. Gallagher was wasting *that* engineering genius on a hunk of ice. Why, the man could work up to captain, would he abide the rules!

But, when I returned, my own ship didn't look as pretty as she used to look and though I still saw to it that my men only went port-side in threes, I began going alone, in full uniform, despite the risk.

The whole thing worried me, and it worried me more as the months passed and tales began to be traded from bar to bar.

At first Gallagher and his glacier were a roar of laughter that swept the spaceways. But it was more than just a roar of laughter. The spaceways had their first independent shipper, and it was a proud thing.

Soon there wasn't a man on a planet that wasn't searching for an old Antolaric of his own. But the corporations weren't exactly napping, and they weren't about to let their monopoly of the shipping lanes fall to the tune of second-hand drives. Within days there wasn't an Antolaric to be found that didn't have a company label attached. Though the spaceways had an independent shipper, he was the only one, and it looked like that was permanent, for though the Antolaric is a fairly simple drive to build, it takes power to build the machinery to do it. That was where the corporations' monopoly began to show. Power to build machinery, outside of corporate hands, was a scarce thing in the planets, for Earth had no intention of letting her colonies do more than supply raw materials for her own manufacturing.

In the long run, there was only one independent shipper in the starpaths, and though Gallagher and his glacier were a laugh at company expense in any port, the company colonies weren't allowed to trade with him. How many of the black-market tales were true and how many apocryphal, no one knew. The tales grew as such tales will. One thing was sure: Gallagher had plenty of time and plenty of money to satisfy his sociable nature in the bars up and down the space lanes.

Those tales had the ports and the colonies laughing, but they didn't seem funny to me as I sat in my comfortable captain's cabin or when I went into the ports alone in sheer defiance and came back to my ship unchallenged.

II

That was how it was for the better part of two years. There were tales told of cargoes that weren't waiting for their normal bidders when the company ships appeared and of how the black market thrived on goods and services they hadn't had before. Tales told of feats of daring and of impossible adventure; they made of the company ships a ludicrous caravan of imbeciles.

The tales grew and the laughter grew, and the corporations ignored the laughter, waiting patiently for the original of the tales, Gallagher, to make a wrong move. But they knew better than to make a martyr of him meanwhile. Corporations are eternal, while a human has a short span, as one lawyer argued.

But the corporations were smarting, although they pretended to be above the problem. The colonies were restless, for now the hatred of the colonists for the corporations had something to fasten onto.

Then Gallagher hit the galactic funny bone. It began in a brothel in a port town.

A man who set out as an independent prospector in the early days could fail and get killed or become a spaceways bum. But when a woman who went with him, or alone, failed, or if her man was killed, there was only one place she was likely to wind up. It wasn't that the girls were a special class there, but you did find the kind of horse sense that had at least survived in the roughest pioneering man had ever set himself.

When Gallagher bought out the house and took them all off to a planet of their own, there was sympathy behind the guffaw that went up. When Gallagher promised them he'd separate out the sheep from the wolves along the spaceways bars, and bring them a batch of able men to help homestead their planet, there wasn't a man who was ashamed to volunteer, and after Gallagher had culled the volunteers, there wasn't a man who went who wasn't proud to be selected.

I had the bad luck to make planetfall where Gallagher was doing his culling, and I lost an astrogator and a machinist third class to the cause. It made me mad, chiefly because underneath I nearly approved of what they were doing.

I put on my dress uniform and I walked into the port town, too mad to risk driving a skimmer. I looked up Gallagher where I knew he was to be found, in a bar.

"You got two of my men," I told him without waiting for the amenities.

"Sit down and have a drink," he said. "We'll discuss this politely."

I sat down and somehow I didn't seem as little by his side as I had the first day we met. Maybe it was because I'd made a habit of going into ports alone when it wasn't a secure thing to do; maybe it was just because I was a captain in the starways.

We had a drink and then another before I spoke again.

"You're going to pay a price, you know," I told Gallagher, my gruffness ready and waiting for him to upbraid me on the uniform I wore. "The corporations won't let you get away with this forever." It wasn't what I had in mind to say, but it was what came out.

"There's the price of anything," said Gallagher, "and then there's its value. Let's look at the value, and then we'll discuss the price." The way he said it made sense, and my gruffness began to slip away.

"Where's the value?" I asked, and knew myself a liar in the asking. "Where's the value? All you're doing is making yourself the laughing stock of the spaceways."

"Takes a free man to laugh," said Gallagher, "and it takes laughter to make a man free."

We didn't speak again after that, but we kept ordering the drinks. First he'd pay the round and then I would. But we didn't speak, and all the time those words of his were echoing back and forth between us, just as if we were saying them over and over to each other.

When I climbed into my bunk that night the words were still there. "Let's look at the value," the words kept saying, "and then we'll discuss the price."

That was that for a long time, and Gallagher was a thorn in the side of the corporations, but not a very big thorn. They continued to ignore the irritation.

As for Gallagher, he had a thriving colony to ship for, and the shipping itself was almost more than he could manage with his one glacier. Little by little, the responsibility was beginning to interfere with the habits he preferred, and he was said to complain loudly of the fact.

I listened to the tales whispered through the bars and knew most of them to be apocryphal but some to be true, and I wondered how people found them funny.

I remembered the way the *Starfire* had come to be a thing alive when he had engineered her, how the port inspector had ordered the drive reworked to its old condition when I'd reached Altura, and how she'd never responded with that particular aliveness again.

I thought of the small farm I'd buy myself on a company planet where they'd accept colonists when I retired, and it looked empty and uninspiring, for I was an old hand in the spaceways now, an old hand by two years. I'd been on corporation planets.

Colonists, you see, weren't exactly indentured servants, they were just in debt before ever they left Earth and obliged to work in the company mines, or whatever else supported the corporation colonies, to pay off the debt. By the books, it took two years to pay for passage to a company planet and another two to earn passage back, if you wanted to go back. The company pay-rates were set accordingly. But meantime you had to live, and the company owned the stores; your credit was good at the stores.

I had known about colonists and I had known the conditions under which they lived and worked. Earth is crowded these days, and any chance to get out into opener spaces would be a bargain to some people, I told myself. If I saw things that didn't match up with the advertisements that the corporations used to recruit their colonists on Earth, why a person should investigate, I told myself, before making a move like that!

It hadn't troubled me on my first few runs, at least I thought it didn't trouble me. It hadn't troubled me the first few times I had to drop crewmen into colonies as troublemakers, to join and survive if they could. I told myself that didn't trouble me; the safety of my ship came first.

Then my schedule called for a stop at Stellamira, to deliver supplies and to pick up a cargo of starstones. It was my second stop at Stellamira. The first time there had been one of my first commissions, and I'd dropped a rebellious crewman there. Stellamira had an unsavory reputation in the starways, but I knew the profits that the corporations made from starstones, and that it was an important colony to them. Starstones were wicked gems, with a hypnotic quality; they were sold and used as tranquilizers. The planet where they were mined was bound to be one of the worst for human life, for it was a new planet.

I orbited the *Starfire*, let down on the pad at Free Port, and made my way to the company headquarters, sleek, dry and air-conditioned after the heavy humidity of the landing area. Tall, graceful buildings flanked the edge of the port itself; the area was landscaped and walled. It made a striking contrast to the open pits that I had seen scarring the landscape as I came in.

I was welcomed with the quiet hospitality that is accorded rank and shown luxurious quarters. Then I was given a social schedule for the two days I'd be in port that was quite elaborate, and that underscored the need of the local personnel for visitors to entertain them.

But I had seen Gallagher's lander at the port as I came in, and I excused myself from the festivities the first evening early, and headed for the gate that connected the corporation area to the colonists' area, hoping to find him. Perhaps it was curiosity, perhaps envy, perhaps simply a need to talk to a fellow from the old country and to hear a brogue again.

I reached the exit and was surprised to find a heavy gate and a guard, and that I must sign out before leaving. The guard impressed me as a nice, alert young man, but a bit over-concerned for my welfare, since he stressed to me several times that the colonists were a rough lot, and implied that it was beneath the dignity of one of my rank to associate with them.

I found I'd wasted fifteen minutes with the guard and still not gotten anywhere towards signing out, when one of the men who had officially greeted me on arrival showed up.

"We're sorry our company displeases you," he opened. "We've usually quite sufficient entertainment, for visitors of your rank. Is there perhaps something missing? Or possibly," he added with a leering twinkle, "you'd like me to recommend? If you're after rather . . . bawdy entertainment, there's Suzie's. Her place is just inside the colonists' area and is set up for the entertainment of ships' officers as well as crew. Suppose I escort you?"

I smiled at him, rather grimly. It was on the tip of my tongue to say I'd seen Gallagher's lander and wanted to see if I could locate Gallagher himself, but something warned me against it. I merely said, "I've a curiosity about the colonists."

"Oh?" His face looked grimmer. "Then," he said, "I shall insist upon sending along an escort, though I shall not volunteer myself. We do have a bit of trouble now and then."

I drew myself up. Though I'm not tall, I do command a ship and can adopt the manner of authority necessary to such a command when it is required, whether with equals or subordinates. "I think," I said, "that I am quite capable of managing myself, even," I added to appease his concern, "among rabble. I am not unarmed," I lightly touched the laser gun at my hip.

With that, I turned and strode through the gate, nor did I bother to sign the paper on the guard's desk. I simply turned my back on the two of them and walked through, seething at the necessity to pull rank to do as I pleased in a Free Port.

Just beyond the gate I found myself quickly submerged in a surge of pleasure-seeking humanity. On my right was Suzie's Place, proclaiming itself with neon lights and a rather luxurious entrance. Beside the entrance was a small sign, "CORPORATION AND OFF-PLANET PERSONNEL ONLY." It rather startled me, and I looked at it again to make sure I'd read it aright, but it remained, innocuously unobtrusive, but unmistakable.

I shrugged and looked around. Opposite and beyond were bazaars and shops, grocers and the like. It was much the same as you will see in any of the free ports of space, I decided, and probably not one whit rougher. Not only because of the sign, but because the executive had suggested it, I ignored Suzie's Place, which looked much the most inviting of the honky-tonks, and made my way around the corner that it created.

The crowd was thick and noisy, yet I noticed people shrugging away from close contact with the uniform I wore. It was an odd reaction, since in most free ports a captain's uniform is a prime target for all the peddlers of this and that that hope to fast-talk a buck out of any rank they see.

I'd made my way past Suzie's and rounded the corner to find a less luxurious side to the same building, and centered in it a set of old-fashioned swinging doors that spelled *bar*, though they were probably copied out of an old Western. By their sides, was a small, innocuous looking sign that read "Colonists."

This was still Suzie's that I'd been told to visit; yet it was a different Suzie's than the entrance nearest the gate. I was tempted to turn back entirely because of the dirt, noise and smell and perhaps the crowds that inexplicably shrugged away from me instead of ganging to sell me wares. Actually, I wanted to go back to the cleaner atmosphere, to the quiet, to the—the womb of my own kind and their environment, but instead I turned to the swinging doors.

As I started to push my way through I met resistance, and looked up to see a tall, bearded fellow staring at me over the doors.

"S'matter, sonny," he said in a belligerent tone, "can't you read?"

"I beg your pardon?" I said formally, and stepped a half pace backwards, simultaneously tugging the door out from in front of the bearded man who had been pushing to hold it shut. My action caught him by surprise, and he came tumbling out. With a sidestep and a push at his back as he went by, I managed not only to get through the door, but to leave him sliding into the dirt outside.

That immediate arrogance, I decided as I walked in, might have been a mistake, though I'd not have changed it even at the moment. It was a long and crowded barroom, with tables set along its length. The bar stools were filled and there were standees to boot. A hush was over its length, every eye on the door and on me as I strode through. Several figures at various tables were slowly rising to their feet, and I was debating whether to stand where the wall beside the door would still shelter my back, or whether to continue my firm stride forward, when a voice bellowed over the crowd.

"Ho! It's Captain Dundee of the *Starfire*. Harald, will you join me for a drink?"

There was Gallagher, seated with a woman and two men at a table near the far end of the room.

My hands loose at my sides and ready, though with no gesture to indicate that I recognized the hostility around me, I made my way straight to his table and saw, from the corners of my eye, the men who had started to rise slowly sinking back into their chairs. As I approached, the two who had been seated with Gallagher rose and left; and Gallagher waved me to join him and the tall, rather hawk-faced woman beside him. It wasn't really a hawk face, I realized as Gallagher rose to introduce us: the nose was decided, the chin firm, but not excessively so. It was the intensity of the face that gave it that appearance. Her eyes were eyes that saw what they looked at; deep, interested eyes.

"Suzie," said Gallagher, "this is Harald Dundee."

She smiled, and her whole face was smiling. Suzie? I was astonished; this was Suzie's Place. A place of entertainment is the euphemism, although it's an exact statement. There was a bar, music and dancing, gambling and girls downstairs; the bedrooms were upstairs, obviously. Suzie was its mistress, but she didn't have a blousey look. She was dressed in a red shirt and tight, black slacks; she wore makeup, but not much.

"How do you do," I said. It seemed rather inadequate. I was surprised to meet such a woman, and I don't think I hid it well.

We were interruped at that point, which was just as well. The murmur and background buzz in the room died abruptly, and Suzie, Gallagher and I all looked around to see the bearded man standing in the door looking around for me. He spotted me as quickly as I spotted him, and headed towards me. Then he noticed who I was with, hesitated, and came forward again.

I wasn't exactly spoiling for a fight, but he looked like he was, and I was relaxing my tensing muscles to be ready. His belligerence faded as he approached, but he came with obvious purpose.

"Come join us, Seth," Gallagher invited as he got near enough to hear. "This is Harald Dundee, Captain of the *Starfire*. Seth Thompson, Harald," he added.

The man extended his hand and I reached out to grasp it until I realized the gesture was not one of greeting. He spread the fingers wide, and two were missing. "We've met," he said shortly, "in an engine room."

I remembered. I hadn't recognized him through the beard, but I did now, a burly giant, slow of speech but strong. There had been a brawl in the engine room, and it had been he who had swung a wrench at me. I'd really had no reason to have been there, as far as I knew then the fight had been between two ratings, and I had thought that I'd only happened to be passing in the corridor outside. When I'd stepped through the bulkhead to see what was going on, I'd seen nothing but a hand and a wrench, swinging towards my skull.

My reactions had been fast then, too, and I'd stepped back and slammed the bulkhead door. It hadn't closed completely, and it hadn't blocked off the scream, but when I'd opened the door again there was no fight, and no one around, only a trail of blood. He had gone to the medic, but he had claimed injury on duty, telling of a wrench slipping and his fingers getting caught in some machinery, so I could have dropped it there. But I hadn't. I'd had him jailed, and when we'd landed at Stellamira I'd had him left there.

Not satisfied with that, I'd let the other engineer ratings go, one by one. A captain may not always know what goes on in the minds of the crew, I'd told myself, but he can be fairly sure that when he walks into a setup like that, there was something cooking that wasn't good. I'd blacklisted every one when I bounced them off my ship. It was a hard policy, perhaps, but one according to the books.

Gallagher was waiting silently. "We've met," I agreed shortly.

The face had scars that hadn't been there before and it was working now in a controlled anger that I could well understand, whether I could agree with it or not. Gallagher was silent, and I stayed silent too, watching Thompson's face working, watching the anger of the man, and wondering what the odds were if it came to blows again. There were Gallagher and Suzie and the rest of the barroom; there were too many unknowns. Even if it were just the two of us, it was his size, strength and nearly berserk anger if it broke, against my quickness. I kept myself relaxed, but I was ready. It may have been seconds.

Then his face began contorting, and that I couldn't read at all, so I just stood, loose and ready, until words began to come out, and I relaxed. A man like that will talk or fight, but not both.

The words were slow and halting, and they came past a heavy barrier of emotion. "You're here now, Captain," he said, and his tone was ugly but the decision had been made and I could listen more and watch less. "You're in my world. I think I want to show you what you dropped me into when you dropped me here, blacklisted so I had no way off."

Then, quite suddenly, his face broke into a grin that was more weird than the anger that had preceded it. The anger was gone. He turned to Gallagher almost happily. "The captain had good reason to drop me," he said, the words still coming as slow as the man's thinking processes. "We wanted his ship. He was young, and we thought we could get it. Then we'd have been real free men in space, like you are, Dublin."

At that he paused again, and his face contorted with thought. "Only we'd have been pirates, not like you," he said. His honesty had me on his side completely.

There was a long pause and nobody spoke at all. I could feel Gallagher and Suzie waiting, and I was waiting and almost wondering what was coming, but it was like stepping out of a hot bath. You just wait a second, not really thinking.

The big bearded face turned back to me, and it held a new, a rather surprised expression. "You lived and kept your ship," he said, "no thanks to me. But I lived and that's no thanks to you. Now you come with me; I'm going to show you how I lived. I've waited to find you again just once. I was going to kill you when I did." His head swung back and forth between the three of us. "I reckon that Gallagher and Suzie have made a difference in me. They've made a difference to all of us, and now I'm just going to show you."

He was serious, I realized, and I would refuse at cost. What that cost would be, I could only guess. I looked at Gallagher and I saw a sort of proud expression on his face, like one gets when one's dog shows he knows and Suzie had a happy sort of look.

Seth must have hated me, completely and absolutely for about two years. Then I realized it must have been more than hatred. It was an anger and hatred so deep that it probably kept him alive. Yet he was foregoing his day in some queer reasoning that had to do with Gallagher and Suzie.

I looked at each of them in turn, and the queer, proud look they had. Then Gallagher nodded to me and turned to Seth.

"Sounds a fair proposition to me, Seth," he said genially. "A good look at Stellamira should be a part of any captain's education. But if you don't mind, I think I'll be coming along. I think I want the captain to see what's here; but I think, too, I want to be sure he gets back in one piece. He'll be a good witnesss . . . later."

I didn't know what he meant, but I didn't really care. I knew I had little choice in the matter.

Suzie was rising from her seat. "I'm going too," she said, which surprised me. Suzie has never failed to surprise me, and I guess she never will. She just doesn't fit any pattern I've ever known.

That night my senses were shocked as they had never been before, for the conditions under which the colonists on Stellamira lived were unbelievable: cattle are better cared for.

It's a sterile planet; hot to the edge of the degree that a man can stand, and not having evolved life in sea or on land, which meant that, although the atmosphere was sufficient for a human, everything else had to be imported.

That first area was the pleasure area, the Free Port proper. It was crowded, noisy, dirty, bawdy and horrible, but livable, if you could call that living. But the living area wasn't fit for beasts. The stench itself was enough to make one ill: the quarters were ramshackle huts, the streets were dirt and filthy, and the faces of the people, crowded into a small area, were haggard and hopeless.

"But why don't they build themselves better quarters?" I asked aghast. "There's rock, if nothing else, for building."

"If you want to eat, you work. If you work, you work fourteen hours a day. There's not enough water, not enough food, and you work for both of them, from the time you're eight or ten years old," Seth said. "Mining can be done pretty early."

Then there were the mines themselves and the men,

women and children working them. I won't try to describe the mines; I wish I could forget them.

Starstones are a big product commercially, and there were rare minerals as well, which meant that the mining of the planet was invaluable. But it takes a lot of mining to make a cargo worth carrying through the spaceways; and the mining left no time for comfort or luxuries such as proper living quarters.

There was no escape. One can't escape into a planet that's as inhospitable as Stellamira and survive. As to saving and buying passage back, the company couldn't afford to have eyewitnesses going back to Earth. If you scrimped and saved and starved to keep the pay that the company provided, it was stolen from you in the long run. There was one other choice than putting up with it: that was suicide. I gathered that the suicide rate on Stellamira was as high as anywhere.

It was a stinking, sweating, slave-labor life, with a honky-tonk of a Free Port the only luxury to be had. There was not enough water, not enough food and too much work, right in front of the company executives living in luxury.

No wonder the company kept the ships' officers in its own compound and guarded it! No wonder the colonists were feared and hated in company quarters! No wonder you ran the risk of murder and sudden death coming among the colonists, if you were of the ranking company personnel. The colonists had been tempted here with promises of wealth, and now they were prisoners, to all intents and purposes. They were free men, the company would tell you, free to go anywhere on the planet they wanted to, if there were anywhere a man could go. They were free to work for the company or not work for it and starve. They were free to leave when they liked, if they could pay the passage. They were free to die.

By the time I said goodbye to Gallagher, Seth and Suzie, I was boiling mad. I promised myself that a report on this planet and the conditions it supported would go straight to the U.N. Space Commission.

Gallagher laughed when I told him that. Seth snorted, but he seemed more eager for it to happen. Suzie just shrugged. I asked Gallagher why he laughed.

"The Space Commission?" he asked. "You can rub their noses in it for a bit, perhaps, might even get some results, for they do manage to look away mostly, but this stink is enough to get up a nose that's forced to smell it. In the long run it'll do you no good," he said.

"Aye, but I'll only be starting there," I told him. "I'll carry it as far as it must go, to the news media—"

"The controlled press?" Gallagher laughed heartily this time. Then he sobered. "You're a young man, Harald," he said, "with still an ideal or two left under that uniform, and a lot to learn. It won't hurt you to try. I wish you well."

Seth, however, was grimly satisfied. "You dropped me off here, Captain," he said, "to live or die, and I don't really think now you knew what you were condemning me to. If you should report this to the Space Commission, we'll consider old scores settled."

"It's not for that I'd be doing it," I told him with a grin. "But you're right; I'd no idea that I was condemning you to *this*. This," I said grandly, waving my hand to indicate the entire and habitable part of the planet, "is beneath the dignity of the human race, and must not be allowed to continue." I had faith in my captain's stars in those days. I headed back to the company compound, head high, chin out, ready to administer to rank what I'd administered in my time to file.

There was no trouble at all in returning to the corporation compound. The guard nodded me cheerfully in. As

I entered the lobby of the main building, I found the executive who'd seen me out with such concern wandering about as though he'd just arisen from a refreshing night's sleep.

"Ho, Captain," he said, "did you enjoy your night among the *canaille?*"

My chin went up, my eyes glinted hard. "*Canaille,* is it?" I said. "They looked like human beings to me, human beings, enslaved and degraded." At that point the liquor I'd been imbibing with Gallagher must have got my tongue, for I went on in the fury that was seething within me. "This planet is a disgrace to the starways, and the U.N. Commission will hear about it, in detail, when I return."

His eyebrows went up then, and the sarcasm was light in his voice. "Oh? The good captain was displeased?" It was a soft voice, and it stung to the heart of my disgust.

I described with great accuracy and detail just exactly what I had seen, and I quoted the laws on the Space Agency books that protected colonists from such treatment. My tongue was loose and ready, and I described not only what I had seen, but the detail of my plans for presenting the problem on Earth, not just to the Space Commission, but to the news media, the underground and the official media. If I got a hearing in the more-or-less black-market news area, the other media could not ignore the problem.

He listened, and he must have questioned me in that light, faintly sarcastic tone, for some time. If I'd been less sure of the privileges of rank, or had taken a better look at the consequences to him and his ilk of my doing what I was saying, I'd perhaps have been more careful. But my tongue was loose and my confidence long.

It's hard for a young man to realize what one man will do to another, and even when he sees it happening, the security in which he was born and raised may give him the indifferent armor of knowing it can't happen to him. It never occurred to me, frankly, that it could happen to *me*.

I went to my luxurious quarters and slipped out of my jacket and side arm; but instead of going to bed, I got out paper and pen and began to draft a report on Stellamira. It was a violently worded start, though I was trying my best to couch the violence I felt in the formal terms necessary.

When a knock came at the door, I opened it without hesitation. There were three guards on the threshold and the rating in charge said simply, "Come with us, Captain."

"Who's called for me?" I asked, my naïveté still self-assured and confidently unalert.

"The brass wants to talk to you," said the rating with what I took to be unintended brusqueness.

". . . wants to talk to you, *sir*," I said. Ratings must be taught from the start.

He looked at me startled, caught my eye and dropped his. "*Sir*," he said sullenly. "The orders are immediately and as you are."

Now a rating cannot question his orders, and though I was in no mood to talk to anyone, I wasn't sleepy either. Perhaps, I decided, I *was* in a mood to talk to someone in authority. Perhaps I could get some action immediately, even ameliorate conditions so that I could tone down my report. I followed the guard.

A ground car took us through the gate into the port part of the colonists' area and through it to its outskirts. Then it pulled up before the local police office.

"Are your officers *here*?" I asked in surprise, still unsuspicious.

"This is the place they said," the flunky replied without any form of respect again, but I ignored it and went in without protest.

I found myself bustled into a cell by company police.

I was a prisoner. All my shouts for information, all the shaking of the bars that my fury indulged in, were to no avail. What the future held I could only guess. It seemed forever before the colony manager finally appeared. Then I wished I didn't know.

"You think you could get away with something like that?" he asked without preliminary. He was a hard-eyed little man with a face like a weasel and deep circles under his eyes, gray lids drooping over them.

"And just what charges do you think you're holding me on?" I asked in turn, cold with helplessness and fury. "Your Earth managers shall hear of this!"

"My orders are standing, direct from your Earth managers, mister," he said. "Direct, with details of what to do. They don't name you except as Joe Doe, but they apply. They're . . ."

"To let me out of here immediately," I said furiously, but with a hollow in the pit of my stomach.

"Oh, yes," he said, and his weasel face grimaced. "Oh, yes indeed, almost immediately. We just put you here temporarily. Easier that way." He stopped then, deliberately, and stood watching me. I could feel myself shaking, and I tried to control it. I hoped he couldn't see them.

But the crooked grin told me he had seen, and translated to his pleasure, and I knew him for a sadist.

"The doctor'll be here to examine you tomorrow," he said slowly, taking his time to refine my reactions. "You'll go to the psych ward. Obviously insane, you know, probably dangerous, certainly dangerous to your ship and crew."

Then his voice grew hard and ugly. "After a few doses of shock therapy," he said, with a yearning in his voice under the hardness, "you'll be amenable, quite amenable, amenable enough to ship back to Earth. You'll be cared for the rest of your life, so you needn't worry."

Then abruptly he grinned, and there was a pleasure in that grin that watered my knees. "I'll be there, watching you," he said.

I'd read about a sadist's grin, but I'd never seen it before.

He left then, and the barred door at the end of the corridor outside my cell clanged shut. Then a bolt clicked. It was the most final sound in the universe.

Time stopped; it just stopped. There's no feeling like it. It could have been hours or days, minutes or years. The light filtering through the high, barred window didn't change, so intellectually I knew that no time had passed. But I knew it internally even more.

III

How long it was by a clock before I pulled myself together I still don't know. The light from the window hadn't changed, but eternities had passed.

Then I began to explore the cell, looking for a way out. I examined every crack in the paint, every scratch on the wall, every corner, every seam where floor met wall or wall met ceiling. Given a reason for doing so, I think I could probably give a microscopic description of that little company cell.

There was also the jail. I set myself to recall every detail I'd seen. It was a small building, all on ground level, located at the brow of a steep hill. I pulled myself up to the window. The hill fell away below; it was about ten meters to the first shelf, which was covered with boulders.

The jail was solidly built. It was not of the filmy construction typical of the colony. It wasn't built to permit escape.

It was with a feeling of hopelessness buried as deeply as I could bury it and a stubborn optimism that I set firmly on top of the hopelessness, that I started to work on the only plan I could dream up.

I scraped up all the grit and dust there was on the floor of the cell, and there was dust and grit, though it seemed too clean to me, as I tried to gather a pile. Then I took my shoelaces, for they were the best grinding surfaces I had, and I worked the heaviest grit onto them. Then I hooked them around the bars of the window and began grinding, back and forth, reaching above my head and working with a ferocity that took little heed of blood-drained, aching arms and numb fingers. I continued rubbing, trying to make that dirt act as a grinding agent.

I wasn't making much progress, but I was doing the only thing I could think to do; and I couldn't just wait to be made into a vegetable.

The first shoelace was beginning to fray, and it had been dark outside for some time when there was a quiet laugh above my head, and I heard the lightest of whispers. "Leave it, Captain. Let me give it a try."

It was only minutes, then, before the bars began to slide out of sight, one at a time, neatly cut. I didn't know how he cut them, and I still don't. I didn't care. The hand that stuck in the window and beckoned, holding the last bar, was the greatest sight I've ever seen. I didn't waste time, and I didn't make a sound, hoisting myself to the window and sliding my head and shoulders out.

The figure beyond was holding the edge of the window and leaning aside to give me room to join him on a short mooring tube, a plastic, expandable Bourdon mooring tube. It was just big enough for one man to hang onto with a rope harness. The figure was clinging to the tube with a regular climbing belt, but there were no spikes on the shoes. That would have been fatal to the structure itself. Instead, I could see dimly that a loose lacework of rope had been draped over the tube providing foot and hand grips for its climber.

"Climb on down, Captain," the figure whispered. "I'll be with you in a minute." Then he clung to the window while I made my way down the rope network.

When I reached the ground and let go, I stumbled, then got to my feet and looked back up. He'd leaned back on his belt and was seaming the bars back in so that the method of my escape would not become immediately apparent.

I stood at the bottom of the tube looking up, trying to see what the other was doing, when another soft whisper reached me. "This way. Quickly, Captain."

It's hard to tell, on a barely moonlit slope when someone whispers, where they are or what they are. I looked around, my eyes adjusting, and could make out two figures working on some equipment. Then the tube behind me began hissing down, and the man who'd cut the bars was beside me as it flattened to the ground. He ignored me and began strapping the collapsed tube together, while the other two began detaching what must have been a compressor from the lead-ins.

But a fourth figure was tugging at my sleeve, and I turned and followed it down a steep way through the boulders to a point where we reached a rock wall behind some buildings. We jumped down from the rock wall, and I could just make out a skimmer there, in an angle behind one building and an alley just beyond.

"Hadn't I better help with the equipment?" I whispered.

The figure shook his head. "No. Gallagher's waiting." I realized then for the first time that it was a girl beside me, and then that it was Suzie. "Get those clothes off and put these on," she said. "We may need a captain's uniform some day."

I took the clothes she shoved into my arms and looked around for a place to undress. She giggled, and then whispered fiercely, "Right here, right now—and fast. We need those clothes; you need these; and there's not much time."

I did as she said, though my modesty was offended. As I stopped at the skivvies she gestured those off too, and I obeyed. While I was naked as a jay the first of the men landed beside me, reached back and was handed the heavy equipment, then the other two landed and started putting it into the back door of the building.

As the packaged mooring tube went past, Suzie shoved my uniform, shoes and skivvies on top and they were taken in, too.

I had a bit of trouble with the garb she had handed me in the dark, but I got on the old pants and shirt and a kind of sweat shirt affair—not too clean, I judged from the odor—as well as a pair of sandals. I glanced at the legend painted on the door that had closed behind my benefactors, and could just make out in the dim light, SURPLUS SALES.

As I was buckling on the sandals, Suzie leaned forward and passed something damp across my face and hair. It was both damp and slightly sticky. "Have you ever been an actor?" she whispered.

I had been taken by surprise by the physical contact, and started to reach up to feel my face, but she grabbed my arms and said, "Wait a minute till it dries." Even as she spoke I could feel the damp, sticky stuff cooling and hardening.

"I . . . uh . . . no, I've never tried acting," I stammered.

"Well, that's okay. It won't take much. Come on." She went to the skinner, opened the door and gestured me in. I saw Seth at the controls as I bent to enter. Then I felt a light tap on the back of my neck.

I came to, knowing I was in a ship in orbit. My head was throbbing, and I hadn't opened my eyes, but I knew I was in orbit by the feel of things, so different from a planet. I'd spent too many hours with those feelings not to recognize them.

I opened my eyes, and knew I was in the control cabin of Gallagher's *Glacier*. There could be no control cabin quite like it, of course. In an ordinary ship, one might have to guess, but Gallagher's control cabin is hand-rigged, and there's an unfinished quality about the consoles and other controls that no manufacturer would tolerate, though the wiring itself was something ships' engineers dream of.

I was in the navigator's chair, leaned back for acclera-tion or comfortable sleeping; and there was no one at the controls; we were on automatic. I located Gallagher himself when I sat up and looked around, in the tiny galley that opened off the control room, whistling cheer-fully under his breath.

The stiffness I half expected either evaporated or wasn't there as I stood groggily; the throbbing in my head dis-appeared. My face, though, felt stiff, and when I touched it a fleck of blood came off.

"Go wash your face," Gallagher told me cheerfully. "You're not dead yet."

He gestured toward a small refresher next to the gal-ley, and I looked into the mirror there. My face and hair were covered with blood. I looked like I'd just been murdered, or just committed murder. It was synthablood I realized, remembering the damp, sticky stuff. I began dousing water over my face. I needed it for more than the synthablood; I needed to bring myself out of the grogginess. I started out being careful not to splash water on my clothes, then noticed the old sweat-shirt affair I was wearing, and didn't bother.

I was mopping up with a towel when I looked up to see Gallagher lounging at the bulkhead, grinning. "You've changed some, formerly-dapper Captain," he said happily.

"I've been in some changing places," I noted, and found myself grinning back, though I couldn't decide why I felt so happy. There were enough problems I could see ahead to keep a man worried, like getting my lander and the men in it back from the planet, and getting the *Starfire* to Earth so I could report the renegade Stellamira Company. I was out of the trap now that would have prevented it, and I wanted to get on with the job.

"Who were those people who sprung me out of the clink?" I asked. "Suzie was with them."

"Suzie and her crew? Well, you could say she was with them. It's her gang. They're what you might call a corporate underground. They do me a bit of a favor now and then, like getting you out of the clink, and I manage to return the favor, now and again."

"Well," I said carefully, "I owe them somewhat more than a favor. But I plan to report the Stellamira Company to the Earth Space Commission and change the conditions there. Perhaps that will do a bit towards evening the score. Do you know what those company bastards had rigged for me?"

"I've a pretty good idea." Gallagher was looking at me in a skeptical way, but his voice went hard, with a fury under it. "I've seen some of their results. That's what Suzie and I were sort of planning to change. And I don't think we can wait for you to report to the Space Commission, Harald. Springing you is going to make things pretty hot down there."

"Oh?" I was concerned. "But how can you and Suzie

change it? It will have to be reported, of course. But perhaps, if I can be of assistance in ameliorating conditions meanwhile—I certainly owe them anything I can do. She's an odd one to be mixed up in something like that."

Gallagher's skeptical look changed to one of amusement. "Suzie? Yep. An odd one, you might rightly say. Never quite met anyone like her for guts or brains or practical ability. She runs that place of hers like a stage manager, and besides what comes to the house itself, she's rumored to have slept personally with half the guys on the planet, corporate and private. I think she does it for fun as well as for purpose, though I think purpose would be sufficient motive, because she knows what she wants to accomplish and that's the best way to do it. The girls she takes in are her kind; they're doing what they're doing because they're bachelor types with a goal in mind. If they're not that type, they don't get into Suzie's. They're the only ones on the planet with freedom to organize what needs organizing and the ability to do it, too. But even if they have the goals she has, a gal can't come in unless she has the bachelor attitude which," he finished dryly, "is somewhat different than what you find in a normal house."

I looked at him, puzzled, but I changed the subject. "What did she hit me with?" I asked, rubbing the lump at the back of my neck. "And why?"

Gallagher chuckled. "I reckon she didn't know whether you could handle a bit part as a quick study, so she had to make you into the one kind of actor who can't go up in his lines. She and Seth got you onto the landing field as a drunken crewman that had had one too many. The guards all frequent the place too, and if Suzie says jump, they jump. She knows too many answers about each of them personally for them to question her, even on Stellamira. As for your other question, what she hit you with, why, I imagine she used a little Syrette known as a roller's tap. It's good for using on drunks, whether you want to roll 'em or not, and not particularly harmful if you don't mind a long sleep."

My face and hair were now clean, but my clothes still stank. I'd been standing there, listening to Gallagher with both ears and not particularly noticing a tugging at my senses until it had been going on, probably, for some time. Now the tugging finally got my attention and I noticed that the feel of the ship was somehow wrong.

Automatically my mind slipped into what I think of as captain's gear, and I began paying attention to the details of the feel of the ship. The gravity was wrong. Instead of the smooth spin that one should feel in orbit with a slight displacement that spacemen automatically compensate for but never quite get used to, there was a quiver.

I listened for the throb of motors, and I barely heard it. I listened with each of my other senses in turn, but it was only the little balance point between my ears that said something was wrong with the gravity and the faint quiver.

"Dublin," I said, "there's something out of kilter with —I think your gravity control, though it might be more serious."

He nodded slowly. "Thought you might notice, Harald." His tone was satisfied. "You're not all by-the-book, I guess. There's a little seat-of-the-pants left in you. Yep, the gravity's a bit out of kilter. We're enlarging the hull, making holds for a cargo of about five thousand people. You better begin getting familiar with the ship anyhow, so come along. I'll show you."

The mention of five thousand people should have alerted me, but it didn't. I wanted to see the ship, and the reason for looking was immaterial at the time. Gallagher headed through the bulkhead at the back of the control room, and I followed.

We stepped into what should have been a straight, simple corridor, tunnel would be a better word, and I recognized the handiwork of his mice. But it wasn't straight and it wasn't simple; it was bent and twisted like a child's jump rope that had been dropped to lie as it fell, twisted and turned, with bumps, slopes and curves. It was a crazy child's toy of a corridor, and I sucked in my breath, thinking that the bumps might be leaking. Gallagher just stepped out along it like it was the normal way to build a corridor.

It was even more of a shock when we reached the first of the engine rooms. It contained a king-sized power converter unit, about four meters long and one and a half meters in diameter. The thing was nosed over at the heavier end, and out of level in respect to the servicing catwalk next to it; and there was a thin trickle of water seeping out from in front of the contact surface that was swept up by a pump and circulated, presumably to a better location.

I stood and stared. Then I found my voice. "Why in hell," I asked slowly, "did you install it that way?"

"Didn't," said Gallagher. "It creeped."

I stared at him in amazement, and he began to explain, almost sheepishly. "Ever hang a weight by a string tied around a cake of ice? The string will melt through the ice, but the cake of ice will stay whole. The ice welds itself together behind the string. Well," he went on, chuckling under his sheepish look, "this ship, her parts and specifications creep and move around like she was digesting 'em. I reckon I spend more time reorienting machines and chambers than I did building her in the first place. But she keeps ahead of me and has 'em screwed up most of the time. It's kind of a family battle, you might say."

I looked at the ice, melting against the converter unit; and I listened to the warmth of his voice as he spoke of "her." She seemed warmer to me. It was as if he had invited me into his home and introduced me to his crazy wife; I was startled at first, but there seemed a love between them that made her seem warm, comfortable, loving and more beautiful because of it than the dolls you normally meet.

But I couldn't think of anything to say, so I asked, "Plastic flow?"

"Yep."

"But, how do you compensate?"

"Nope," he answered, "compensate's not the right word; rebuild's more like it. We expand or shrink or change according to circumstances. You get used to change as your only constant after a while," he said tolerantly. He reached out and touched a switch, but nothing in particular seemed to happen as he went on. "In general, anything that has to be moved rapidly I've coupled with the proper type heating surfaces so that it can be done fast, like this one," he said as the converter unit began tilting very slowly and moving back into a level position. The little pump that had been taking water from the melting ice in front of the unit began taking more water as the unit realigned.

"Things like the corridor we just came through—well, they're not too essential, so I just wait until they get reasonably uncomfortable before I bore a new one and fill in the old one."

I was worried; an unsteady converter is something to worry a man. "But if the converter—if the converter keeps doing this, then everything in the ship must move around or float around or . . ."

Gallagher guffawed, and his laugh echoed and tinkled in the ice cavern. Finally, he said "Well, yes and no. The cabins and things float, and like I showed you back when you first came aboard while I was building her, I just melt water from behind them and pump it under pressure in front of them to squeeze them back into place. But she does have one habit that's harder to manage—she expands radially, leaving a hollow in the center. Boy, does she get fat! Then I have to really go to work, put a plastic skin over her, melt the outside and pump it back inside. Five times out is about as big as I can let her expand and still keep her in kilter, before I have to pause and shrink her back down—put her back on a diet, so to speak. But this time, I'm ballooning her on purpose. That's what we're doing now, giving her a bigger belly so we'll have room for the people."

"People?" The word came through to me finally.

"They'll have plenty of room in the hold we're making, but not much in the way of comfort. The equipment that we'll take—it's to go into a second hold—will be for building the new planet, not for making planeteers comfortable."

"What people?" I asked, though I was beginning to get an idea of what he had in mind.

"The people of Stellamira, of course," he said in surprise. "You saw how rough it was there before. Well, it's twice as rough today, on account of your escape. We weren't planning this for another three months, but I reckon the deadline's sort of called."

"But, but Dublin! I'm going to report it to the Space Commission. It will be . . ."

"Sometimes," he interrupted, "I get to thinking you've got good sense underneath all that company learning of yours. But other times," he went on, keeping me from speaking, "I get despairing of you. Just how are you planning to get to Earth to report the situation as you call it, even if that would do any good?"

"Why, the *Starfire* . . ."

"The *Starfire* took off nearly twelve hours ago, while you were in prison. The ship is in the command of her executive officer, with word that you've been taken space hazy and were confined to a hospital on Stellamira. They were planning to ship you back on the next ship through, and you'd have been nuts all right by then, real nuts."

"But spacemen only go space hazy after . . . the sort of accident that leaves them in a suit too long, or . . ."

Gallagher looked at me kindly. "Space nuts," he said softly, "is a disease that is manufactured in the psych wards, and only there. It's a convenient way to get rid of a man, and it's never been and never will be a real hazard of real space. A guy can go space nuts in a suit temporarily and get over it. What they call the space psycho is the one they manufacture. You were supposed to be it. Now," he said, dropping the subject as though it were completed to anyone's satisfaction, "you are, like it or not, stuck on the *Glacier* or stuck on Stellamira. You've got that much choice, and only that much, and I'm not even going to ask you which you choose. So come on, and I'll show you what we're doing to hold the people that we're going to take off that devil-ridden planet tonight."

He walked to the back of the engine room through another bulkhead, into another child's toy of a tunnel, and pushed through another bulkhead at its side. That bulkhead opened into a sort of spiral slide that led down to an ice floor much farther down than I had expected to find in the ship; it stretched a good kilometer from forward to back. It was a hold, circled around the central corridor, and the floor of the hold was about forty meters down.

It wasn't so much the size of the hold, but the way it was rigged that got to me. There were ropes, not just a few ropes, but grids and nets of ropes. Gallagher swung out along them confidently.

"Can't have people just sitting on the ice in here," he said, "and I didn't have enough material for proper decking. So I reckon this is about as good a crash deck as anybody could rig."

The plane of interwoven "decking" that we were traversing was at an angle of about forty-five degrees to the current direction of gravity. Suddenly Gallagher sat down and allowed himself to protrude somewhat through the fairly wide mesh.

"They can lie down like this and not be particularly uncomfortable whether we're on spin gravity or drive gravity. It's almost as good as a hammock."

I'd been carefully matching Gallagher as we made our way across the thing, trying to keep my mind from actually confronting what he'd told me about the *Starfire*. Now I tried the webbing. It looked comfortable, but in actual practise it wasn't. I stretched out, and the ropes were soft, but there weren't enough of them. I could prop my feet and not slide, or I could even let my feet dangle through. But I couldn't get the idea that it would be anything but an awkward way to travel.

"Don't think I'd be comfortable here," I said, and Gallagher swung back up into position for leaving.

"Doesn't make the best accommodations you could think of, does it? But really, the company didn't leave us much choice. We managed to get this rope from one of their warehouses. It's actually cable they use for mining. It's soft and plastic, but extremely strong. Anybody that can manage to bring himself along a hammock or something of the sort will be ahead of the game, and lord knows those people have already had enough problems without facing them with a mode of transportation like this. But it was the best we could do with the materials at hand."

Beyond the ropes, there were men working around the floor of the hold, and there was a glare from infrared heaters strung in a seemingly haphazard manner around the floor. A blast of heat rose from that surface that I certainly wouldn't expect to be compatible with ice. The melt was running off in channels and being pumped, I assumed, to the outside.

Gallagher stood on the ropes surveying the scene. "We've got it nearly big enough already," he said with some satisfaction. Then he turned and started back to the bulkhead; I followed. But now I could no longer keep my mind blanked. The *Starfire* was gone. I had lost my commission; I was a space nut, theoretically, if not in the bleak actuality that had almost happened. But I was *not* a space nut, and I *was* captain of the *Starfire*. I was determined to find a way to get to Earth to reestablish myself properly.

We reached the bridge, and Gallagher flung himself into the captain's seat, but I remained standing.

"You're taking the people off Stellamira, evacuating it?" I asked, rather forlornly, I'm afraid.

"What would you do, abandon them to the company finks who are out for blood now you've been rescued?" Gallagher's voice was hard.

I shook my head. "Even so, it's piracy," I said, "or something like it."

"It's a rescue mission," he said shortly. "That planet's murder, the way it's being run."

"The way it's being run could be changed," I said weakly. "It beclouds the issue, just hauling them off like this," I added stubbornly. "The company would have the right to send armed ships after them."

I paused, and then in spite of my better sense I went on. "The colonists have rights, including the right to leave, fair enough. But they *do* owe a debt to the company, and if they just leave without paying the debt, then the Space Commission has to go after them, or the company can take military measures of redress. And there are other planets in the same fix, or at least nearly so. So if you becloud the issue, legally that is . . ."

Gallagher looked at me curiously. "You're right," he said, "in a sort of half-assed legal way. There's some might even hesitate because of that fact. But they're being treated like animals, and that no man can tolerate."

"They could acknowledge the debt," I said desperately.

He thought about that for a minute, then his face broke into a huge grin. "Sign an I.O.U? By God, Harald, that they could! On the planet I've in mind for them, they can set up and repay the debt before any Space Commission that ever existed could even get through the first investigation, much less issue permits for armed intervention. With me to handle their shipping and their marketing for them, they could," he added.

Gallagher generously offered to let me stay aboard the *Glacier* during the evacuation proceedings—*war* would be a better term for it. "No use you and your ideals getting mixed up in a pirate operation," he said soothingly.

I refused point blank. "It's a legal operation, handled, I'll admit, somewhat illegally; but there will only be violence if the colonists' right to leave is obstructed." I said. "I'm proud to be part of it, and will be able to report the details more exactly, as an eyewitness, when I appear before the Space Commission as soon as I can find transport to Earth."

"Your faith in the Space Commission is touching," he answered sarcastically, but he made me second in command aboard the *Glacier*, and gave me the coordinates of the planet he had in mind for the Stellamirans before we went down. "Just in case," he said, "a Gallagher's luck turns black."

IV

There are no guns on a planet where the populace is as subjugated as it was on Stellamira, except those in the hands of the company police; and, since officials tend to think of weapons in terms of guns, the populace was considered unarmed.

A preconceived notion like that will do more to keep authority comfortable and unsuspicious than any other factor, and Suzie had seen to it that a complacent attitude prevailed.

A man with a laser gun is absolutely helpless when he's writhing under a jolt of ten or twenty thousand volts of electricity being applied by a contraption that is essentially a battery-powered water pistol. No one in authority noticed or cared when the colonists started making their kids water pistols with two tiny jets spaced four to eight centimeters apart. The tiny atomic batteries they have these days are so useful for powering things like flashlights that authority didn't bother about them either. Yet tiny batteries are equally useful for powering high-energy circuits if the circuit is pulsed and applied to a dual stream of slightly salt water. It makes an efficient little electrocution circuit. The power isn't enough to kill, but it can make a man dance while you knock the pistol out of his hand with a stick or other nonconductive agent.

There was also a ghastly weapon, borrowed from history, a combination of palmitic acid and naptha, originally called Napalm. It hadn't been particularly difficult for the colonists to get the materials for that either. For palmitic acid they substituted common soap and for the naptha, light oil that burns freely. There were plenty of those around, the fuels commonly used in ground cars, oils and gasolines.

They had come up with a brown, sticky jelly which, if you got it on you, was very difficult to get off and would burn where it stuck. A small paper sack of the stuff thrown at almost anything, personnel or building, would stick and burn a hot, deadly flare, for three or four minutes.

Then there were rocks. Stellamira is practically made of rocks. Man, woman, boy and girl, the Stellamiran colonists had formed the habit of taking out their frustrations by throwing rocks. It was target practice. They threw rocks on the way to and from the mines; they threw rocks in any free time they might have; they made games centered around throwing rocks in the bits and pieces of time they had free. The games had names and were competitive.

The complacent belief that they were dealing with unarmed colonists was a major factor in the revolution. The authorities were not really alerted until they were already defeated.

It started while we were on our way down, timed to the instant when we would be just outside detection range but well on our way to port. The internal timing of the revolution had been planned in detail; it was only the date that had changed.

The company armory and communications systems were the first targets; the riot control equipment was in the armory; and the guards and their corporation executives depended on communications from telephone to walkie-talkie. The colonists didn't depend on communications: with the kind of furious purpose there, all that was necessary was advance planning so everybody knew the general outline. After that, runners were sufficient.

Suzie gave an impromptu party that night; and since the thing had been planned for a year, she'd made a habit of impromptu parties. They were accepted as normal. That was at the glittery part of Suzie's. It was mostly for off-duty guards, though a number of executives always came.

At the height of the party, as had become a custom, some of Suzie's girls were dispatched to take refreshments and the pleasure of their company to the guards at the armory and the police station.

The dope went into all the drinks at the same time. Where a guard didn't drink fast enough, there was a sufficiency of the roller's taps around to finish the job, and the girls were alert and watching to see which was needed where.

There were a few of the guards and even one or two of the executives, that the girls had decided were "franks" instead of "finks," and for this Suzie was prepared, too. A big lipsticked *F* went on each forehead. The official franks weren't trusted too far, though. They were marked and locked in a small room at Suzie's until take-off time.

Almost as the guards went down to the dope and the taps, the girls inside opened the barred doors and colonists assigned to those jobs moved into the armory and the police station.

At the same moment, a group of colonists were frantically digging down to a main communications and power cable. The power cable was left until last. It was the communications cable that they tackled, and the two best technicians among the colonists had been put on that job, surrounded with an armed mob for possibly-needed protection.

They didn't cut the cable. That would have presented the finks with a simple problem, recognizable for what it was. Instead, they set up a random pulser that caused the automatic equipment associated with the land wires to go berserk. The random pulser kept initiating a few hundred simultaneous calls, and it not only put the communications lines out of order quite effectively, it tied corporate brains up at a critical point.

Then too, a self-powered, random-pulse sweep generator was turned on. Walkie-talkies, planetary and off-planet communications were instantly jammed, except for a single narrow band that would allow the port control facility to stay in contact with Gallagher's *Glacier* and the landing tugs as soon as the port was captured.

It was then that the power cables were cut; and that alerted the corporation to the real danger.

The war was on; but the armory and the police station were already in the hands of the colonists and a good many guards were out of action.

There were two major points that the corporation would, by its nature, defend first and with the greatest ferocity. Of these, the first would be their "treasure house," the warehouses where the starstones and rare earths waited for shipment. The second would be the port itself, where twenty freighter tugs waited to load incoming ships.

The port we had to have, but the "treasure house" was so much dross to us. The minerals would be too difficult to handle or to sell. The corporate executives should have known that, but Suzie and Gallagher gambled that the instinct to protect the treasure would be stronger than any logical reasoning they might have.

So the attack on company headquarters was a two-pronged instead of a three-pronged attack. The colonists came in through the entrances at the port and at the colonists' area, but they left the way to the warehouses open. Like sheep, the corporates ran to the treasure house. It was beautiful. They followed the instinct to guard the treasure and they followed the path of least resistance. The two were the same.

It was comparatively easy to keep them there, although the fight was not over.

There was one odd advantage the colonists had; that was the short focus of the corporate lasers. To be effective, a laser has to be focused, and it's a delicate job requiring at least half an hour. Therefore, they're prefocused. The people who had armed the guards had considered a short focal range to be optimum, as it prevented accidental destruction of company property under riot conditions.

A ground skimmer gave the advantage of range, since one could come at a target at sixty kilometers an hour; but the skimmers were in the hands of both sides by the time things were underway.

We set down, and the others scattered to their assigned tasks, whatever they were. Gallagher had given me orders to stay at the port; to see that the freighter tugs were operational and to supervise the actual evacuation. The port was swarming with colonists, and though I had a red lipstick *F* on my forehead, I had little else to tell them I was on their side. I wasn't in uniform, which may have helped.

I headed for the nearest tug. Nobody opposed me until I reached it and was opening the hatch, when about sixteen cobbers all had their hands on me at once. There was scatterlight, but that's an eerie kind of light, and it felt like a million people grabbing me.

"Gallagher," I shouted, "gave me orders—"

The hands became gentler, and I was set on my feet, unharmed as yet. Instantly I went into captain's gear. "Can any of you men handle a tug?" I asked. "We've got to get these tugs operational."

A big fellow next to me, examining the *F* on my forehead, grunted. "Don't know you, Cobber," he said grimly.

"I'm Dundee, formerly of the *Starfire*. I came down from the *Glacier* with Gallagher."

The big man gestured to an only slightly smaller one

nearby. "Get in the tug with him, Brant. If he does anything wrong, kill him."

That was all. I climbed in the hatch, Brant right behind me, but before he slammed the hatch shut I saw a company car shoot onto the field, gunning people down and heading straight our way.

I jumped to the pilot's couch and switched on the warmup, calling to Brant at the same time. "Strap down. We'll get the atomic motors bearing on that skimmer."

There wasn't time, but it didn't matter. Brant seemed to trust that answer, for he strapped in. As the screens lit they showed one of the strangest sights I've ever seen. Instead of running away, the big man and his gang had run towards the vehicle. A wave of men seemed to surge towards it, as others on the field answered his shouted instructions and joined. There were bright flashes of guns from three or four in the car, but then the skimmer was onto the wave of people, and every man within reach grabbed at its tail and flipped. The thing flipped over, its momentum barely slowed, and skated along on its top losing speed rapidly. The men ran to catch up. As they reached it, they jumped onto it, and the next time I saw the skimmer clearly, it looked like a can that had been stomped flat. There were parts of guards sticking out all over it.

By then the tug motors were warmed, and I got it up on its ground effect. Brant was standing over me at that point, not sure what I was going to do. I eased the tug carefully past the crowd and back to the one port entrance where the other skimmer had come in and where others might follow it. Then I set the tug down with its tail facing into the entrance. As the next car burst through I was ready and waiting foı it, with the tug sitting firmly, ground effect off. Under that condition I could feed about half power into the forward thrust jets without moving the vehicle. As a second skimmer came into line with the jet, it was picked up as though by a giant hand and rose nearly forty meters into the air, flipping as it went. Nobody had to stomp it as it came down.

I looked around then, and Brant was grinning. He was a heavy man, with a lined face; every line creased with dirt. He looked alive and the grin was as fierce as it was happy.

"Think you could handle this post?" I asked him, putting all the authority I knew how to put into the question.

"You show me how just once more, I'll handle it," he said.

I took ten minutes to check him out. I wasn't sure when I left that he completely understood my method, but I made him go over the sequence until I was sure he had it pat. If determination would do the job, he'd do it. So I climbed out and began looking for the big man who'd first accosted me. He seemed to be in charge.

In the soft light, with a large number of people around, one would think I'd have a trouble finding one man, but I didn't. I wandered until I found a youngster who was looking around for his next job. "Where's the big man in charge?" I asked.

"Bill?"

I nodded and he seemed satisfied. "This way," he said and took me straight to the man. It seems he was one of the runners.

I walked straight up to Bill. "I need pilots for these tugs." I said, as though I were in command, not he.

"Nice job with the tug," he commented. Then he turned to the youngster and gave him a list of names I didn't bother listening to. I pointed out a tug. "Have them meet me there," I said and turned to leave.

The big man's hand clamped down on my arm, and I turned back, ready for trouble.

"I don't know how good any of them are as pilots," he growled down at me. "If you've got a way of checking them out, check them out. They're the best we've got, but we haven't had tugs to practice on much, you know."

I nodded, then added lightly, "We don't really have a space academy here to choose from, do we?"

Instantly his face became hard. "Don't underrate 'em, mister," he said fiercely. I thought for a moment that the hand on my shoulder was going to shake me like a rat. "A slummer can't get into the academies; all he can get into is a colonist's berth. But that don't mean he can't handle a skimmer and translate on out from that, with enough drive behind him. I'm sending you the guys that have had the drive."

"I'm not underrating," I said, "but I'm not planning to mess up the tugs before we get the *Glacier* loaded, either."

He nodded then as though I'd satisfied him, and released my shoulder. I don't think it was a shove he gave me as he let go, but his hand was so powerful that it shoved when it was being gentle.

The men that reported, as fast as they got the message and could get to me, were actually beyond my expectations. Two of them I'd already seen on the *Glacier* and on the lander coming down. In spite of what Bill had said, they'd all actually handled the tugs at one time or another, when the corporation had needed more than the one or two pilots it kept on hand. I checked each one out; I kept most of them, for I needed twenty and I didn't have many more than that. I proved wrong about one, but I didn't find that out until he got one group of passengers safely aboard the *Glacier* and was landing for his next set. He may have known what he was doing; it may have been a malfunction. It was also possible that somebody in the tower had managed to readjust one of the short-range lasers and had done some damage. I saw the machine stagger while it was still two hundred meters in the air and then veer off course.

I speculated later that it might have been sheer luck or real guts on the part of the pilot, but I'll never know. After the tug staggered and veered off course, it dropped a little and gained speed. When it passed through the executive tower it must have been doing a thousand kilometers an hour; it was probably as much the sonic wave in front of it as the actual mass of the ship that blew the tower apart.

I understand the colonists officially decided later that the pilot was a hero and had done it on purpose, but I've never really been able to make up my mind. He could even have been dead of a laser shot before the sequence of action took place, though it seems unlikely that ship was guided.

By then the revolution was basically a mopping-up operation, and my part in it had settled into a routine of getting passengers and all the luggage they could carry into tugs and into the *Glacier*. I decided to leave the tug guarding the gate where it was, just in case. That left us with eighteen freighters plus Gallagher's lander, and we kept them moving. It was probably more to the credit of the people who had taken over the traffic control system of the port than it was to my own efforts that we were able to keep the tugs moving, one after the other, at a slow but steady pace. I don't yet know whether it was days or hours later when we began loading the tugs more and more with equipment and less and less with people.

I began to get foggy and was shoved aside to a corner to sleep for a while. When I woke, the job was still going on, and I started doggedly back to it.

One of Suzie's girls barred my way. "Not yet, Captain," she said. "You go over there and go through that chow line first."

In astonishment I saw tables and fires. Food was being served with hot drinks, by Suzie's girls. They were efficient and cheerful. There were deep circles under their eyes, as well as bandages on their bodies. One girl was on a crutch improvised out of a board and some rags for padding; she was working right along with the rest. I realized that Suzie's girls would have been the ones best organized on the planet, the ones handling the mechanical details, such as food and record keeping. Next to the food area was a group on old boxes with notebooks and paper.

There were few refugees left on the field, and they were trickling one or two at a time into the continously loading tugs. But now the tugs were taking mostly heavy equipment, ton after ton of it: mining equipment, air powered drills, self-propelled atomic supplies, bulldozers and graders. There was both deep-mining and strip-mining equipment, to say nothing of ton after ton of ropes, explosives and less-complicated machinery that would be useful in settling a planet.

Eventually, I turned to check what was to be loaded on the next ship, and found there wasn't a full load left to go. I got the loading started and then put in a call to Port Control. I told them that no more than two of the tugs aloft were to be allowed to come back. The rest were now ordered to secure themselves onto the *Glacier* after they unloaded. We weren't going to strip the port completely. One of the two tugs I allowed to return was to remain with the one still sitting at the gate.

Aboard the last tug we loaded the remaining personnel: the control-room men, the loaders themselves and three of Suzie's girls who hadn't gone up yet. Gallagher had gone up some time before. I looked around for Suzie.

She and Seth were at a distance, working over something on the ground; it looked like a radio antenna of some sort. I called to them. Suzie waved absently, intently standing over Seth, who was pushing down on something that seemed not to give. Then it gave, and at the same moment my attention was distracted by a number of explosions in the port area.

I ran towards Suzie and Seth, who seemed to be gathering whatever piece of equipment they'd been working on.

"The war's started up again," I shouted even before I was near enough. "We're too few down here now. Come on."

Seth already had most of the equipment in his arms, and was trailing Suzie as she turned to go past me, walking fast and hard. I turned with her, and she looked up at me.

"That wasn't more war," she said, her eyes bright. "That was us. We've just destroyed the evidence of how the *spontaneous uprising* was engineered."

That startled me, but I didn't have much time to think. Suzie and Seth ducked into the hatch of the final tug, and I was turning to climb in when I realized, more by instinct than anything else, that there was one person left behind.

I turned to wave at the tug sitting next to the skimmer gate, to see, through the gate, a group of about twenty skimmers come roaring down the lane towards the port. Apparently some of the company finks had realized that nearly everyone was gone, and that, as we were evacuating the last of the people, we would be vulnerable. They were out to make the most of it.

There was nothing I could do but watch and hold my breath. Then, as the first of the skimmers came opposite the tug, it went hurtling into the air from the blast of the thruster, and I found myself breathing again, though the air had an acrid sting of smoke. The paint of the tug behind me was scorching, and I realized that the corporates had had time to refocus their lasers. One after another, six of the skimmers, going too fast to stop, were hurled into the air; they landed in a heap. The other skimmers managed to stop.

The tug I was beside began maneuvering to put its blast towards the gate, but not on it, for that would have isolated our tug. The rest of the skimmers saw it and were backing away. The hatch of the tug by the gate flung open; a figure emerged from it and started to run towards me.

Brant was almost beside me before I turned to climb into our tug and stumbled over the scorched and crumpled body of one of the girls.

I stood and stared. The laser shot must have missed me by micrometers. I almost wished it hadn't. She looked like a small doll, thrown into the fire and lying, half consumed, beside the ashes.

Then Brant was pushing me from behind. I stumbled on into the tug, sick with rage but knowing that my job was to get the last ship up.

The trip to the planet that the colonists decided to call Refuge was rough, but uneventful. Yet it had one detour that came as a complete surprise to me.

It was rough for the refugees, but they seemed to think the discomfort a small price to pay. I did not hear a single complaint; the management that they organized kept the complaints to themselves, if there were any. At Gallagher's suggestion, we left them alone. "They've got to handle their own problems," he told me. "Best they start right now." We went down together, about once daily, on inspection tours, but that was all.

Suzie's girls had a smallish compartment forward of the big holds and aft of the bridge. I had wondered vaguely what the relationship between the girls and the other women would be when they were all together in the hold and was rather relieved at the separation. I gathered, too, that the girls' compartment was closed to business, which seemed quite sensible on shipboard. Some problems, I told myself, have to work themselves out in more spacious areas.

I had a lot to learn.

Suzie herself shared Gallagher's cabin, and Seth bunked in with me. Seth was Suzie's right hand man, and her devoted servant. It was a strange relationship; more that of a dog to his mistress than anything else, and I'm rather sure it wasn't anything else. He was the brawn for her brain, and quite content with the role. I think it fulfilled him far more than any other relationship could have done.

Gallagher was setting our course; Suzie was in the copilot's couch. I was in what might have been termed the navigator's couch, a couch with just a place for writing, without controls. Seth was in the tiny galley fixing coffee. We were all bushed, but far too exuberant to relax.

Suzie was lighting a cigarette as she said quietly to Gallagher, "Set your course for Durango."

He looked at her in surprise. "Thought we'd get the colonists to their planet, then you and the girls would take some time off at Betsy Ann with me," he said. "It's time for a vacation."

Suzie shook her head. "Durango," she said. "We're going to escape from you. You forced us to go along when you evacuated Stellamira, so there'd be no witnesses. But we found some guns and stuff and hijacked you and made you drop us there."

He nodded slowly. "It's a good story," he said, "and you'll be welcomed, because the local talent isn't much and it isn't many, and it isn't set up like you set up. I worked on Durango as an electrical engineer for several months a while back. But why bother? We can whomp up a good story when you're ready. Anyhow," he added savagely, "one revolution ought to be enough for any one or all of you. You could–"

She smiled. "That one," she said, "was for my husband. The next one will be for my baby, and then there are all the other kids we might have had. The company killed them as surely as they killed Jack and the baby. The rest of the girls feel the same way. It's not a single corporation we're after, it's the system. It's the system that killed our men and our way of life. It's the system that's got to go.

She went on, and her voice had a dreamy quality to it. "It's not even that the system has to go. It's the system we're going to kill–us–with our bare hands if we could. With our bare asses since we can't. We're murderers and we're pragmatists, but the murderer part comes first, with each and every one of us."

I was staring at her, dumbfounded, as she leaned back, seemingly relaxed, smoking. She was slender and quite beautiful in her intent way.

"Dublin," she said quietly, "you're just a revolutionist. You're a revolutionist because you don't like the system, and because revolution is more fun than any other game. You're not a killer, but one revolution won't satisfy you, any more than killing one company–and the Stellamira Company is dead. Its assets," she chuckled, "are disbursed. It won't be able to come back, though another company will take over. Until we kill the system, other companies will take over.

"Killing the system will satisfy you. You're just a revolutionist. One revolution will only whet your appetite; it's addictive. But you'll be satisfied when the system's licked.

"That's the difference. You'll be satisfied and turn to something else. We, all of us, will be finished, when that happens. What you do after you're finished is something I haven't started to think about yet. Maybe I'll come to Betsy Ann then. It's a long *then;* don't wait for me."

"Oh, I won't wait," Gallagher answered lightly. "Maybe I'll even let you finish this one off before I kidnap you out and make you fight 'em my way."

"Hell," Suzie said. "Your way's fine, but it's not nearly as efficient. You're envious because you aren't equipped to be as efficient at the revolution business as we are, and the idea of women running the show still shocks you a bit." She started to laugh, and Gallagher started to laugh. Then Seth's voice came from the galley.

"Gallagher could get into your revolutions the way I have," he said. There was laughter under his slow voice. "There's always room for a man in a house."

At that they began to laugh, deep, satisfying laughs. It wasn't funny to me. It was bloody, horrible and sad, and we'd just left a real blood bath in which people had been killed. It was killing Suzie was avenging. It wasn't funny.

But underneath I could hear Gallagher's voice from my memory, *It takes a free man to laugh, and it takes laughter to make a man free.* Perhaps that was it. But they weren't free; they were bound to a life harder than any I had dreamed of, a life of revolution and murder. It wasn't funny.

Then I put my oar in. "I guess I'd better go down to Durango with you," I said. "I could have been kidnapped the same way you were, and helped with the hijacking. Then I could get a ship back to Earth and report to the Space Commission. . . ." I trailed off, for the laughter had stopped and they were all looking at me kindly, like parents interrupted in a grownup discussion by a childish question.

"Harald," Suzie said gently, "you'd be clapped into prison the instant you set foot on Durango. They'd signal your company, and the company would reply, and you'd be in irons. You haven't the—talents—we have to make you welcome any other way."

"But how am I going to get to Earth and report so that this whole situation changes?" I asked. "That's the real job that's got to be done."

Suzie opened her mouth, then closed it again. Seth started to speak, but while he was organizing his words, Gallagher interrupted. "Time enough," he said with a finality in his tone that ended the discussion. "Time enough, when we get to it."

V

We dropped Suzie and her gang at Durango and the colonists at Refuge. We were driving for Beta Antolaris.

They call it Betsy Ann. That's the name of the second system that was explored by Dr. Antolar's original survey, back when the Antolaric drive was first invented. It's also the name of the planet, the one that Gallagher colonized.

Beta Antolaris is a nine-planet system, comparable in most respects to the Sol system itself, including a large ring of asteroids in the fifth orbit. It surprised me that Gallagher didn't go directly in to the third planet on approaching the system, but instead put us into orbit around one of the outer giants and radioed for a taxi.

"But why orbit so far out?" I asked, "and why not use your own landing craft?"

Gallagher frowned at me. "Since when have you tried any interplanetary jumps with a landing tug? They're not designed to do anything but very minor maneuvers in space. It would take too long to get it in, and you know it. Anyhow, the taxis are running fairly regular, and it won't take one much out of its way to come past and fetch us.

"As for orbiting out here," he went on quickly before I could interrupt, "why, the *Glacier* wouldn't have a life expectancy of two years, if I orbited her often around a standard planet." The phrase startled me, coming from Gallagher, despite the fact that it's the usual term for a planet in all respects similar to Earth.

"It would melt?"

Gallagher shook his head. "Evaporate," he said. "I sort of think we may be on Betsy Ann for a while, and it's better to leave the *Glacier* here in deep freeze."

I did a quick calculation in my head and nodded. "So you can extend a parking orbit quite a long time out here," I said, "and not be using any power."

While I sat thinking, Gallagher was inching us into orbit, correcting and recorrecting in an attempt to perfect our swing around the ice world. Then, just as he was making a final maneuver, there was a feminine voice on the radio and a red light on the control panel.

Gallagher reached over and switched on the radio transmitter. His voice crackled out, "Damn it, sheer that taxi away until I get this berg properly in orbit. You're overloading my detectors."

"Sorry, honey, but has it occurred to you that you might be overloading my detectors, too? I was doing a scientific—"

"Scientific be damned. I'm glad you're here anyhow. You can give us a lift back to Betsy Three."

"Okay, Gallagher."

Gallagher hadn't mentioned his name, and how the pilot of the other ship knew who it was, I wasn't sure. Of course, Gallagher was the only one in space that was running around in an iceberg for a ship, but it hardly seemed to me that anybody on a security watch would simply take it for granted that it was Gallagher's ship. I said as much, but Gallagher only laughed.

"You're perfectly right, Harold, if that were all of it. But I assure you that we've got just as good IFFs on our ships as any that the corporations have on theirs."

I felt deflated. Of course, no traffic pattern would be set up without proper "Identification, Friend or Foe" transponders, if only because they make the operation of computer controllers much simpler.

To hide my discomfort, I began fiddling with the dials on the telescreen that showed a picture of nearby space, and almost at once I managed to overlap the red blinking dot with an actual picture of the taxi. Suddenly I strained forward. "Hey, that's not a taxi. That's—"

"A nickel-steel meteor," Gallagher finished for me dryly, "though you can't properly call it a meteor, until it actually touches atmosphere."

I held onto my voice for a moment, but then it came out in spite of me. "Crude construction," I said, though not haughtily. I'd learned at least that much. "Seems like you like to use space debris for transportation."

"Nothing like using what's handy," he answered laconically, "though it won't be a ship long."

He pushed the button for a final maneuver and then checked the orbit. Satisfied, he turned back to the radio and lit up the screen.

It lighted to show a freckle-faced girl probably not over sixteen. The rest of her, under a tight pair of coveralls, gave her about twenty years, possibly a few more.

"Okay, Cricket," Gallagher said, "you can taxi on in now."

"You forgot to turn on your homing signal," she told

him cheerfully. "Should I home in on you as a derelict for practice, or are you going to make it easy for me?"

"Didn't think you'd need a signal after that last contact," he said, switching it on. "However, you have it now. I'd hate to try your guesstimating too far."

The ship ranged in fast and soon we were shoving out the air lock. A few *spuuuts* on our suit rockets put us up against a tiny corridor cut into the meteor; it was hardly more than a slit capable of accommodating us one at a time. Not far back, the corridor went through an air lock and then broadened into a chamber. There was the girl at the controls; nobody else was in sight, and there was no exit except the one we'd come in by.

She was a pretty thing, but seemed very young. She gestured to us to strap down on foam mats on the floor beside her couch, since obviously the ship was not equipped for the convenience of passengers.

Gallagher took off his helmet and I followed his lead.

"Good to see you back, Dublin," she said, as he stretched out on the foam mat, strapping down. I followed suit.

"This is Harald Dundee," he said, "former captain in the Solspace Merchant Fleet. He's stopping off for a visit on his way through to Earth to complain to the Space Commission about how one of the colonies was being run."

She nodded noncomittally in my direction and said, "Hold on." She shifted us into drive, a type of drive I wasn't expecting. I felt like somebody had just stepped on me with a twelve-foot shoe. The foam beneath me squeezed thin and dropped me into a pocket that I couldn't have gotten out of if I'd wanted to.

It went on that way for the best part of twenty minutes and then slacked off to a more standard pressure. Then the girl locked the board, got out of her acceleration couch and said, "How about some food?"

My system was telling me how many things it wanted to get rid of before it went through something like that again, and I made a quick dash for the 'fresher.

The whole structure, as far as I could tell, was a prefabricated unit that could accommodate three people in a pinch, but was designed for a one-man operation. I realized that it was simply shoved into a hole that passed through the center of gravity of the asteroid.

"This thing isn't really designed as a ship, is it?" I asked as I joined them in the tiny galley.

"Well now, that depends on how you look at it." Gallagher waved his hand around the compact compartment. "The power unit here is well designed for the purpose. But the purpose, as you may have guessed, is to come out here and pick up chunks of nickel-steel that we need back on Betsy Three. It's not particularly difficult to bore a hole in just the right place and set the drive unit right into it. Then it becomes a rather slow and cumbersome ship. But take the same drive unit without this hull, and it's a damn' fast pice of machinery."

The trip wasn't as brief as I had expected it to be, because we were using one of the most basic drives that have ever been built, a simple rocket-power device operated on nuclear energy. It took us nearly two weeks in the cramped quarters to get to Betsy Three.

Gallagher and the girl knew each other so well that they didn't bother to use names and it took me two days to find out that Cricket's name was Mary Joinson.

After discovering her name, I asked her a question. "How do you land these things anyhow?"

"We fly them down, of course."

My estimate of weight came up and hit me over the head at that point. It didn't matter how many gees it was good for, one simply didn't land fifty or a hundred million tons of steel all in one chunk.

As I thought about it, I broke out in a cold sweat. A

chunk of steel that size wouldn't have area enough compared to its mass to slow down appreciably in any atmosphere I'd ever heard of. Even if it came out of orbit at a considerably lower velocity than any I thought would be practical, the thing would make a big dent wherever it hit.

"I think I'd rather get out and walk," I said.

"Well, okay. If you insist, we'll give you a parachute."

Somehow the landing operation that would be upcoming got to be a standard joke. I kept advancing theories of how such a chunk could be landed, and they kept shooting holes in them. By the time we had reached the planet and Gallagher and I were told to lie down on the acceleration mats, I was in a real sweat. I was convinced that there was no way at all to land a chunk of steel and that we were all on the verge of suicide. The fact that Cricket had landed such a craft, by her own statement, a number of times, helped intellectually, but it didn't do a thing for the autonomic sensors in my stomach that kept telling me I was about to die at the hands of a girl-child who was at the controls of a real spaceship, instead of the toy one she should have been playing with.

She didn't say much. She just alerted somebody that we were coming in.

Gallagher seemed relaxed.

As a method of easing my nervousness, I kept trying to stare at the unpainted wall of the tiny chamber, but my eyes kept straying back past Cricket's youthful figure towards the dials. There was nothing for me to hear but the susurrus ventilating fan and the ship's radio.

I had forced my attention back to the wall, seeking some imperfection to focus on, when I was brought back sharply by a raucous voice on the radio.

"Ground Control to Taxi X-9. That's a good orbit, Cricket, but you're about nine kilometers too high."

"Okay, Ground Control. Dropping nine kilo."

I gasped and clenched my teeth as Cricket's nimble fingers danced across the board and I felt a crunch of drive thrust that nearly put me through the floor, followed by the sensation of the ship swinging in free fall; then there was another crunch. The reassuring chatter of the radio penetrated my self-centered attention.

"That's good. Locked on. We've got you, Cricket. Cut drive." With each radio phrase there was Cricket's calm reply.

I didn't understand those particular communications, but that didn't bother me. We were safely in orbit now, scarcely a hundred kilometers above the surface. I was relaxed and waiting for the order to unstrap.

Things went wrong with the feel again, and my gaze jumped to the dials.

"We're falling!" I gasped. "Falling like a rock!"

Gallagher's voice penetrated my preoccupation; he was calm and unconcerned. "Relax, Dundee. We're being landed by a new system we use on this planet."

The girl was obviously going to do nothing. While I reassured myself that she and Gallagher were aboard, too, and surely not risking their lives in what appeared to me suicidal inactivity, there was, obviously, something that I didn't understand. I clenched my teeth and tried to convince all my senses that the ship was under some kind of control I didn't know about and that all was well. Intellect doesn't control the sweat glands or the adrenals, though, and I was slippery with sweat and jittery with adrenalin, and tingling.

I suddenly realized that I was tingling with a tingle induced from an external source and that I'd been feeling it for some time. The tingle was building up to a resonance point in the meteor itself; the whole thing rang like a gong. The sound went on and on, and then tapered off into a tingle again. And I heard Cricket's calm voice speaking into the radio.

"First resonance point."

My intellect got a bit more control over my autonomic system then. Whatever landing procedure was in use was at least familiar to those in charge. There was some faint hope in the back of my mind that we weren't about to be killed.

The R.A.I. began to show a distinct decline over the last few moments and was no longer tripping into the red; and my gaze went to the navigation scope.

The planetary image that it presented was roughly that of a half moon, with a terminator, probably the dawn line, almost directly beneath us. We were swinging into the night side.

As I watched, the progress of the terminator across the planetary disk slowed and slowed, and there was still a bare limb of light showing by the time it paused and moved slightly back. The main visible feature of the planet had become a lightning storm immediately beneath us.

The storm began to swell with our descent, and the intermittent flashes of lightning that had at first appeared to be a bar fanned out into a coil, a shaped funnel, beneath us. Again, my whole being was assaulted by the audible effect of the meteor going into resonance with some external force, and then we were beneath the top of the storm and I could see that it was not a storm, but an orderly network of electrical flashes coiling around us and pulsing as though we were riding a loudspeaker.

The sound went on and on, and in the navigation scope faint features of the planetary surface were becoming visible; the bowl-shaped horizon was swinging up and around us.

Then we were down with only the faintest of jars. The altimeter read zero.

I must have been shaking and white as a sheet, but through my daze I heard Cricket's voice.

"Okay, Ground Control, we're down. Check ejection orientation."

"Ejection orientation is on target," the radio assured her. "Proceed with ejection."

I was trying to find my voice to ask Gallagher what they were talking about, when a heavy blow slammed into the entire surface of my body and I was crushed under acceleration as though I were being launched by a primitive rocket.

Then we were falling. There was a distinct splash and a reorientation; the control room settled into a quiet bobbing motion on its side. Gallagher, Cricket and I were strapped to our mats and couch against a wall, the controls were on the floor, and the bulkhead was the ceiling.

I stayed there shaking, until the inner bulkhead swung down and the handholds on its outer surface were ready to serve as a ladder.

A voice called down, "Okay, you guys, you can come out now."

Gallagher and Cricket had got themselves unstrapped and were stepping carefully across the controls. I couldn't seem to find the buckles, and with a tinkle of laughter our young captain reached over and helped me unstrap as though I were a typical passenger.

"Come on, big boy," she said, "time to get your ground legs working."

Then Gallagher heaved himself up the ladder, and the whole cabin swayed in response to his motion. My feet nearly swayed out from under me.

"Steady as she goes. We'll be out of this tube in a minute."

With a steadying hand, Mary helped me towards the bulkhead, and I scrambled up, finding a short rope ladder within my reach and a walkway at the top of it.

Outside, I realized that the walkway was on a crane, its huge arm extending above me. Magnetic grapples were firmly secured to the tiny, tubular cabin which was floating in a small body of water. The cabin was scarcely more than a piece of stovepipe expanded to accommodate the cargo of people.

The meteorite itself was nowhere in sight.

VI

The place was alive; there seemed a special zest in the air. There's a difference in the people too. On Earth, one was a citizen of this or that and a member of this or that, but spoke of *they* when referring of the factors that really control life on the planet.

On Betsy Ann, every individual owned the planet; it was theirs. They didn't speak of *they*, they spoke of *we*. It has a different sound.

We were sitting in a workmen's canteen, on a rise overlooking the port, or industrial complex; I'm not sure which is the better term.

I was beginning to understand the theory behind the landing, not only meteors of the size we'd come in on, but also of interstellar ships, even if they are as delicate as eggs. I was as impressed as a schoolboy; I'd been expecting a primitive economy.

It *was* a primitive economy, in a way, for it was spotty. There hadn't been time yet to produce tools for consumer goods, but they were underway in directions Earth hadn't dreamed of for generations.

The landing system was from what Gallagher called their *solar tap*. They were tapping the electric potential that exists between a planet and the belts of ionized particles caught in the planet's magnetic field. The landing system was part of a larger system that produced, from one site, enough electricity to power the entire continent on a broadcast basis.

Earth hadn't had broacast power, though it was known, because the production of power was geared to installations that didn't have sufficient potential to use the airwaves for more than communications, such as Tri-D. But the power potential in the solar tap was so great that it could be thrown away on an inverse-square basis and still run anything thousands of miles distant, from a manufacturing complex to a skimmer.

The landing system was a gigantic web of laser beams, angled upwards and focused to create a huge electrical discharge spiral that used magnetic induction and repulsion to bring the meteors in. They could bring in any metallic ship as well on the huge spiral, even though the interstellar ships were comparatively fragile, for the gentle cradle of the magnetic induction-repulsion system could raise or lower ships as evenly as a freight elevator might bring down a crate of delicate electronic equipment.

The solar-tap landing system was a magnificent sight, and as long as I was on Betsy Ann I never ceased to be caught into a tremendous awe and delight when it was turned on. It wasn't turned on now. Only the one beam from atop the central pyramid pulsed its broadcast power and sang its deep-throated song.

There was a central pyramid supplying power on each of the three continents of Betsy Ann, I was told; those would soon be supplemented with satellite pyramids needed to create landing systems on each continent. Meantime, the equipment needed to convert Betsy Ann from a desert planet into a lush, green one could operate anywhere on broadcast power.

"But why haven't they gotten this on Earth?" I finally asked.

"Stop-motion thinking," Gallagher answered, "Bureaucratic, cosmocorp, governmental thinking. Anyhow, Earth's already built a steel-frame civilization, and she'd have to use some real know-how to introduce a tap without frying people because of the resonance factor. It's best to stick to stone or plastic buildings when you're using a tap."

"But where's the meteor we came down in, and what's your plan for it?" I asked. "That's plenty of steel."

"Over there." He pointed to where I could see a glow in the sky at the center of the port complex. "We can use steel; we just use it with know-how."

I stared at the glow in the sky. "Surely it couldn't have been that hot?"

"The glow? That's not the meteor, that's the melting tap in operation. But the meteor did come in at a red heat, at least in its surface layers. You see, we land them in the furnace. As soon as everybody's clear, they change the frequency of the induction current and start melting them down. It saves quite a bit of time, and time's our most precious commodity. The energy we're not worried about; that we've got in plenty. But it takes time to reheat, and if the ejection mechanism doesn't work, it's a two or three hours' setback to lose the heat that was built up during descent, so that we can get the people out, and then we have to reheat the darned thing so we can melt it down."

"Isn't that a rather expensive way to get steel?" I asked.

He grinned. "You're just not used to the idea of real planetary power," he said. "Those meteors can be brought in, melted down, and ready to use for tools at a cost per ton of, say, a hundredth of a solar credit."

"There are lots of corporations on Earth," Cricket interposed, "that would gladly pay S¢100 for the same ton, delivered on Earth."

It was a strange economy there on Betsy Ann. There was broadcast electric power, a great improvement over the puny atomic power stations of Earth. Yet we were sitting in a primitive cabin, a crude construction of logs laid together to surround a restaurant space and heated by a wood fire in a stone fireplace. Crude as the surroundings were, I was comfortable. The open fire was a cheerful thing to watch after the starship cabin. In contrast, the lights were globes of gas ignited by broadcast power.

The people, too, were oddly contrasting. I found that I, a captain and a graduate engineer from Earth's best academies, was one of the more inept in some ways, though I did manage to shine in others.

Not much time had passed when a man wandered in, was introduced and joined us; I didn't think much of it. He was tall, stooped, thin and about forty. Dr. Strathmore was his name and the title surprised me. I hadn't expected doctors among the people there, but my surprise passed quickly. He asked questions with a voluble curiosity that was unexpected in a total stranger.

While we were talking, three others walked in. Later others came in, singly and in pairs. They were all introduced, several of them as doctor this or that. I gave up trying to get the names straight. They were all firing questions about Earth conditions, whether there were any changes in attitude, what changes there had been in colonial trading policies and the like. The questions were coming so fast I didn't have much time to think about names.

Then a rotund man walked in, and I recognized his face from the Tri-D even before he was introduced. He was Dr. Lamar Jacobs.

"But—but you're a PhD., Doctor," I said. "You're the

head of the Institute for Astrophysics! You're in the lunar laboratories!"

He smiled cheerfully. "No," he said, "I'm on Betsy Ann. I've been here almost a year."

Gallagher was laughing, and his laughter rang through the small cabin, joined by others. "You think these were all medical doctors?" he asked finally through his laughter.

"Of course," I said stiffly, getting embarrassed. "It did occur to me that you had quite a large number of medical men here, but then, I don't know the size of your colony."

The colony had been growing. Once Gallagher had founded an independent colony, the colonists began to arrive. How each one got there was a separate story; why each one got there was a separate story too, except for the one thing they had in common: they wanted to live and work freely.

They wanted to be free of the perpetual secrecy, regulation, and frustration of the impersonal systems that dominated Earth.

The ones who had come to debrief me and to find out what talents I might have that would prove useful were mostly scientists and engineers. But every type of person in a civilization was represented by those who had found their way to Betsy Ann.

"There's a sort of rule of thumb that we've found has worked out in which way people get here," Gallagher said. "If you're a conservative independent, let's call it, you head for a planet and get word to me. But if you're crackling mad at the way civilization's grown on Earth and its tame planets, if you're a no-holds-barred, let's-get-out-there-and-see-what-we-can-make-happen type, if you're mad because the government and the corporations control space—then you pirate a ship and head for Betsy Ann."

All the time, Cricket sat there as though she belonged, her little-girl appearance belied by the ability with which she joined in the technical conversation. Her light, bantering tone added as sparkling and warm a note to the surroundings as the glowing lamps.

When the owner of the canteen came over, bringing a guitar and handing it to her, the contrast was even stranger. She curled up, then, over the guitar and forgot anybody else was around while she crooned to it, tuning it. Meanwhile, the conversation went on, slightly muted, as though in respect to the guitar and its mistress.

Finally, Cricket began humming and strumming, and then, in a slender voice, she began to sing.

It was then, I think, that I despairingly fell in love with Cricket Joinson. It was despairingly because I realized I was old-fashioned, because this was a modern world with modern technology and I was Earth-bound in spite of Earth's rigid senilities. Gallagher had said, *Let's consider the value, and then we'll discuss the price.* All I'd been looking at for many years was the price; I had given no thought to the value of things. I sat feeling hopelessly without value because I had refused to pay the price.

Then I took myself to task mentally. They could have freedom, but my job, I told myself severely, was to get back to Earth and force the facts of the colonies down the Space Commission's throat, to make them listen and change. I didn't say it aloud; I was quite sure they would laugh at me. But I felt that would be my contribution to a new civilization, and when it had been made and if I still felt the way I was beginning to feel, then perhaps I would have paid the price of entrance into Betsy Ann, for I felt I must pay before I had the right to join them. I wanted to pay the price in a manner that included a loyalty to Earth, although it had shown itself to be stupid, backward and intolerant.

I continued to answer the questions as eagerly as they were asked, and my answers were all pitched to show reasoning behind the muddleheadedness that they showed. I think the men questioning me were impatient with that for a long time before Jim Strathmore spoke up.

"Dundee," he said kindly, "stupidity always has its rationale. That makes it none the less stupid. Let me put it more strongly," he went on quietly. "Suicide always has its rationale, its justifications, its reasons. It's still suicide.

"Earth," he said, "is committing suicide. We all know the rationale. We've all escaped from Earth. You can buy it and say 'poor pathetic Earth is acting stupidly,' or you can refuse it and say that if Earth wants to be pathetic, the only way to stop the trend is to establish a terminal so strong that Earth has to forget suicide and get on with the business of competing. Now, if Earth continues to commit suicide to the bitter end, well, it will be dead. But the race of man won't be dead, because we're here. So, though we can't prevent suicide of the planet, we can prevent suicide of the race, and we're doing just that.

"If Earth wants to notice that there's life to be lived and competition to be had, then she can rise from her sickbed and get back into the business of living and growing and being vital."

I was shocked. I hadn't thought of Earth as a "poor, pathetic planet," though I may have thought of the crowded millions there as pathetic people. When Lamar Jacobs said that the poor, pathetic people of Earth were that way by their own refusal to change the situation, and that they were trying to create colonies of pathetic people in their own image, I was inclined to agree with him.

I learned a lot that night, although I was answering the questions. I learned a lot in the next few weeks, and though one hijacked ship came through and I knew I could go out with the ferry and take passage back to Earth, I made excuses to myself and stayed on Betsy Ann.

Cricket ferried me around the planet on her business which seemed to include a lot more than just piloting meteors. Much later, I learned that she'd been shunted off her normal routine to go on errands for the purpose of ferrying me about. Gallagher seemed to take my report to Earth more seriously than I thought; he wanted to be sure I'd make a full report.

I saw the Beta and Gamma tap stations. Since Betsy Ann is mostly desert, the most vital work I saw was where tap-powered machines were digging dams in desert areas, to stop the water that's always below the surface of a desert, and force it back to the surface.

I also saw the method, probably copied from Gallagher's *Glacier,* by which they brought drinking water to the port and other centers. They froze ice ships at the poles and floated them down to the desert areas to melt there. This supplemented the dams and wells until the systems were completed and could take over the job. It was a far less expensive method than getting clear water from sea water.

But it was the landing system of the big Alpha Tap that held me fascinated. When it went into operation at night, the faint play of lights that were the melting tap would dim and pale and for a period of perhaps two minutes the lamps of the area nearly went out as well.

Then the horizon would light up again, and instead of the pale single streamer that flickered, instead of the omnipresent *chee-ops; chee-ops* that was the song of the tap in its normal operation, the huge, ladderlike structure of beams would flame into the sky, and the chorus of the other pyramidal structures would join into a deep subsonic roar like the after rumble of thunder, interspersed with harmonics that were more like a drum than the oboe note of the single tap.

On the flaming ladder against the night, a darker mass would slowly make its way, a giant figure stepping up with improbable smoothness, lifted by the powerful chorus of light and sound, until it reached the top of the ladder, a bright point. Then its trajectory would curve, and it would sweep off and away, out of sight.

The ladder had a pull to it, a pull that was as strong as space itself and as irresistible. I longed to be out in the starways, to climb those golden rungs and fling myself into the freedom of space. The sight of the tap gave me a longing for the farther stars, for infinity, perhaps. It was an unreasoning reaction. Safety is on a planet; space is dangerous. But the pull of that ladder was a deeper pull than I could withstand. I knew I would be going out again.

Once, when I'd stood enmeshed in the powerful web as it lifted a ship out to the stars until sight and sound of it were gone, and the low, pulsing beat of the *angor-watt; angor-watt* had been replaced by the *chee-ops* of the single tap, I turned to find Cricket beside me, staring not at the tap, but at me. There was an expression on her face that made me take her in my arms, oblivious of the canteen and the people there.

"You'll go with me?" I asked. "I have to go."

Her voice against my chest was muffled. "Not to Earth," she said, "not to Earth for any reason."

I let her go then, but I felt a loss.

Ships were going out to Refuge now with some regularity, and although most of the trading was one-way, with Betsy Ann sending goods and accepting Refugian script, since they'd not had time to produce a return trade ability. Yet the returning ships were carrying things needed on Betsy Ann, and I learned that the black-market traders in the colonies were accepting the Refugian script at nearly face value, in spite of the fact that it was known that Refuge would pay Stellamira as its first priority. That spoke a lot for Gallagher and for the feeling that was permeating the starways, a heady feeling. I think the Refugian script was actually considered a better long-term value than that of the company colonies; those who could were banking it for future use.

Gallagher was not handling the trade now. Betsy Ann had its own ships, and though they could only trade in the black market, the black market was a flourishing thing. It had its dangers, but ways were found.

Gallagher himself was still on Betsy Ann, though I saw little of him and actually forgot to ask what he was about.

I was both surprised and pleased when he walked into the canteen one night while Cricket and I were having coffee; we had just returned from one of her business trips.

"The *Glacier's* setting course for Durango," Gallagher said without even a greeting.

I felt the smile on my face freezing. I had been excusing myself from finding a way to Earth, but my course was set. I had set that course myself, I told myself, and I couldn't deviate.

I held my longings firmly in check, and I held my voice light and bantering, while I said, "Thought you'd forgotten all about Durango, Dublin."

He looked at me queerly. "When you've got a goal," he said finally, "you can rush the goal and lose, or you can take your time and make plans and get them ready. That gives you a good chance. I've been tooling up."

"If you'll have me," I heard myself answering, "I'm going along." I felt rather than heard Cricket let out a sigh, and it could have been one of relief. I don't know.

Gallagher looked from me to her and back to me. "Thought you were set for Earth and the Space Commission," he said.

I guess that's when I first took a good look at what I was doing and why. I hardly recognized my own reasoning or even my own voice. I was watching at a great distance a change revealed that had already taken place.

"Going to the authorities on Earth is a waste of time. "I think," I said slowly, "that I've got sense and guts, though it's late showing. If you think so too, I'll go along."

I stopped then, but there was a silence, and the silence continued. Finally I went on.

"There's the price of anything," I quoted Gallagher slowly, "and then there's the value. I been sort of fooled about the value, or maybe I wanted to be fooled—the price is pretty high. But I think I'll opt for the value and pay the price, if I can find a way to make the trade."

Then Gallagher threw back his head and laughed, a loud, happy, deep laugh that had a satisfying ring to it. Cricket was laughing too, with tears sparkling in her eyes as she laughed.

And I sat there trying to see what was funny. It didn't seem funny to me at all, just a matter of pride and value and price I knew would be high.

Gallagher rose, still laughing, and he looked down at me, and though I almost resented the look, it was pleasant deep inside.

"We lift in two hours," he said. "You two won't need to bring anything except a few clothes. Heavy duty clothes," he added, "boots and field wear." Then he turned and left.

VII

Déjà vu is a strange phenomenon. I've never had it before or since, but during the time we spent on Durango it occurred again and again. Maybe it was continous.

It was as though we had been there before, doing the same things at the same time and the same places over and over again, to the point where I knew what was happening just before it happened.

I seldom had any feeling that I wanted to interfere with what was going on. But even at the times when I did want to and did interfere, it was as though I'd done it before and was destined to do it again.

Durango was one of the more settled planets, more settled by three or four generations. It had small but thriving cities, and a compromise between the company cities and the independents that broke into open warfare on occasion, but that was mostly quiescent hostility. It was in many ways like the relationship between England and its American colonies in early history. The company owned the planet by right of grant from the Space Commission, so it had the right to tax and to police the planet. But the colonists of the second, third and fourth generations were no longer indentured servants because a son was not responsible for the debts of his father. Earth wanted to keep the colonies as sources of raw materials, and to reserve for herself the right of manufacture. Durango would have been much better off to manufacture her own needs, but it wasn't permitted.

By law, the independents who had won their way free of any indebtedness to the company and preferred to support themselves rather than work for the company had the right to do so; they were equal under the law and were taxed on the same basis that company employees were taxed. Of course, company salaries were set to take care of the taxes, and the taxes were extracted before the salaries were paid. The taxes made any independent industrialization prohibitively expensive.

So, by the book, it was a free trade economy. An independent shipper could land and take off and had the same rights as company shipper. Even the tariffs paid on goods shipped were the same. But the company owned the planet and collected the tariffs, so that though they were prohibitive to an outsider, they were a matter of taking money from one pocket and putting it into another to the company. There was also red tape, which could be cut or snarled at company convenience.

Gallagher and I landed at the port; Cricket stayed with the *Glacier*.

Then came the red tape, and it wasn't too surprising that it was snarled. Talking to one blond clerk was like talking to a computer, one that seemed to keep losing track of what it was talking about. I finally realized, after a few hours, that her program read something like, "Keep them talking until Intelligence sends further instructions." Evidently, Intelligence needed plenty of time for whatever it was deciding, checking, or planning.

"Well," said Gallagher happily, "it seems we've got a week here, Harald. All I really wanted to do here was to go over to Suzie's Place, anyhow. Why don't you come along with me while you decide what to do about the charges against you before the Space Commission?"

I rose stiffly and nodded. "Sounds like sense to me," I said. "Maybe I'd better investigate my rights a bit before I walk into the compound where the Commission has jurisdiction. I'll clear those charges," I added grimly, for the idea of the charges had been eating into me.

It was a grimy, down-at-the-heels port town, far different from Stellamira, because of the difference in planetary hostility. It was more spread out, and the company areas were not so strictly divided from those of the colonists. The segregation arose chiefly because the company officials lived in large places in the suburbs and the colonists in town. There were no ghetto walls. Crossing a street could take you from one area into the other; the differences were obvious, but the street was the division point.

Suzie's Place was in the center of town, but it was an all-colonist establishment. It was early evening, and a neon sign over the swinging doors announced that the place was open for business. From out on the street the sound of a jingling piano and of raucous conversation and laughter could be heard.

We pushed through the swinging doors and spotted Suzie by the piano. Gallagher waved at her and galloped across to where she stood, swung her up and kissed her roundly. I stood back and waited. When he'd set her down she turned to me and gave me a warm kiss on the cheek. Then she turned back to Gallagher.

"So you've decided to forget that I hijacked your ship into a small detour?" she asked him loudly, without the slightest apology.

He bowed from the hips. "When a lady wishes to be taxied to the place of her choice, who am I to do other than see to it that her wishes are obeyed?" he said with a grin. "But the hire of the taxi must be paid, and I've come to collect my fare." With that, he picked her up unceremoniously and headed up the stairs with her, Suzie giving a few little kicks of token protest, but obviously pleased.

I didn't know what was expected of me; but I didn't

have long to wonder. One of the girls, the one who'd been on a crutch at Stellamira and who seemed to walk with a slight limp still, appeared at my elbow and offered me a drink. We made our way to the bar. I took the drink and played with it, and we made polite conversation. It was made clear to me that a trip upstairs would be available, but I refused that and continued to play with my drink. Our conversation remained light, although we had shared danger together.

Though the company was good, it was a long wait, and I may have grown a trifle nervous. I sat outwardly calm and feeling warm with the bonds between me and the girls who came to chat with me one by one. My back, as I sat at the bar, felt naked, and the hairs at the nape of my neck felt stiff and standing. I felt watched by cold eyes and sure that there were company spies in the room.

When Gallagher came down, he was obviously tipsy. I was sober, having played with one drink all evening I had assumed that he, too, would be careful. I was furious, but I hid it well.

"Come along, Harald," he said jovially, swatting me on the back so hard I swayed over the bar with the blow. "Come along, for the hour is early yet, and we've a bit of pub crawling to do before the night is out."

I rose, unsteady from the blow, and grasped his arm. "Maybe we'd best go back to the lander for a bit of sleep first?" I suggested, cautiously.

He threw his head back and laughed with a bellow that turned every head in the room. "Go back to bed, and me so long away from the space lanes, so cramped yet from the months of settling in colonists who are serious and sober and God-fearing? Why no, Harald. You sleep if that is to your liking, but me, I thought I'd see the town, maybe even beard the governor in his lair." He leered down into my face, and I became really worried.

We made our way boisterously to the street. He stopped everyone we passed to exchange a greeting or to gainsay an offer of a drink.

He took me by the arm and led me through the main part of the town. I realized that we were being followed.

I made it my policy to try to steer Gallagher to the most brightly lighted spots, for I'd more than a suspicion that the company goons who were following us had nothing better in mind than getting us into a dark alley and leaving our bodies to be found there. But it became more and more obvious as we made our way along the streets that the town was full of dark allies. The joints were getting scarcer and scarcer, with longer stretches of dark pavement between.

Then, with a great shout, Gallagher dragged me off the main thoroughfare.

" 'Tis Tiny's place we're forgetting," he said as he headed me up one of the darkest alleys we'd passed.

We were into the alley before I'd quite gathered my wits.

As the darkness surrounded us, Gallagher's tipsy gait left him, and he moved like a cat.

"Hold this over your nose," he whispered, and thrust a light-weight square of greasy cloth into my hand.

The greasy texture caused my hand to hesitate on the way to my nose; I was almost too late following his instructions. There was a faint tinkle behind us, near my heels and a faint hiss, and I forced the square of cloth firmly over my nose and mouth.

It seemed anticlimactic that we strolled on at a reasonable, unexcited pace, then stopped and waited, scarcely ten meters from the entrance. I was about to take the cloth from my mouth and ask Gallagher what was happening, when a half dozen figures appeared in the mouth of the alley.

Cautiously, as though feeling their way, searching and unsure, the men came into the narrow way after us and then began to disappear, dropping one by one.

I'd not been noticing Gallagher's faint count, ". . . and five and six. Okay, that took care of them, but there's more of them outside." His voice was low. "They didn't all come in, and by now they'll have the other end of this alley sealed up too."

You could touch the walls on each side of the narrow way by stretching, and Gallagher did just that, feeling along until he reached a door on his left. He centered on the door and then began scrabbling with his fingers along the pavement. Abruptly, he began heaving on something, whispering at the same time, "Give me a hand."

I moved beside him just in time to catch hold of the rim of a manhole cover. The two of us heaved it up and balanced it on edge next to the hole.

"Down you go."

My feet found the rungs of a ladder, and I made my way half way down, then reached back a hand to support the lid as Gallagher moved onto the ladder beside me, then carefully replaced the lid over the hole.

"Safe to breathe yet?" I asked softly.

"Keep the cloth over your nose a while longer; I used strong stuff. We've got to move quickly now, for they'll be all over that alley in another fifteen minutes. The gas may hold 'em off that long."

We felt our way down the blackness of a tunnel scarcely a man's height; the wires, pipes and various boxes that my fingers passed over told me its use.

Then ahead of us there was light, and the passage broadened into a dimly-lighted, underground room.

"Junction terminal," Gallagher said succinctly. I was

about to move ahead when he held me back. "It'll have personnel relays in it," he said, "and I hadn't time to get hold of the necessary electronics to knock one out."

We paused only a few meters from the lighted room, and I was wondering whether it would be wise to go back. Apparently Gallagher was thinking of something else, for a small flame appeared in his hand, and he began carefully tracing some of the cables that ran along the wall beside us.

"This should do it," he decided with the air of a man talking to himself, as his other hand came out of his pocket holding a small knife. He made short work of slicing through the protective plastic cover and picking out a couple of the color-coded wires beneath. These he peeled carefully without breaking, and then twisted them together.

"Okay. That'll give them enough to worry about for a while."

"How do you know you didn't just short out somebody's telephone?" I asked.

"Advantage of being a floating engineer," he answered "I spent a couple of months working on this underground system between space hops once. That's when I got to know the problems here on Durango. I just shorted out the alarm that will tell them every warehouse in the neighborhood, as well as all the tunnels and other guarded areas, have been invaded. We just became an army," he said grinning.

"But won't that mean they'll have people swarming all over these tunnels looking for intruders?"

"Not really. They'll search the warehouses first. Then, after ten or fifteen hours they may find out exactly what happened. But come on, I'm not sure we've got that long."

There was a plan to the tunnels that was undoubtedly logical and easily remembered by anyone who ever worked on it. But for me, it was a matter of walking and crawling, twisting and turning. Eventually there was another manhole cover. We heaved it out of our way, and crawled out into another alley.

"Took you long enough," said a nearby feminine voice. Suzie was leaning out the door of her skimmer, and Seth was in front at the wheel. I felt myself pulling back, as though to avoid that roller's tap at the back of my neck, but Gallagher replaced the manhole cover and got in, with me right after him. The skimmer took off, slowly at first, turning and twisting through areas of fewer and fewer houses until we were away from the town. Then Seth threw it into high speed operation; and I turned to Gallagher.

"The company was just hoping we'd go back to our lander," he told me happily. "If they didn't have it booby-trapped, I don't know company minds. They want us dead, but they want us dead unofficially. When we didn't head right back for it, they decided to take further action, but there's enough independence in this town, that they didn't want to be open about it. And we had to take the heat off Suzie's Place by being long gone from there before we disappeared."

"But if they've got our lander," I felt foolish asking, because I thought I already knew the answer, "how the devil are we going to get off of here?"

"That's what's been worrying a lot of people for the last few years," Suzie answered me. "We've got some independence, some of us, and we've got parts of the planet more-or-less under control. But how to get on and off—well, that's gotten more difficult every week since the Stellamira uprising. The port's theoretically free, but time after time independents have had accidents at the port."

"But if you've got ground control . . ."

"Ground control means you control an area. But the

company controls the space around that area. Any time they've a mind to, they can drop something on one of our installations, and who's to say it wasn't an accident? Controlling the ground and being able to use it—well, that's two different things."

But it was a standoff, because the company couldn't use the planet either. With two and a half million independents scattered around the planet, there wasn't a safe thing the company could do, any more than there was a safe thing the independents could do.

In all my experience I've never had a ride like the one I had that night. Seth drove with a sure control that was beautiful to watch, and I soon got over thinking of him as the stumble-word I'd remembered him to be. But at our speed, even sure control wouldn't be enough, unless he knew the country like the palms of his hands.

The upper speed limit of a skimmer on a straight run over a flat plain is reputed to be five hundred kilometers an hour, though no one in his right mind would drive one half that fast on anything rougher than a mirror.

How far or how fast we traveled that night I don't know, but the next morning we were well into a range of mountains that are not even visible from the port; we had passed over totally unimproved territory.

There was a tiny cabin that we got to just at dawn, and there we stayed. I'd thought it a stopover point when we first arrived, but it was not. It was to be our headquarters, I discovered, from which we were to organize a revolution.

At least, it would be headquarters for me; for Gallagher, Suzie and Seth it would be headquarters when they were there.

I was put in charge of creating an intelligence system from among the guerrilla fighters. It was decided that no one who was not directly concerned know about their activities. Should my intelligence men or I be captured, we could not give away what we did not know.

Gallagher and Suzie were seldom there. When they were, it was to drain me of all the information I could give them, with them both keeping their mouths shut for fear of giving me information, and me doing my best to throttle my own inquisitiveness.

About two and a half months later, when I was thoroughly engrossed in the business of gathering data and drawing a picture of company activities on the planet, I got two pieces of news that frightened me.

One of my most reliable runners came in with word that a strange craft had been seen outback. It had been near the areas where I knew, but had not been told, that Gallagher and Suzie were operating.

It was a huge, silent vehicle, nearly two hundred meters in length according to the report, with a shape like a stingray. It had come slowly drifting out of a cloud bank and had silently progressed up the valley. The vehicle had been reported from at least a dozen good sources, and all the descriptions were nearly the same.

The companies seemed to have had something really new, and probably very dangerous to us.

Word of this had to get to Gallagher at once. I debated sending the runner on to him, thought better of it, and decided to go myself. But before I got to the skimmer, I heard another skimmer coming, and I waited.

There were five of them, but Seth's was in the lead, and so I knew it was all right. I saw that Gallagher was driving the second skimmer and knew I could report directly to him. Suzie was driving the third. But when I saw who was driving the fourth skimmer, I ran to where she'd pulled up beside the cabin and opened the door for Cricket.

She came out and into my arms, and it may have been quite a while before I was thinking again.

Then, hanging onto Cricket's hand, I dragged her to where Gallagher, Seth, Suzie and a man I didn't know were unloading hundreds of cartons, and I began to tell them about the new craft.

I noticed that Gallagher was barely listening. I took a big grip on myself, dropped Cricket's hand, and got between Gallagher and the skimmer he was unloading.

"You've got to listen," I said, "this is important."

He smiled at me, then. "Yes," he said, "it's important; it just happens we already know about it. I didn't mean to be impolite."

"Well then, for God's sake, tell me what it is," I said desperately.

"Why, it's a new kind of landing craft, for landing people and freight from interstellar ships," he said. "It's far more efficient than the landers we've been using."

"It's too big," I said flatly.

"It's two hundred and twenty-eight meters long," he told me, "and it can carry one hell of a lot of freight and equipment."

"It can't be a lander." There was doubt in my voice now, though I knew that a vehicle that size, making little or no noise couldn't possibly be launched with an inertial drive.

Gallagher looked at me solemnly. He said softly, "It's an L.T.A."

I must have looked blank, for he went on, "Lighter than air, it floats."

"Like a balloon?" I asked inanely.

"Yes. And radar won't pick it up, because radar circuits reject anything that slow."

I could have gone on questioning Gallagher as long as he'd have let me, but it was at this point that the real blow fell.

A skimmer came over the hills, and Suzie and Gallagher ducked inside the hut. It skidded to the ground and I headed towards it. The hatch opened and Jane, the girl with the limp, jumped out, and came towards me as fast as she could go.

"Earth's sending a shipload of Space Marines," she called, panting.

I turned to find Gallagher, but he and Suzie were already coming towards us as fast as they could.

"When?" he asked.

"They got word to me at the house last night. It's already lifted from Earth. I got away as soon as I could. Nobody knows why, but the gossip is that you've been in the outback so long, and Stellamira was so drastic, that they're going to take a hand in settling the matter. The excuse is that Durango has been plagued with outlaw raids and has asked the Space Commission for assistance in subduing the outlaws."

Gallagher looked grim. Suzie was standing back with a waiting look on her face. Cricket must have come up while I wasn't noticing, for now she slipped her hand into my arm.

"What are we going to do?" I asked, trying to keep the hopelessness out of my voice.

"What *you* are going to do," Gallagher said fiercely, "is to change your intelligence network over into a distribution network as fast as it can be done." He waved back to where Seth and the other man were still unloading the skimmers, "Get those things to every independent you can get them to. They came in on the L.T.A. lander you spotted, and we've got them now, but they've got to get to where they'll do us some good. By the time your men get these distributed, there will be more. You've got a week; then I'll come get you."

Jane looked at Gallagher, and her face was strained and tired. "What's my job?" she asked.

"Take a load of these, all you can carry, to the house," he said.

Then he, Suzie and Cricket ran to the skimmers from which the last of the packages had just been unloaded, and they took off.

I felt empty, looking after them.

Slowly I walked over to the piles of packages. There were three kinds: a huge pile, nearly two-thirds of the lot, of one kind, a smaller pile of a second kind and a very small pile of the third.

I opened one of the cartons from the big pile and relief flooded me as I pulled out one of the tiny guns that it contained. The thing fitted my hand as though it were tailored for me, and it had the sort of beauty that comes from precision parts intricately fitted together.

Carefully, I slipped it into my pocket and went to the second pile. Those cartons held communicators, thousands of them. I didn't even pull one out. They solved most of the problems of my information network, I knew without examining them.

I turned to the third pile, and when I opened a carton there, I think my heart broke. They contained lamps that could be powered only by broadcast power.

Once I'd seen the globes, I didn't have to pull the gun from my pocket to know that it, too, was a broadcast-power device. Later I tested all three devices.

It seemed the corporations had discovered solar taps and were about to turn one on. Even with some of their supplies, we would be much weaker than they.

VIII

My sense of *déjà vu* was strongest when, a week later, I jerked from the papers I was working on in the cabin about twilight. Abruptly worried, I ran outside. Then the feeling disappeared and life was new and exciting again.

The L.T.A. lander hung about a hundred meters away and six meters off the ground, with Gallagher climbing down a rope ladder from an underslung cabin in its middle and eight men from it anchoring it to trees.

I was still gawking when Gallagher reached ground. "Time to go now, Harald," he said.

I shook my head. "You may do as you like," I said, "since you seem to have captured the means to do it, and I hope you're taking Cricket with you. But I've helped start something here, and just because they've gotten ahead of us, I'm not about to run like a scared rabbit—unless everybody else on our side can run, too."

Gallagher shook his head. "Damn it," he said, "the Earth cruiser will be landing Space Marines in a couple of days now. We've got things to do meantime. Take my word for it, we're not running like scared rabbits. I haven't time to argue; come along."

I came. He wouldn't even let me go back to the hut to get the papers I'd drawn up with the latest information. "You have everything we'll need in your head," he said, as he practically shoved me up the ladder.

Cricket was in the control room. Suzie was there, too. Soon Seth and seven other men who had been helping him tie the lander to the trees appeared, and I realized we were rising. The craft surged away from the ground like a thing alive, but so gently I could have stood on tiptoe and balanced with the greatest of ease.

For a time we made our way through a long, dark canyon. When we were out of the mountains, Gallagher let the craft really rise, and we were up and away into the higher atmosphere.

Eventually the ocean of atmosphere through which we had risen became tenuous, and Gallagher cut in drives that were still quiet, but that produced a different motion in the ship. Again we began to climb.

I had waited for hours to ask the questions I wanted

to ask. I had thought to ask Suzie or Cricket, but they were stretched out on foam-rubber mats, sleeping, as were the eight men. Now Gallagher woke one of the men, turned over the controls to him, and stretched out. He was undoubtedly dead tired, but I had to know. I moved over beside him.

"How'd you capture it?" I asked softly.

"Didn't," he said. "It's ours." His voice was sleepy.

"But . . ."

"Told you I'd been tooling up for a revolution while we were on Betsy Ann; it was part of the tooling up."

"How'd it get here?"

"Came with us."

I was stumped. Gallagher had shrunk the *Glacier* back nearly to its normal size before we boarded her at Betsy Ann. On the way from Betsy Ann to Durango I'd gone with Gallagher all through the ship. There hadn't been any large holds, and those there were were practically empty. There hadn't been a thing in the way of materials for a revolution, and that had both surprised and distressed me, though I'd kept my mouth shut at the time.

Evidently the authorities on Durango had been stumped too. They'd sent up a boarding party a few days after we'd escaped from the port, and had been greeted only by Cricket. They'd inspected the craft from end to end, and then left, finding nothing but a bit of automatic machinery on board, and a few passages and cabins.

They probably figured that Gallagher was leaving the *Glacier* in synchronous orbit for use as a radio relay through Cricket, and that by letting it alone they could tune in on the communications.

It hadn't occurred to them, any more than it had to me, that there might be holds that simply did not connect either with the surface or with other parts of the ship, bubbles in the ice that could be opened into the rest of the ship or sealed from it by the ice mice.

One more question I asked. "Have you built a solar tap base on the planet?"

"Wasn't time," he answered in a far-away voice as he fell asleep.

I worried the matter a long while, then fell asleep myself so that when we reached the *Glacier* we were ready for action.

Gallagher didn't pause in the control room when we reached the *Glacier*. He headed aft. Seth and Suzie stayed in the control room, but Cricket followed Gallagher and the seven men, and I tagged along.

We entered a big hold open to space and to the planet below. Down the length of the hold stretched a gigantic gun barrel, aimed straight down. I shivered.

The gun was obviously one of the most powerful laser beam generators I'd ever met, but Gallagher and Cricket were ranging it in a way that would, it seemed, make it useless as a weapon. I was puzzled, but said nothing as they worked.

Finally, Gallagher chuckled quietly.

"Okay, Cricket. Check the sweep."

Cricket leaned forward and flipped a switch. The laser began putting out a middle C *cheeee*.

The sound sent shivers down my back, because it meant to me that an enemy had been sighted and was in range, though there seemed to be none of the tenseness that one would find in the control room of a war vessel swinging on target. There was nothing but a planet out there for a target.

The ridiculousness of shooting at a planet with the ineffective sting of a fine-focused laser began to creep up on me. The focus on it was so fine that it would probably make no more than a centimeter hole in whatever target it hit, and though that's enough to play havoc with a space vehicle, it would be less than the sting of a mosquito as far as the planet was concerned.

"Set power pulse to three seconds."

Gallagher's voice was slightly edged, but Cricket's came back in a singsong that showed no overtones of emotion.

"Power pulse on three seconds by off point five seconds."

"Initiate pulse."

Cricket didn't have to respond to that because the machinery did it for her. There was a slow, rhythmic, *mmmm-pop, mmmm-pop* from the power supply that went on and on and combined with the *cheeee* to form a now familiar repetitive pattern, the song of power that I had heard on Betsy Ann: *cheee-ops; cheee-ops.*

"I'll be damned," I yelled. "This thing's an upside-down solar tap."

There was a choke behind Gallagher's laugh, and his voice had a sweep and flow that spoke of tensions releasing.

"We're way above the radiation belts," he said, "but the oscillating lens of our zoom focus makes an ionized path from Durango's ionosphere to its ground, and that's all you need for a tap. We didn't have time to build a pyramid down there, so we turned the tap upside down."

Then I realized that we had won, that the battle was over and we had won.

There would not be a company electric plant on the whole planet of Durango that hadn't quit working in the last thirty seconds. Though broadcast power and hydroelectric power can work side by side, our side had set its power to be antagonistic to the other.

"Not even the spy-satellite system will be worth a damn now," I heard Cricket's satisfied voice say.

"And the port?" I asked, though I knew the answer.

"The port? Oh, much more than just the port!" It was Suzie's voice this time, and it held a deep, internal quiet. "The port's knocked out of course. The effect reaches out several planetary radii. I'm quoting Gallagher," she added, "but he knows. It reaches out several planetary radii, and any ships that come close will be easy prizes, for their electrical systems will be knocked out, their motors and their instruments and—they can't even come close without our letting them."

I could see her face through her helmet, and she was beautiful. The lines were smoothed out, and there was only a quiet triumph and a peace such as I have seldom seen on a human being.

"We've won," she said. "We've won for Durango and for all the planets. We'll not be slaves again."

I stood there looking at them each, Cricket, Gallagher, Suzie and Seth, in their suits in that ice chamber by the big barrel that pointed out to a planet. It took a minute for what Suzie had said to sink in.

Won for all the planets? But of course, when you can establish a power tap from outside, no corporation can keep the outside from coming in. They wouldn't have to set up pyramids on Durango or any of the other planets. They'd simply set up a satellite to take the place of the *Glacier* and they'd surround it with smaller satellites to make the Jacob's ladder, and they could land their own ships.

The deep ringing voice that I heard, the *cheee-ops, cheee-ops, cheee-ops* of an upside-down tap was a freedom bell ringing across the starways.

I looked at Gallagher and I felt that it's men that make history, not history that makes men, for it takes a man to dream freedom so hard that the stupidities are brushed out of the way. It takes a man to burst through the static forms that keep their shape by being rigid, the forms that can't change because any major change destroys them. It takes a man to replace that static stability with a dynamic stability that can change, adapt, grow and evolve.

It was then I began to feel the laughter that was bubbling up from my toes, and I knew finally what it is that makes a free man laugh. There's a price for anything, and there's its value. But the value I saw then is beyond price. The question of price simply drops out of the equation.

I looked down the barrel of the cannon pointing power for a planet and a pathway to the stars, and laughter enveloped me.

There comes a time when a man's got a right to lean back and laugh.

Walt and Leigh Richmond's POSITIVE CHARGE is a collection of technological and fantasy tales of man's vast, puzzling, and often perilous future. Here you will find:

An electronic saboteur . . .

A shepherd whose flock threatens galactic domination . . .

A robot faced with unemployment . . .

A substance repelled by *both* poles of a magnet . . .

A stranded explorer who can't prove his identity to the rescuers from space . . .

. . . and much more!

Turn this book over for second complete novel

WALT and LEIGH RICHMOND

have also written:

SHOCK WAVE

THE LOST MILLENNIUM

PHOENIX SHIP

POSITIVE CHARGE

WALT and LEIGH
RICHMOND

AN ACE BOOK

Ace Publishing Corporation
1120 Avenue of the Americas
New York, N. Y. 10036

POSITIVE CHARGE

GALLAGHER'S GLACIER

Printed in U.S.A.

CONTENTS

M'LORD IS THE SHEPHERD

M'Lord received the message on Moonbase One with a feeling of complete dismay. This species was 50,000 to 100,000 of their years from the type of development Galactic Central was asking for!

Yet the message was specific. The Korm'aans, according to present calculations by Computer Center, would begin a sweep through this spiral arm of the galaxy, and Galactic Central would need a developed people as an ally.

Get them into condition to receive Galactics without fear in two hundred of their years, capable of offering their resources freely, capable of assistant labor?

Forced stimulation was one thing, and he'd watched it tried. It could work, though normally it simply killed the stimulated species.

"The greater good for all the peoples of the galaxy demands that we take a chance on sacrificing this species," the message added, a sop to his conscience, since the message was an order, not a request. "We will then have either an ally of a weak but unhampering variety, or a planet of the proper Z characteristics from which we can operate unhampered by a developing and possibly resentful native intelligence."

The methods were left to him. By all the knowledge of Computer Center! What stimulus could one apply to a species barely into the Iron Age to get them to an intelligence level where they could even stay from underfoot in a mere two hundred years, especially when each member of that species required a full one-tenth of that time to develop to maturity and the useful life-span of individual members was a possible thirty years?

Obviously, it would have to be a nerve stimulus and it would have to be broadcast to affect the entire species.

It would be electronic, of course. But they weren't even capable of electricity yet, much less electronics. That, in the pattern that their development showed, would be at least 5,000 of their years in the future one couldn't introduce a broadcast electronic stimulus from within the culture immediately. That would be sure death, though Galactic Central did say they'd as soon have the planet returned to the primitive.

No, the stimulus would have to be confined to wires so that it could spread slowly and so that it would act as a stimulus only when a member of the species was within a few miles of the wires. Too abrupt an introduction of a stimulus would be surely fatal, and central had specified an attempt to develop the creatures.

I, their shepherd, must take a chance on ruining the flock that shows such promise, that I have spent my career in nurturing! He knew a moment's sadness before he set himself to the task at hand.

The best stimulus, of course, was the sixty-cycle-alternating current. It must be introduced in such a way that it would grow through the culture, until finally each member of the species—at least the major groups—were subject to the nerve-impact most of the time, but also in such a way that it was possible to escape it. This would give the most aware a chance to withdraw occasionally and give their nerves a rest.

One couldn't introduce the stimulus from within as AC current at sixty cycles. It was best to introduce the battery and let them play with direct current for a matter of fifty to seventy-five years. There would be no stimulation there, and Galactic Central might consider the time wasted, but one had to give a species time to play with and prepare for the type of battering

am that was inherent in being subjected to a constant ixty cycle nerve jolting whenever they were within an ppreciable distance of wires carrying the frequency, you planned to see that those wires webbed the culıre almost inescapably.

With a sound that might have been translated as a igh, M'Lord summoned his teslars.

A seventy-five year interval since the introduction of he battery on Alterra had passed, and M'Lord realized vith some disquiet that he now had no further excuse or delaying the introduction of alternating current.

The species had done well, had taken the new toy anded them so unobtrusively and made it their very wn. They had examined its possibilities with more eenness than even he, who had devoted his entire working period to their care, had expected. Just the introluction of the battery must have had a stimulating ffect on the creature—or perhaps his teslars had dropped few unauthorized hints—for still on his own, the creaure had jumped from the Iron Age to steam, smelting, elegraphy.

M'Lord was proud of the Alterrans.

Yet he was probably to be the instrument of their lestruction, he knew. Galactic Central was getting far oo impatient for him to dally longer. The stimulus itself nust be applied. Under that stimulus, the nervous sysems of Alterrans would either respond with a surge that vould take them far beyond their ability to cope with hemselves or those nervous systems would wither comletely, leaving the Alterran an animal subject to his nvironment. If that occurred, he would be shortly viped out, for in developing his ability to alter his environment to his needs, the creature had sacrificed his bility to survive as an animal.

However, the computers still extrapolated from

Korm'aan strategy the probability of a move into this spiral arm.

M'Lord summoned his chief teslar.

This job must be handled delicately and the chief teslar would undertake it himself.

A quarter century more was gone on Alterra, and still the necessary alternating current had been introduced only as a potential. The potential was strong; the ground work had been well laid. But the first of the two centuries was passed, and the Alterran was still within his normal framework: slightly altered, slightly advanced, but still essentially the same creature, with no potential of the necessary drastic change. With these slow methods, the overall webbing of this culture with the wire that would carry the effective sixty-cycle alternating current wouldn't be accomplished for another quarter century!

M'Lord had reason to worry. The species might be his charge, but Central was beginning to bring pressure, and the galaxy was Central's charge.

When the signal interrupted M'Lord he brushed the communicator with an unusually brusque response.

"Chief teslar reporting, sir."

M'Lord visuated his chief. It was remarkable how the make-up fitted. "Even I wouldn't know you from an Alterran," he grumphed.

"Sir, the Alterrans themselves have barely noted even my presence," his teslar communicated proudly. "I could not avoid being noted to a slight extent, or being credited with some developments, of course."

"You've done a careful job, teslar, but a remarkably slow one. So slow that it will be twenty-five of their years before results begin to show."

"Sir, may I be allowed free saying?"

"Speak."

"We have miscomputed them in including too large a resistance-to-development factor, sir. They are self-stimulating to a degree I had not thought possible. We have noted their violent reactions against progress, and the force with which individuals with new ideas have been put down. But we have failed to note equally the force with which those new ideas and developments are put up. As they say on Alterra, it takes two to make a battle.

"Again, we have noted the negative resistance factors that culminate in wars, but have failed to note the equally strong positive factors involved. While we've watched the wars, we've failed to notice that individual arguments and group arguments are almost a way of life with this species! They argue. How they argue! Self-generated arguments at the individual, the group, and the cultural-center level at a constant. Because of this, our applied stimulus might work as a release on their self-stimulus, both positive and negative, and act as an addition rather than as a basic! So much so that I– Sir, complete free saying and no retribution?"

M'Lord visuated the teslar fiercely. "You're bordering on ultimate insubordination already! But yes, free saying and no retribution."

"Sir, I altered the concept to a degree. I—as the Alterrans would say it—hedged your bets. I have arranged that one major portion of their culture only, the strongest, shall get the full sixty-cycle stimulus. In the remainder of their centers, I have introduced the probability of the far lesser stimulus of fifty cycles."

"You dared!"

"Sir, we have not sampled their brain recordings for quite a period, and the patterns have advanced. The sixty cycle may be too strong, even for the period of time allowed."

M'Lord leaned back. His own sympathies were with

this species, although it was a weakness he could not admit.

"No retribution," he said, "for altering the plan. And it is possible that you have introduced a better potential. However . . . however, if the course of events does not justify . . ."

"Yes, M'Lord."

But even his chief teslar's re-estimate proved to have been made with too large a negative factor.

Within ten Alterran years a sketchy, initial wire webbing was in place in most of the planet's major centers, and the effects were astoundingly immediate. Within twenty years there was little of the culture that was not heavily webbed, and it was apparent that there was no danger whatsoever that the creatures' nervous systems would succumb to the impact. Not only the sixty-cycle subjects, but even those subjected only to fifty-cycle stimulation were now reacting with impossible leaps in technology and computational abilities. The life span of the individual to as much as a normal sixty-five to seventy-five years, while the maturity span, formerly an optimum thirty exclusive of senility, now was about fifty years.

The effects were so immediate and so completely unpredicted that recordings were rushed regularly by special transport to the computer at Galactic Central, which began altering its entire series of time-potential-probability sequences to include the new time-potentials now being demonstrated. Galactic Central sent special observers.

The third decade following the initial introduction of the stimulus had nearly passed before the final factor fell into place that required reclassification of the species.

Unemotionally, the computer removed Alterrans from ?he classification *sheep,* to be coddled for potential ?lave-service to the Galactic peoples to the classifica?ion *predator.*

Almost as the reclassification was made, a command ?irective went by emergency beam to Moonbase One. "Alterran development must be reversed immediate?y," the directive read. "Apply stupidifiers at once. If ?ossible, impose from within, if necessary, emergency ?ction may be taken and stupidifiers imposed from with?ut. This species is a greater hazard than Korm'aan. ?o time can be wasted."

M'Lord acted at once. Ultrahigh-frequency radiation ?n a broadcast basis was indicated. It could be intro?luced from within with no time wasted. Low fre?uency broadcasts had already been developed by the ?pecies as an entertainment medium and a war was ?naking on the planet, so that a means of detecting ?nemy craft with high-frequency radiation bombard?nent, which would hit the creatures as well as the tar?gets, was natural.

The low-frequency, long wave-length entertainment ?roadcasts had had little if any effect on the nervous ?ystems of the Alterrans, although the waves of radia?ion passed through their bodies as consistently as they ?lid through the instruments built to receive them. The ?ong wave lengths were far too large to be, at any point, ?ontained within the body, and neither were they at?uned to the body's own frequencies. Therefore, they ?eft no signal with the body's nerve systems.

Quite the contrary would be true of the ultrahigh?requency, ultrashort wave broadcasts as they filled the ?tmosphere with their signals. These wave lengths were ?hort enough that each wave would be contained in ?nicrosecond intervals, complete within the nervous sys?em. Whether or not they attuned the bodies own sys-

tems, they would leave an impulse on the nerves—an impulse towards unspecified action, so that the nerves would tense for action and be unable to direct the tension and so relieve it. Again and again the ghost impulses would bombard the nervous systems, and the systems would alert. Nervous breakdown was inevitable, nervous breakdown and complete myasthenia.

Radar was introduced within less than half a year on a formula his teslar had left sleeping as a precaution. The effects were, again, immediate, but the development failed to slow.

Within two years it was apparent that radar would not be sufficient. The radar bombardment was constant, the myasthenia general throughout the species, but Alterran development barely relaxed its headlong pace, much less reversed.

"They should be worn out, completely frazzled, on the way to primitive conditions and in a state of breakdown as a species! There's a proportion of breakdown, but only a proportion, and they're carrying that proportion and still heading into space!" M'Lord's chief teslar was as drawn and whorled as his master.

"Apply hypnosis." M'Lord's communication was firm with a conviction and an authority he no longer felt.

"Hypnosis, sir, requires the centering of each individual's attention. That is an individualized process, sir."

"So?"

"So it cannot be imposed from without, and there is no time to develop it from within the culture!"

"Radar was developed by this species in time-elements measurable in increments of their years."

"But this must be individualized, so that each member of the species is subjected—"

"These creatures are on their way into space, in a

condition of destructive compulsion unknown in the galaxy. You will find a method!"

The chief teslar was hesitant. "Perhaps, then, a major hypnotic is justified? A complete stupidifier, one that centers each individual's attention on a pattern of lights flickering at a frequency near enough that of a main brain-wave frequency to capture and alter the brain-wave rhythm? But that would be catastrophic, sir!"

His master grouched angrily, as much distressed as the teslar. "It must be so!" he affirmated.

The teslar bowed his head. "I grieve with you, sir, if you will so permit me." Then he unslouched and communicated firmly. "We will introduce an instrument for screening transmitted entertainment in the home. It can be set to a flicker rate near one of the creature's main brain-cycle patterns so that, watching it, he will unconsciously match the brain cycle to the flicker rate and will become hypnotized. This will be easy, sir, in the areas where we have introduced sixty-cycle electric currents. This frequency is nearly a divisor of their major brain pattern. However, in the fifty-cycle areas—well, the hypnotic effect will not necessarily be as great, but the stimulation here has not been as great either, and the stupidifying effect of the applied hypnotic need not be as strong."

The initial development of optarad required a period of several years, while Galactic Central altered its plans for containing the spiral arm of the galaxy from defense against the Korm'aan to defense against the new species. Plans were sufficiently detailed to include methods for enlisting the Korm'aan in common cause against the Alterrans.

Then optarad was in production, the frequency of its light pulse set at a rhythm very near that of the dominant brain wave of the species.

The introduction was highly successful. Within a decade the daily habit of attention-centering on the instrument was nearly as broadly spread as the use of electricity.

The hypnotic stupidifier was at work, aided by the nerve-frazzling broadcast of the ultrahigh-frequency radar signals.

Relaxing for the first time in one hundred and fifty-seven years, M'Lord waited for the commendation he felt sure would be forthcoming from Galactic Central. Radar had had around twenty years to take effect, the new optarad hypnotic frequencies had been played into the eyes of a vast majority of the leading Alterran creatures for five or more of those years.

"My poor sheep," he thought regretfully to himself. "We turned you into predators, and must now put you to sleep. Yet, perhaps I may find a way that you be allowed to safely graze content and peaceful at last."

The entry signal blinked, and M'Lord brushed the come-in response with a sigh.

"Chief teslar reporting, sir."

M'Lord visuated his chief, who seemed rather excited. "Well?" he grumphed.

"Sir, the hypnosis is not sufficient. Sir, it is numbing their brain centers—but the brain capacity seems to be far larger than was indicated by the small portion they were using. As one area of each brain weakens, the stronger of the creatures adapt by putting another unused portion of brain into service to replace it. At the same time the weaker are reduced to apathy so that they are no longer in the way. These creatures, sir, are heading into space in spite of the hypnosis! Sir, our predictions fail by a factor of . . ."

The communicator blinked the red emergency, and

M'Lord watched his own nerve ends flare as he pushed the begin button. The communication spat out:

"All plans whorled. Computer predicts these beings will have galactic mastership within approximately five hundred galactic years. The Korm'aan have made common cause with us, and you now serve as ambassador to both. Entreat for us free living and no retribution. . . ."

IF THE SABOT FITS . . .

16:31:39 EST. The University's educational TV show, *House of Blocks,* was being broadcast to the town and taped for national distribution. On the screen, Boff, with his clownishly ineffective manner, turned to the stairs against a checkerboard wall behind him and raised his foot to climb. But the stairs were no longer going up; they were upside down. Foot raised, Boff stared at them in wonder, and the children in a myriad homes and apartments howled with laughter. Boff moved his foot uncertainly, and the stairway changed position so that it was going up the side of the wall.

16:31:39. An electric drill whirred in the hands of a workman drilling a hole in one of the steel ribs of a new skyscraper. It paused and whirred again.

16:31:39. An experimental circuit set up by a young electronics enthusiast responded erratically to the line transients reaching his home from all the various switches, drills and other electrical appliances close enough to affect the device. Each transient produced a click which, if listened to carefully, sounded like some secret code. The boy listened in fascination.

16:31:39. A computer clucked happily and produced a check for the largest sum that its register was capable of printing. The automatic mailing machine slurped up the check, slipped it into an envelope and slipped the envelope into the mail. It was all done without touch of human hands.

16:31:39. A computer in a chemical factory initiated the dumping of a 10,000-gallon tank of perchloric acid into a mixing vat already full of other chemicals.

16:31:39. A repairman at Schultz Super Electronics Service watched an odd, steplike mark of pulses wan-

der across the face of his oscilloscope. It was doubly odd, because the oscilloscope, though operating, was not attached to anything. Its lead lay loose in the clutter of materials on the bench.

16:31:39. A canning factory on the outskirts of the city ground slowly to a halt as its computer issued an impossible order that jammed sixteen conveyers simultaneously.

16:31:39. Twenty-five telephone callers hung up disgustedly as each realized he had reached a wrong number. The library computer delivered a hot sex novel to a spinster in search of a good murder mystery. All the street lights in town flickered on for a moment, then flickered off again. The air-raid siren wailed.

The city was rocked by a tremendous explosion from the MiRite Electrochemical Works.

By the time the fire from the explosion was out, the local detective complement of the police force had been supplemented by the nearest FBI agents. MiRite was a highly secret government-contract firm. Quiet calls had gone out for reinforcements. Reports were flooding in by then to police headquarters, and Chief Pat Flannagan was already over his head in esoteric jargon.

"To put it more cogently, Chief, somebody got an electronic signal into the computer at one of our most important and most secret projects and caused it to blow up the works. You remain in nominal charge, Pat," Dick, the FBI man who'd been in the area for some time, assured the chief kindly, "but we're going to take over the job."

Pat nodded sourly. "Glad enough for you to do it; takes a load off my mind."

"Oh, it's your responsibility for the record, and you'll get the credit when we catch the saboteur."

"And what if you don't catch him? Do I get credit

for letting somebody wreck a secret project I didn't even know was here?"

Dick laughed genially. "We're still not admitting it; and the only kind of trouble you can get into is if you let on there's more to it than an explosion in a factory. You don't even suspect sabotage, for the record. You just go out and tell the reporters that are already asking questions out there that it looks like somebody got careless at MiRite, and the stuff they handle won't abide carelessness. Tell them you'll give them all the details as soon as you work them out. But first, I want every dick you have in plain clothes out there guarding the perimeter of the site. We'll take care of the inside with our own men but I don't want it to be easy to get inside."

Pat nodded, issued the necessary orders and strode out to the desk where his sergeant reigned. The local news service and two wire men were waiting.

"Did the sergeant give you the details about the amount of damage, boys?" he asked smiling.

"Yeah, Pat," answered the local man, "but—"

"Well, I can tell you about what caused it, but not the exact details yet. Seems somebody got careless . . ."

"Yeah, Chief," one of the wire men said impatiently. "Did somebody get careless at the canning factory too?"

"The canning factory?"

"Strauss & Rand, out on River Road."

"What about Strauss & Rand?"

"They've got a mix-up it'll take 'em about twelve hours to straighten out. Nothing serious, except a lot of man hours and overtime."

Pat turned to his desk sergeant with one eyebrow raised.

"Nope, Chief, we haven't gotten anything from Strauss & Rand."

Pat turned back to the newsman. "What on earth has

a jam-up in the canning factory to do with what we were talking about?"

"I don't know," he said. "I just heard it had happened, and it was the same time as the explosion. So I thought there might be a tie-in."

Pat smiled in relief. "Forget it," he said. "So my aunt's pet cat might have caused that explosion, too. It didn't. Somebody got careless." He went on about the investigation into the causes which underlie such carelessness. Then he said, "The insurance investigators are doing most of the work in that, but we are cooperating with them fully," he said pontifically. "There will always be human carelessness, but it is up to the authorities to see to it that safeguards are taken against a repetition. . . ."

It was nearly dawn before Pat left his desk; he had been reworking his schedules so he could give the FBI the most efficient help possible. That MiRite was top-priority government secret even his plainclothesmen guarding the perimeters mustn't suspect. He'd been warned; and he handled the details of assignments and reports himself as far as possible. By now, he realized, the town must already be swarming with FBI men, but even he would not know who or what they were. He'd catch some sleep, he decided, then come back and make himself available if he could be of any use. Maybe he could get some inside information. Not that he cared, he assured himself. It wasn't his problem; but he was interested.

No sooner had he opened the front door than his son, Tim, was tugging at him in the dark hall to come upstairs to his "ham shack," actually his bedroom; it was filled with electronic equipment.

"Up early, aren't you, Son?" Pat asked quietly after he'd closed the door behind him.

"I've been listening for you, Dad. Didn't want to

phone you. Figured you'd be busy over that explosion, and it may not be important. Well, I got signals on my new circuit today that—they were code signals, Dad. I didn't want to worry Mother about it, but I thought I ought to tell you."

Pat grinned fondly down at his son, ruffled the blond curly hair so like his own, a gesture he could only make these days when the boy was sitting down. *Growing fast*, he thought, *up to my chin. He'll be a six-footer, too. And the same bulldog-type face.*

Then he realized what the boy had said, and it lined up suddenly with his day's work.

"Code signals?" he asked cautiously. "What made you think they were different from ordinary Morse code? That's all over the airways."

"They weren't anybody's Morse code, Dad. They didn't sound like Morse. They seemed to come in groups, but not quite random groups; and I had the source isolated. They weren't coming in over the air, but off the power line itself. I thought they might be computer or teletype signals like I know the electric company uses, but they didn't seem to fit that category either.

"I was running a check on line transients. It occurred to me that a statistical analysis of the detectable line transients would be something I could turn in to my Senior Math class. The teacher's a nut on statistical math and we're supposed to do a paper applying math to some form of analysis."

"Are those signals something new, or have they been going on for a while?"

"Well, gee, Dad, I don't know. I just got the circuit set up today, about 4:30 this afternoon. There they were, and then they went away. And . . ."

Pat grinned. "Might be important at that," he said. "Could you describe them more exactly?"

Tim's relief and pleasure showed in his face. *He*

must have been worried that I wouldn't take it seriously, Pat thought.

"I taped them; I was taping the transients. Here, I'll play them for you," the boy said, but his father shook his head.

"Wouldn't mean a thing to me. Let me have the tape. I'll let one of our guys listen to it that knows about those things. And, Tim, don't mention it to anybody else, will you? Get some sleep. Even if tomorrow—today—is Saturday, you need your sleep."

Tape in hand Pat left the room and again closed the door quietly. But instead of going to his own room, he headed downstairs and out of the front door.

Back at the office he yawned, sent for some coffee and then called Dick. *Wonder if he picked that name consciously or subconsciously,* he thought, knowing it wasn't the man's real name.

On Monday Joe Newton stopped by the Post Office as usual before going on to his small machine shop. He was preoccupied, his mind already patterning out the day's work, a special order for a small and intricate part. He unlocked his mailbox, pulled out the one envelope and took a look at the return address. *Good, the check from . . .*

A voice at his elbow said, "I'll buy you a cup of coffee while you open that." It was a statement, not an invitation, and Joe turned, startled.

It was a stranger; the man was neat, wearing a necktie. He was a businessman, Joe decided. "Why the hell should you?" he asked truculently, then realized he was being truculent, and half grinned.

"You were sent the wrong check," the man said. "It was mailed before we discovered the error, so I came along to get it when you got it."

Joe walked slowly over to a long table against the

wall in the nearly deserted lobby. "Let's take a look," he said.

The check slipped easily from the envelope and he looked at the name first: Joseph Newton. Then his eyes slid to the amount and widened: $9,999,999.99.

Slowly he grinned. "Seems to be made out to me," he said.

"The check was an electronic error," said the man sourly.

"Yeah, in my favor. Boy," he said, "that's some error!"

"I'll take it," said the man.

Joe eyed the other narrowly. "Mister," he said, "I don't know you from Adam, and I don't think I care to."

"I am the claims agent for the firm's insurance company. My papers . . ."

"Papers be damned. This paper says I'm a millionaire." Joe had no illusions that the check could be made valid, but he didn't like the other's attitude. "I think I'll cash it."

"You can try." The man was developing a truculence of his own.

"Well," said Joe thoughtfully, "I think I should get a reward for honesty, *if* I return it."

"We can settle this legally, if you prefer." The man's voice became nasty. "I have your proper check here."

What the hell, thought Joe, *I'd just get involved with lawyers.* He'd been hoping the check would get here this morning; he needed the cash.

Suddenly he shrugged his shoulders. "Take the damned thing," he said. Then he looked at it in some awe. "Well, I was a millionaire for a few minutes, anyhow."

Pat was on his way to headquarters, driving slowly, when the sound of drilling penetrated his consciousness. It was high up in the new building with its steel skeleton.

Rat-a-tat-tat-tat, tat-tat, rat-a-tat . . .

Could be, he thought and speeded up the car.

"I'll get the electronics men on it. It could be a lead,")ick said doubtfully. "I don't think so, though. That ape your son made? It was code, all right, computer ode. And it could have done the job."

"Tim's always talking about resonance," Pat insisted. That steel skeleton might have been resonating, and naybe it could have . . . sort of made a code by hance. . . ."

"Thanks, Chief," said Dick, but his voice still sounded lubious. Then he leaned back. "This one's really got s. Whatever code was used threw at least two dozen ther computers out of whack. We've just started on hat angle, because we've just recognized it. I think our son's right. They put it on the power lines strong nough to get past the filters." He grimaced. "I've ot my men checking all the computers in the area, ut I think there's no doubt about it. Whatever else our aboteur may have accomplished, he sure caused a lot f companies a lot of trouble."

"Who else was affected?"

"Well, the chemical plant—there's a man there who ught to get a medal, except we don't want people etting together and comparing computer trouble that ay. The computer there ordered 10,000 gallons of erchloric acid dumped into a vat that already had, h, some other stuff in it. Would have been as big a ess as MiRite, if not as important. This guy noticed, ad pulled the switch in time."

Dick had no sooner left than the sergeant introduced visitor, and a gangling young man walked timidly to the office.

"Yes?" said Pat, putting a soft note into his voice ad switching on the tape recorder hidden in his desk

with a movement of his foot. The man was in his twenties, Pat decided and he was obviously taking his courage in both hands. *Confession coming up,* Pat told himself.

"Chief . . . I. . . ."

Put him at ease, thought Pat. Anybody with the will to confess doesn't really want to be an outcast and doesn't have that professional urge. "It's okay," he told the young man softly. "You can tell me."

"I . . . got some signals last Friday . . ."

Inwardly, Pat laughed at himself.

"Yes?" he asked, this time his voice more man-to-man.

"They came on about the time that—well, I gather that several computers went haywire. And they were—well, a stepladder signal—on my oscilloscope." Then, not sure that everyone besides himself knew what an electronic signal was all about, he hastily added, "An oscilloscope's an instrument for registering . . ."

"I know about oscilloscopes," said Pat kindly.

"Well, Chief, the thing was . . . the oscilloscope wasn't attached to anything. Oh, it was plugged in and turned on, but I didn't have a load on it."

"What kind of signals you get?" asked Pat.

"Sort of a stepladder. It must have been repeating at thirty cycles per second, because that's the way the—that's the frequency the horizontal trace was set to. And . . . well, I've never seen anything like it. But the pattern turned upside down and then right side up, and then just disappeared again."

Pat leaned back. "How come you came to me?" he asked.

"Well . . . I don't know, really. It seemed to me somebody should know about it, somebody in authority, just in case it was connected with—with anything that happened." The young man's face was getting red. "It was so—well, different."

Pat nodded, asked a few more questions, got an exact description of the stepladder and let the young man go. Then he had a messenger take a tape of the conversation to FBI headquarters.

A call from Dick came several hours later. "Thanks for the tape, Chief." The FBI man's voice made it clear that the thanks were of dubious quality. "Now we've got a real stickler. That guy's oscilloscope—we've checked—was and is in a completely different part of town, miles out of the area. He lives in that trailer park about six miles out Pleasant Street. You know the one, Fresh Breezes Trailer Park or something like that? Repairs radios out there in the Schultz Super Duper Electronics or something. Schultz's is in a shopping center there."

"I know the place." Pat frowned.

"Do you know of any computers in that area we could check against?"

"Hmmm." Pat thought briefly. "There's an air-raid siren out there—but no, that's controlled from downtown. Well, there's a telephone interchange not far south of there."

"We'll pay hell trying to check on any effects in a telephone interchange. But I'll see if there's any record from the area on the trouble-call channels for the time."

"You need to know, essentially, how broadly the signals reached? That it?" Pat asked suddenly.

"That's about it, yes."

"All right. There are computers operating in various sections of town, even if not that one. Let's see, there's the library computer; that's outside of normal computer areas, and certainly out of the area so far covered. There are several at the University. And there's. . . ."

He stopped. Who *was* using computers these days? Anyone with any sizable business. Even small business firms used them on a pooled basis. "Tell you what," he

said. "Check IBM for computer locations. Then you can check the ones that would be outside the—former trouble area."

By Friday the puzzle was even more complicated. The signals had obviously emanated from at least a dozen different sources, probably simultaneously, but possibly in a quick sequence of confusing impulses. The picture of the damage done by putting the signals on the power lines could be estimated already in the hundreds of thousands while the potential damage ran into the millions.

Even discounting the MiRite project, the man hours involved in cleaning up the short period of electronic confusion would run—if anybody made official overall estimates, Pat decided—in the six figure bracket. Banks had worked overtime locating unbalances then checked the myriad business firms that might have made computer-coded deposits at that time. Except for the fortunate intervention of one alert individual, a second plant might have been completely destroyed.

There was a chemical firm that had had to dump its entire output of six hours; there were innumerable pieces spoiled in computer-controlled lathes in machine shops.

Pat had sweated all week. If the newspapers tumbled to this, there'd be hell to pay. Nobody that he knew, outside of the FBI and himself, and possibly one or two of his plainclothesmen, had noticed the extent of the malfunction. The banks and various company executives who had inquired about whether their own electronic malfunctions were more than local had been assured that the evidence pointed to an accidental signal, and that measures had been taken. He'd implied that the power company had made a mistake.

And my men, he thought, *have better sense than to gabble.* Even so, he'd had a conference with his own

detectives in which he'd casually brought up, in another ontext, the question of talking about their work. He'd nderlined heavily that idle conversation had dire results.

The afternoon sun was slanting across his desk, and ne leaned back, rubbing the muscles at the back of his neck. *Interconnection,* he thought, *like the power and light grid and the East-Coast blackout, not so very long ago.*

Interconnection. So much technology, technology run by the computer, essentially. We're only beginning to understand the ills to which a computer is heir.

Like the automobile, he thought. When it was first nvented, the streets built for horses could accommodate cars, with a little resurfacing. Then there got to be too many cars, and highways were built, then thruways. Still the cars had come, and the cities were smothering n cars. Now, if one car had an accident, it was a pile-up.

Electric power was also like that. When the technology of power had vanished for a few hours in that Eastern blackout, civilization had stopped temporarily. That blackout had been caused by one malfunction in one spot, a whiplash that started as a ripple and grew as t surged along the long lines, until with a snap it had blacked out technology throughout the Northeast.

There's only six figure damage and no deaths in this particular computer sabotage, he thought. *But ten years from now?*

Sabotage? A pile-up of automobiles isn't sabotage; the blackout wasn't sabotage. And the computer has comparable interconnectiveness . . .

He looked at his watch. It was three P.M., Friday.

Abruptly he stood and went to the sergeant's desk. "Get a car over to the school and have them pick up 'im," he said, brusquely. "Have them bring him home.

Tell him I'll meet him there." Then as he strode to the door, he said over his shoulder, "Tell him it's all right. I just need some information, and he might be able to give it to me." He grinned and slammed out.

Tim was there in fifteen minutes and Pat was waiting for him in his bedroom.

Tim moved some of the stuff on his bed to give himself room, then sat down on it thoughtfully. His boyish face looked intent and serious. Pat resisted the impulse to go over and ruffle his son's hair but the feeling of pride and affection that went with that habitual gesture was welling through him.

"I . . . I guess I don't know, Pop. You mean the code I picked up—last Friday, wasn't it?"

"Yes. That was computer code, pure and simple computer code. And it affected almost every computer in town. But," Pat grinned, "that's top-secret information and I'll have you in Leavenworth if you breathe it."

"I know better than to talk, Dad." Tim's face was serious.

"I know you do." Pat made a decision. "That signal caused the explosion at the MiRite plant." Tim looked surprised, but the expression quickly passed. "It nearly caused at least one other major explosion. It affected almost every computer in town—and I find, to my surprise, quite to my surprise, that there are more than a thousand computers in this town. That doesn't count the little, everyday machines like radios and vacuum cleaners and telephones and traffic lights." He glanced at his son. "Gets awesome, doesn't it? You could call them robots, instead of computers, if you wanted to. We're a computer technology these days, Son, without even knowing it."

"And you think it was a computer that put a signal on the power line here that day?"

"I don't know. I'm not really thinking. I'm just guess-

ing. It was a computer code signal, and it was on the power lines. But the power lines for different parts of town are isolated one from one another. It was on all the power lines in town, maybe at the same time, but certainly at about the same time. It was probably a saboteur," he added sadly. "I was sort of hoping that that was a wrong guess, but the more I think about it, telling you about it, I guess it had to be a saboteur. The damage ran into the hundreds of thousands, if you add it all up." He grinned, "But nobody but us . . . cops, have thought to add it all up. Everybody thinks it was just their computer, or just a few."

"Well . . . uh. . . ." Tim stood and thrust his hands deep in his pockets, frowning, in unconscious imitation of one of his father's gestures. Then he walked in a preoccupied manner to the bench where the rig was still set up. "Without the roll of tape I gave you, I haven't had enough tape on hand to finish my experiment, but if I picked the signal up here . . ." He pulled one hand from a pocket and flicked the device on, watching as the bench oscilloscope warmed up, and the little green trace began wiggling its way erratically across the face of the tube. "It had to be a pretty powerful signal. We're in a residential district, an isolated network, and that signal was coming through real strong."

He leaned forward and pointed out some of the sharp, erratic peaks that were being displayed on the screen. "These, the stronger ones, originate mostly right here in the neighborhood: automatic refrigerators switching on and off, thermostats, people switching lights on and off, that sort of thing."

Then he leaned forward and gingerly disconnected the leads to the scope, held them out and nodded towards the screen. "That pattern, if you listen to it, sounds something like a bad filter capacitor in an ordinary radio. It took me a long time to find out what it

really is. You see, I'm actually acting as an antenna. And the scope is just nonlinear enough to pick out the pulse pattern from that TV station down on Broad Street. I wrecked quite a few recordings before I found out that that silly buzz was the raster pattern for a TV picture."

Tim grinned and reconnected the leads.

"Would you get that pattern on the power lines?" Pat asked, a sudden guess making him alert.

"Yes. Once I'd identified it and started looking around, I found out that that combination thirty cycle and fifteen . . ."

"What?"

"Thirty cycle, Dad. The . . ."

But Pat was already heading for the phone downstairs. It took him almost a minute to get the local broadcasting studio on the line and their head man on the phone.

"This is Chief of Police Flannagan," he barked. "What show's on at 4:30?"

"Why, the educational TV show from the University, *House of Blocks*. They'll be on in five minutes, Chief."

"All right. You get your men ready to cut that show off the air as fast as it can be done, if necessary. Get your men ready, then stay on this line. If I say cut, don't take even *seconds* to do it. Do you understand? Shall I send a man up there to enforce the order?"

"I take it this is serious, an emergency. We'll obey, of course, and expect . . ."

"Never mind what you expect. Get your men ready." Then he said to Tim, "Get upstairs and fix that scope to catch the signal. If that pattern comes on, yell *loud*."

16:31:39. The University's educational TV show was being broadcast to the town and taped for national distribution. On the screen Boff, with his clownishly ineffective manner, turned to the stairs against a checker-

board wall behind him, and raised his foot to climb. But the stairs were no longer going up, they were upside down. Foot raised, Boff stared at them in wonder, and the children in a myriad homes and apartments howled with laughter. Boff moved his foot uncertainly and disappeared from the screen.

It was a very angry professor who strode into the Chief's office half an hour later. The Chief, his son Tim, Dick, and an FBI electronics expert were waiting for him.

"Thank you for coming, Professor Boffington," Pat greeted him.

"I hope," the newcomer declared, "that you have a very good reason indeed for your actions this afternoon." There was no trace of the ineffectual manner that made his teaching so effective on the airwaves. "Our show is one of the few educational shows that has been able to out-rate the normal TV guff, and you want to sabotage a breakthrough like that!"

Pat nodded slowly. "Professor," he asked, "would you say that the show was worth, well, exploding the MiRite plant?"

"And just what do you mean by that?" The professor was undaunted, still grim.

"It could have caused more serious explosions this time."

"You will please explain."

"That checkerboard pattern you use . . ."

"A new introductory theme which will be built up and used to demonstrate visual patterning, the changes in patterning caused by light intensity and coloration, or even by the eye's—"

"Is run by a computer?"

"Yes. The changes are programmed."

"The computer speaks computer language, and it was speaking to every computer in town."

"Nonsense. Computers are filtered against random signals."

Pat cocked his eye at Tim, and the boy spoke up eagerly. "Sure, sir. They're completely filtered internally against any signal except a type of signal that is of the proper wave shape to operate the computer itself. The computer operates on yes-no impulses, and the internal circuits have not only to be able to handle those pulses but amplify them, and, well, if you filtered *them* out, the computer wouldn't work.

"And then they're filtered externally against normal transients on the incoming power lines to keep the computer from receiving signals from other computers, and to keep it from broadcasting its own thoughts. But the pulse-pattern in which your checkerboard switched around was a computer-code pattern. A lot of TV sets were pulsing to that pattern, reinforcing the code put out by your computer, and it got reinforced until it was more than any normal filtering system could stand. It got through to every computer in town, and it sort of—well, it induced electronic epilepsy. I guess nobody expected a signal of quite that volume to be broadcast from that many spots around town simultaneously."

"But why doesn't it happen all the time? TV is in constant use."

The FBI electronics expert spoke up. "The output of an irregular picture," he said, "is quite random and will be treated by the filters as a random signal. Even if it got into the computer a little, it wouldn't cause much interference. But that checkerboard pattern you use just happens to have a projection created by a computer, and it had exact computer-language elements in it. Once it got through the filtering systems by being reinforced so thoroughly, the computers had no way of tell-

ing whether it was their own personal thought or one from outside. They went a little bit nuts, or, as Tim put it, epileptic."

"You mean it wasn't the computer itself that was putting the signal on the lines through the broadcast, it was from the *pattern* being broadcast?"

"The pulse of the pattern. That's right."

The professor wilted. "So we have to yank last week's tape; it's due for national broadcast next week. We have to kill that part of the show, and we can't use computer-coded effects." His voice was despairing.

"Oh, no sir." It was Tim, leaning forward, intent, serious. "If you'll let me, I can filter that tape for you and take the computer signals out. Well, we ought to be able to design a filter for the system that . . ."

Pat restrained his impulse to reach out and ruffle the boy's hair, but his pride was almost irrepressible as the electronics expert and his son began jabbering in a jargon that was over his head but that seemed to indicate the situation was under control.

Dick, as thoroughly out of the conversation as he, moved quietly over beside him.

"What I don't understand," he said softly so as not to interrupt the others, "is how you managed to get the clues our guys missed? How did you get the connection?"

The grin that Pat had been withholding could break out now. "That," he said, "is what cops are for, tracing the connection between the criminal and the crime."

COWS CAN'T EAT GRASS

HARRY GIDEON stretched his lean, hard frame and looked up at the sky—a light purplish sky—shaking himself awake for the day.

They should be here soon now, the Galactic Survey Team that would rescue him. It was a triumphant thought. He would be here, alive, for them to find. The wrecked scout, the destroyed and burned landing craft, the lost supplies, even the spider bite: he'd survived them all.

The rude tree-house shelter, built of small branches loosely woven into the lower limbs of a large tree, shook and swayed as he rolled to his feet, grasped his rough quarterstaff, and jumped lightly to the ground. Six months ago he couldn't have made that jump, he thought, recalling how he had climbed painfully that first night into this same tree. His frame, then, had been bulky and bulgy, and he had been quite ill—he had come a long way, for somebody who was grateful still to be in the same place!

He made his way to the wreck of his landing craft, scorched almost beyond recognition. He was as always alert to every sound of the forest, automatically identifying the various sibilances and whistlings, for all he was certain nothing dangerous to him sang in that chorus. He was not just swinging his quarterstaff in readiness but actually using it to bend back loose whipping branches and to break a way through thickets wherever the path was too narrow. He skirted the sunlit place where the big snake lived—poisonous or harmless he didn't know—and at last poked his head into the wrecked, but at least partially unburned, cabin to check on the still-functioning passdar receiver, one of the few instru-

ments that had partially survived. With only one of its eighteen gigacycle antennae still operating, it could no longer completely live up to its name—the passive ambient signal could be surveyed for direction, but not for range.

But that didn't matter too much now. Any object in orbit around the planet would generate its own distinctive signal due to the ambient temperature difference from its background, and would emit detectable microwaves. The orbital velocity of the object would provide an easily calculated range, roughly checkable against his own derelict—thus providing a range gauge of sorts.

The blip in orbit that was his own ship, and that he was receiving by its own radio-thermal emission, was down near the horizon and . . . and—yes! There was another blip with it. There was another ship, besides his own derelict, in orbit. The Galactic Survey Team had arrived. Perhaps they had already been scanning for his landing craft during the hours he had slept.

Turning, he ran toward the big pile of brush carefully collected over the last six months—his signal flare. Then he checked himself. Not yet. The passdar image showed that the two ships would be below the horizon within minutes now, insufficient time for the signal flare to put out a large enough cloud of smoke.

Tensely he turned back to the remains of his landing craft to wait out the hour and a half before it would be time to light the signal fire.

Commander Cal Davis of Galactic Survey had inspected the orbiting scout personally, and he knew that it was probable that the explorer within survived when the rock that made the ship a derelict went through. The landing craft was missing, either out at the time

of impact or used as a life raft afterward. Either way, Gideon might have made it down to relative safety.

He stood staring at the projected telescopic image of the planet below. Was it friendly or hostile? If the explorer had reached the planet—a big if, though his landing craft was nowhere to be found in orbit—could he have survived six months alone down there? Atmosphere and gravity were within acceptable limits. The man, Gideon, had sent back word of a probable planet find before the short, sudden, Mayday. But there was no homing beacon from a landed craft, and as yet they had been able to pinpoint no wreck.

He'd search for signs of survival for one more rotation of the planet below, and then land his team for planet analysis whether or not the scout had survived.

"Smoke smudge, sir"— The formal, clipped tones of the observer broke into his thoughts—"coming up about the thirty-eighth parallel. Same place we got a pinpoint metallic reading on the last orbit, just about two hours past the dawn line now."

"Shift orbit," Cal said to his pilot. "Put us as close across that point as you can. Observation, I want the best pics, passdar readings, magnetometer survey, and anything else you can get on that area."

The replies were lost in his surge of excitement. Perhaps Gideon *had* been one of the lucky five percent that managed to survive a lone downing.

"It's a small fire for a natural occurrence, and a large one if it's man-made, sir. And yes, there it is, that's what's probably the drogue chute spread out on some trees. The fire's in the middle of a large, a very large, clearing."

"Magnetometer reading, sir. There's metal down there. Could be a landing craft, though it's pretty scattered."

"Passdar reading, sir. Definitely fragments of metal."

"Maybe Harry survived, sir?"

"Let's not jump to any conclusions yet. That fire could still be a natural phenomenon, or the work of natives." Cal remembered wryly the time when natives on another planet had made an idol of a wrecked landing craft.

"Observation, get a spread of pics around here and put them through the computer for possible good landing sites near the area."

"Yes, sir." This time the perfunctory reply registered with him.

Harry Gideon turned from the blaze of the signal fire and strode off into the jungle in search of breakfast. The survey team would see it, but that didn't mean they'd be here immediately. His landing craft hadn't made it out of the wrecked scout undamaged and had been nearly out of control from the start, his landing site had been a matter of chance, not choice. As far as he had been able to judge from recalled glances at the surrounding areas as he had fought his craft to a catastrophic landing, the nearest proper landing site was a lake four hundred and fifty miles southwest.

But that didn't mean they'd be here in a week, even if they picked that spot to land. Any survey team worth its salt wouldn't risk its members until they'd checked the environment and the ecology and knew what a rescue party in a chopper would be up against. They'd figure he had survived—if they figured he had—six months, and that he could survive at least a month longer.

Then, too, there would be a lot to occupy them: setting up base, putting up weather survey and com satellites, landing and assemblying labs and choppers and full field equipment. They weren't here just to rescue him. As a matter of fact, he would be almost incidental.

But at least they were here now. He could begin

measuring rescue time in weeks rather than in months or years.

Radio messages for him would be covering every band, but that was of no use. There hadn't been enough electronic equipment that escaped burning and crushing to make either transmitter or receiver. His passdar unit, the only operating device left in the entire landing craft, was of the most modern, undetectable type, so even it would tell them nothing about his existence.

Of course he could have built a spark-gap transmitter that would serve as a homing beacon, and now that they had surveyed the planet sufficiently to know that there was no native radio on the air they could use it to home in on. But that wasn't necessary. They'd spot the fire and the drogue chute and probably the metal of the landing craft as well; even if they didn't, they would land and set up a base. Of course, they'd find the planet habitable as he had, and if *they* didn't find him, the colonists would after a colony was established, he could go find them, but not yet. His orders were to stay with his craft until "located or reasonably certain that location would not be made."

Six months ago it would have been a different story, he realized. He would have been frantic in seconds at the thought that another human being was on the same planet. Six months of survival had changed that. Now, there wasn't much hurry at all.

The breakfast tree was right ahead of him. Harry reached into the thicket of small brush and pulled out a long pole with a crook on the end of it that he used for the purpose of collecting breakfast. He was late this morning. The sun-warmed fruit might already be inedible. If it was, that meant a day without eating, so he would look. Experience had taught him that breakfast fruit must be picked not more than two hours after dawn, before it had lost a lightly, greenish color that it

took on during the cool of the night. Otherwise it was worse than useless to eat. It was also useless to eat anything else.

Experience had taught him that, too: no breakfast, no lunch *or* supper. The sensitive changes were brought about, so far as he could determine, by temperature or some subtle alteration in the planet's chemistry. His stomach had been the only laboratory handy, and his experiments had cost him thirty pounds of blubber.

With a practiced eye he scanned the lower branches and found some of the fruit that still looked edible. Tomorrow he would have to be early; this was the last of the low, well-shaded fruit.

There was a ripping roar of wings beating for rapid altitude, but Harry was barely startled. The birds seemed to depend on their startle mechanism, waiting almost until you stepped on them, and then suddenly scattering in all directions. Amused, he watched the last and slowest of the lot go careening wildly through a clearing in the branches. Then he reached up and knocked down some breakfast.

"Sir?"

Commander Davis looked up. Pat Carver, the biotechnician, was young and very earnest and the freckles that sprinkled her upturned nose belied the heavy frown that brought her sandy eyebrows together.

"Sir, my test animals are dying. Not one of the possible local foods seems to be edible by Earth life. It's not that they're poisonous, though some of them are, it's just that they don't provide any nourishment, not a bit. The chemicals are there—the right quantities of carbon, oxygen, hydrogen, phosphorous, et cetera—but they're not digestible. The sugars are tied up as polysaccharides similar to cellulose and other undigestible substances. From the available data, I have to conclude that a hu-

man could not possibly survive on this planet without extensive assistance. And . . . well, a couple of my animals died in convulsions, though that–"

Behind her, the ship's agronomist, Jacques Sinclair, spoke up. "That goes for Earthside plants as well, sir. They can be grown here quite readily by hydroponics techniques, but something seems to interfere with their chemistry–they literally refuse to grow, or starve, you might say, when planted in the local soil. A very few of our hardier grasses have survived, but of these only one type actually tries–a type that's noted back on Earth for its absolute uselessness."

Cal raised his eyebrows. "I thought you only tested for the most useful plant life adaptations?"

"Yes, sir, but as a general check we also carry such pests as crabgrass, and that's the only thing from Earth that really grows well here."

"Hm-m-m." Cal pondered thoughtfully. "I have reports here that there are few hostile species of animal. There's one type of insect similar to a spider that's capable of giving a man quite a hard time. Its bite seems to be deadly, at least to one monkey, though it probably is not more than just serious so far as a man would be concerned. Raw materials are available for any form of civilization. The weather extremes are milder than they would be on Earth. We have found no evidence of intelligent native life, with the possible exception of that fire we observed shortly after we arrived. Except for the food problem, a man or a colony could survive. But unless the food problem can be solved, a colony would be dependent on hydroponics and the chances of a total colony failure would be relatively high from a simple crop failure in case something went wrong with the hydroponics."

"That would seem rather unlikely," Jacques broke in. "We would certainly set up multiple facilities around

the planet, so that even major storms could hardly upset a full-scale colonization program."

"Unless you depend on hydroponics," Pat Carver answered seriously, "I don't think this planet would be suitable for colonization." The bio-tech unconsciously chewed on her upper lip in concentration. "There's just no food here, sir."

"But, carrying their own food, and being wary of spiders, I gather a search crew for Gideon will be safe enough." Cal stretched back in his desk chair. "The matter of colonization actually won't be up to us anyhow. I believe we're ready enough to send out a search party. As you say, we probably won't find him, but we should pick up anything he may have left and our stay here is just about over. So tomorrow morning . . ."

"Request permission to go along!" Both of them spoke eagerly, and Cal glanced up, amused.

"O.K. You two and one med-tech, in Copter Seven. I'll send another copter along as well. But remember, if you find Gideon, every precaution is still to be taken. From what we have learned, his survival is extremely unlikely. But the fire looked man-made and from the pictures, that drogue chute was spread by hand. You should bear in mind, however"—his face took on a stern look as he gazed at the two—"what a variety of life forms might exist in the galaxy. And you should take no chances that another life form might have utilized Gideon's knowledge of how to bring us down in this area. Nor will you ignore any other possibilities, such as contagion."

"Yes, sir." The two seemed solemnly impressed.

It was nearly noon and Harry Gideon was using a stone hoe to dig for the roots of the steak-lunch plant, when he heard the mechanical sound of a chopper crawling slowly through the air along the side of the far hill.

Hastily gathering up a couple of the succulent roots that he had already unearthed, he began a light trot to the clearing where his look-out tree had long since been provided with a piece of the brightest metal he had been able to pull from the wreck.

Without giving it a second thought, he leaped for a low-hanging limb and swung himself into the tree, most of his senses concentrated on the rising and falling sound of motorized equipment that for the first time in nearly seven months broke the pastoral quiet.

Hastily he snatched up the carefully selected mirror of metal, polished on both sides. He had practiced signaling with it for months. The hole in its center would pass sunlight through to the ground or other object below. He could sight through the same hole at a distant object. Using the rear reflective surface, he could also see the dancing spot of light on the ground. By matching that exactly with the hole, he would be reflecting a beam of light at the object sighted through the hole. It was an elementary signaling system, but one that had taken much practice.

In the distance, the chopper was passing, but he couldn't get a clear sight. Frantically he scrambled for a higher branch, but the chopper was past him now.

Harry felt a surge of despair, and then realized that the fading sound of the chopper was being echoed loudly. No—it was another chopper.

Quickly he swung around and began signaling. The chopper paused, seeming like a playful, fat dragonfly.

Harry signaled again, and the chopper blinked back. The standard *dit dit dit, dah dah dah, dit dit dit,* had been answered, and Harry began signaling instructions. L-a-n-d . . . a-t . . . s-i-g-n-a-l . . . f-i-r-e . . . h-a-r-r-y.

The chopper signaled acknowledgement and turned off. As Harry swung down from the tree he noted that the other chopper had turned back.

As he broke into the clearing, an amplified voice from the chopper suddenly stopped him in his tracks.

"Hold where you are. Don't move a step farther." The muzzle of a snub gun on the front of the chopper raised towards him to emphasize the words.

A frustrated grimace went over his face. They were going to play it by the book.

"I'm Harry Gideon, explorer scout," he said, "identity number C-305-9728, spider-bitten, but otherwise unhurt. Request permission to greet the first humans I've seen in seven months." He grinned and waved his quarterstaff.

Only one of the choppers had landed. The other would remain aloft, both for certainty of communication and as sentry, until the exploration party was convinced that it was safe enough to set up a base here.

"Stand where you are, please, and drop your weapons."

Harry almost laughed out loud. "Weapons?" Then he realized that actually the quarterstaff *was* a weapon. Carefully, he laid it down.

"Sidearms, too."

Sheepishly, Harry felt along his belt, and sure enough there was the regulation blaster, a device he had hardly been aware of in the last six months, since it had no practical use in this environment.

"I'd forgotten all about that," he mumbled, and dropped it beside the quarterstaff. They were being very, very correct when "faced by native life," and suddenly Harry began to chuckle at the inanities of going by the book!

"O.K.," he called, "weapons down. Now are you going to say hello to a fellow human, or are you going to keep me standing here?"

The voice that answered him was apologetic, but firm. "Look, if it's you, Gideon—and you don't match your ID description worth a damn—O.K. We hope it is,

and we'll be willing to congratulate you after we've proved it. But our information says you *couldn't* have survived here. It's not possible. Therefore, we've got to assume that you're not you until we find otherwise."

"Well, if I'm not me, who the devil do you think I am? And what makes you think I couldn't survive here?" he asked. He was beginning to lose his good humor.

"The food here won't support human life, all our evidence shows, by the looks of your landing craft, you didn't bring an ecolotank down in one piece. But you've been here for seven months, therefore . . ."

"Nuts. The food here supports human life very well. I eat it. But I sure would like a good steak. Anyhow, how do you propose for me to prove I'm me, tell you stories of Earth, sit on the ground and tell sad stories of the deaths of kings?" There, Shakespeare ought to convince them.

"No. If you've been taken over by some symbiotic life form, or if you're an imitation, you'll have Harry Gideon's memories. At least that seems a reasonable assumption by what we've observed so far."

"Then just how *do* you expect me to prove I'm me? How about if I tell you the number and type of satellites you have in orbit? The types would be a guess, but the passdar scanner says there are a total of eight satellites in orbit, and . . ."

"No, same objection. You could also know about passdar and satellites. Darned if I know how, but we'll think of something."

Harry sat down on the grass, pulled one of the steak plants out of his belt and began to eat it. "This may be a long job," he remarked conversationally. "If you're hungry, I've got a steak plant here. I'd be willing to trade. Maybe you've got some coffee?"

A feminine voice replied, and it was bitterly cold.

"I've seen five test animals die of convulsions from one of your steak plants."

Harry noted the *your* and realized that one speaker at least had made up her mind that Harry had been taken over by a native life form.

The third voice was more congenial. "We've got coffee here. Wouldn't it be safe enough to have him back up and we'll leave a pot of coffee for him and some food?" Suddenly the loudspeaker went dead and Harry could imagine the argument that raged behind the silence.

At last the argument was resolved. The speaker began again. "We will deposit food here and back off. You are instructed to remain exactly where you are until we have done so."

It was only minutes later that Harry was allowed to advance and pick up the first Earth food he had seen since the landing-craft disaster. The synthaburger looked delicious, as did the coffee.

Harry squatted on the ground and began to eat frantically. He was beginning to form a plan.

Nausea hit him suddenly and completely, and the vomiting was followed by cramps so violent that he doubled in agony.

Somewhere out of the blackness there was a voice. With supreme effort he concentrated on the chopper. The muzzle of the gun was leveled at him again.

Anger gorged through his aches. "You're supposed to be humans," he spat at the chopper, "yet you sit there and watch a fellow human die. I survived this planet, but I wonder if I can survive the . . ."

The voice that answered now was steel cold. "I have watched Earth animals die of convulsions from your food," it said. "Now I think I am watching a native of this planet nearly die of Earth food, though evidently

you did not eat enough. What have you done with Harry Gideon?"

His mind was beginning to clear now, and Harry began finally to realize what he was up against. They quite literally didn't believe that he was himself. He had lost his bulgy figure; he was stronger, slender, hard, and too, he thought, a bite of hamburger and a cup of coffee had given him cramps. It must have been convulsions for he had passed out.

Suddenly the whir of a starter broke the stillness, and Harry's attention jerked to the chopper and to a distressed feminine voice: "Oh, no! We *can't* just leave him!" Another that answered bitterly, "We have to."

Then the latter voice addressed him. "I don't think you're Harry Gideon," it said, "but if you are—goodbye—and good luck. Even if the evidence were not as strong as it is, we couldn't take a chance on infecting the whole human race."

As he spoke the rotors of the chopper began to turn slowly, the vehicle rose from the ground.

Harry felt his jaws clench. He, a scout, selected for his ability to meet the problems presented by all possible life forms, was defeated by a type of mind with which he had been born and raised, by the thinking of his own species.

Or was he? A hard core of stubbornness formed. *Think of them as aliens,* he told himself. *Look at them as aliens and find a solution.*

With an effort he forced his body to relax, forced a slow grin onto his face, forced himself to his feet.

"Never mind," he said, turning as though to go off into the woods and speaking over his shoulder, "you may have figured me out, but you're too late anyhow. We're aboard your ship. Every shoe that's touched this planet has taken us aboard. And within two weeks, just as you reach Earth, we'll have you as our own. When

you land . . . ah! We thank you for having brought us a new planet."

He moved on, pretending to leave and then, as if struck by an afterthought, turned back. "You seem hard to convince," he said. "Suppose you take samples of your contaminated blood and take a sample of mine with which to compare it? I don't mind, you know. I'll even help. Toss me a sterile syringe, and I'll take the sample for you; you can handle it with all the best procedures to protect you from any infections you may not yet have gotten. And I'll give you an outline of my—of our—diet.

"And, oh yes," he added slowly, "I'll come by your camp in two weeks to check on your progress."

It took Harry ten days of the two weeks he'd given them as a deadline to make his way to the major campsite. They hadn't left. He'd known they wouldn't, they couldn't afford to. If they *were* infected, they had to remain and destroy him, their craft and themselves, to protect mankind. They were a by-the-book survey team, and they'd play it that way. They had to.

Carefully he scouted the campsite. If they'd found the answer, he was safe. If they hadn't, they'd shoot to kill. There was no way of knowing.

Finally he took a piece of bark and a bit of charcoal he'd carefully prepared from his last campfire, and wrote a message. "Have you found the answer yet? I'm me, you're you. Harry." He wrapped the bark around the shaft of his quarterstaff, waited until the darkest of night, and heaved it into the campsite as far as he was able. Then he climbed a tall tree to watch and wait.

When the answer came, it was blared toward the woods from a loudspeaker.

"Harry Gideon, come in. We have the answer. You're safe."

It might be a ruse, he realized, but somehow he didn't care greatly. He wanted to go home to Earth. The muscles of his stomach seemed to care, though, for they tightened spasmodically against the possible bullets as he strolled toward the main hall of the camp—to be greeted by a bedlam.

"Don't eat our foods yet!" somebody called almost as he appeared. "We'll have you back to normal in twenty-four hours, but it might be fatal now!"

"Why in hell did you have to scare the pants off us that way? We might have committed suicide!"

"A colony *can* be independent here!" This last came from a pert young woman with freckles on her nose. "If you hadn't done what you did, we'd never have found it!"

"O.K." Harry was grinning, his muscles loosening slowly. "But what's the answer? I'm interested, you know."

The voices answered all at once.

"You got bit by that spider thing and it gave you an injection . . ."

"You really *did* pick up an alien symbiote, only it wasn't running you, it was working for you . . ."

"Like a cow. A cow can't eat grass . . ."

Suddenly the whole group was in an uproar of laughter.

"Whoa, there," said Harry, "one at a time, one at a time! Bacteria, alien symbiotes, and who says cows can't eat grass? They do!"

It was the pert one with the freckles who took over. "Yes, of course. They *do* eat grass, but what I meant to say is they don't, not really. The cow takes in the grass, but then a symbiote actually digests it, breaks down the cellulose to sugars that the cow *can* live on.

"But this system isn't even quite that simple. You *had* to have breakfast fruit and steak-lunch plant, and then

you were free to eat an evening meal of anything you liked. The bacteria, here, were on the spider thing's feet, and migrated into the spider bite. They were benign, but they required an enzyme from the green mold on the fruit. That was the hardest part to find out. Even after we discovered the symbiote, it didn't come out right until we caught on to the green mold from the breakfast tree. I had been disregarding that part and picked the ripest fruit that didn't have the mold—but it was the mold that provided the enzyme that helped the digestive system. But then, my animals had also died of convulsions after eating the steak-lunch plant. You didn't, but you would've if you hadn't, because the steak-lunch plant counteracted the enzyme from the mold and completed the cycle."

Harry smiled down into her earnest eyes. "Explorer's luck," he said softly. "I thought it had deserted me that day when I crashed, and had hardly gotten away from the fire when I got bit by a 'spider.' I wasn't sure I'd make it. When I was finally able I crawled back to the wreck of the landing craft to find something to eat and there wasn't a thing, not a single thing that hadn't been burned. That seemed the final disaster, but I always did let my body tell me the answers and it answered that one. Then the ship came and the chopper and it was going to leave without me. . . .

"It was your voice, wasn't it, that said no? It was a warm, kind voice and it held the promise of all the good things of Earth . . . but they were taking it away and I'd never see Earth again!" Harry shuddered.

"Explorer's luck," he said again, still gazing down into the sparkling eyes of the bio-tech. "It's the blackest black on the outside, but it's pure gold in the middle. That's the explorer's job, to turn it inside out."

SHORTS WING

The contraption with which Willy Shorts was fiddling could not be thought of as a woodworking lathe. But Willy Shorts was usually happier contriving something to do a job than he was just using what somebody else manufactured for the purpose. This was partly the result of curiosity about how else things could be done and partly the result of the fact that he'd never been able to make his pocketbook match his taste in equipment.

Whatever its cause, the characteristic was one that made most people quite unhappy; the number of people who thought of Willy as a genius was small compared to those who thought of him as an incomparable idiot from whom any mechanical or electronic device they owned should be hidden, since, if he were allowed to borrow or asked to fix equipment, he would usually convert it into what he considered superior purposes or superior functioning—a view with which the owner did not always agree.

The device that Willy had contrived this time, to substitute for the woodworking lathe he didn't have, was a small motor with a large pully attached to its shaft and a block of wood bolted to the pulley. The object was to turn out a circular disk four inches in diameter from a misshapen chunk of two-by-six.

Having satisfied himself that the wood was fixed firmly to the pulley and the motor bolted firmly to the very heavy workbench, Willy stepped back and plugged in the gadget. A few seconds' test run, he thought, would tell him quickly whether the wood was too far out of balance.

He shoved in the plug, then pulled to get it out again.

But it stuck, and the chunk of wood was obviously not quite in balance. The motor gained speed, and the vibration became a high-speed, hammering chatter. Slowly and majestically, the workbench began walking across the floor.

Frantically, Willy jerked the plug out and five hundred pounds of bench came to rest, having walked halfway across the shop.

Willy stared in awe. It couldn't be more than ounces out of balance, yet the table had been moved by a tiny off-center weight spinning at 3,600 rpm.

Amazing.

Laboriously, Willy tried to shove the workbench back. After the third heave he gave up; it would take at least two strong men. Yet, if the motor were spinning in the opposite direction . . .

Quickly he reversed some leads, and then as an afterthought he went over to the junk box and selected an old switch and spliced it into the power cord. This time he would have more control over the experiment.

Once again the motor swung into life, and once again there was the chattering rhythm of table legs on the floor. The table walked, this time in the opposite direction.

With the bench safely back in place, Willy cut the motor and allowed the table to vibrate snugly against the wall. Above him a small boy's voice said, "*Zoo-oo-oom,*" and Jimmy Skein from next door power-dived down the basement stairs, banked steeply to avoid the bench and landed smoothly at Willy's side.

"Hi," said Willy.

"Hi," said Jimmy. "What's that that moved that?" He pointed to the bench.

Willy reached out to touch the chunk of wood with a respectful finger. "This," he said in an earnest voice, "is a lever that could move the world, properly used."

"Aw," said Jimmy, "it's only an old piece of wood bolted to a motor." Then he added, "Bet it'll never get off the ground!" Converting himself back into a plane he took off up the stairs to the kitchen where, presumably, Molly would offer him cookies while Willy made his way to the book-crammed office of his basement lab.

It was in *Machinery Handbook* that he found the formulas on centrifugal force that he needed: it increases as the square of the speed; it increases directly as the mass of the spinning object. It increases fantastically with the weight of a few ounces of actual material, off balance.

Willy sat back and considered. "Somewhere," he said to himself, "there must be a useful thing that could be done with this."

It was used as a vibrator, of course, but that was an almost apologetic use of a principle that could use ounces to move tons! In his mind, it verged on the indecent to limit such power through lack of proper application.

Willy, with a principle of physics in mind, was apt to exhibit the attributes of a mother with a new-born child. That other people did not see these magnificent simplicities in the same light and did not insist upon admiring, discussing and planning for them, came to him as a constant and baffling surprise. The importance of the potentials, the need for understanding, were so obvious to him!

Possibly it could be used for transportation. But what kind of transportation? One might make a sort of car with four flat feet instead of tires, the feet connected to the body with a coiled spring and each having a controllable spinning weight. Each foot could be picked up and shuffled forward independently, or they could move in unison.

Willy considered again. An automobile with flat feet might find a market somewhere, perhaps for getting around in sand or something of the sort. But somehow it didn't seem aesthetically appealing.

He was still considering when Joe came in, letting in a blast of cold air and shaking snow from his shoulders. Joe the salesman was a character who literally had, at one time, sold iceboxes to Eskimos and had also done other things to win and lose large sums of money, including some of Willy's.

If there were any commercial value in the idea, Joe would be sure to spot it.

So, with a wave towards the coffeepot in the corner, Willy busied himself over the motor again, reversing the starting leads, but without any explanation to Joe. Demonstration, Willy had found, was considerably more effective than words.

Just as Joe was turning away from the coffeepot with a full cup, Willy switched on the motor with its off-center weight. Majestically the huge bench began advancing on Joe.

The coffee cup shook, coffee spilled. Joe stood riveted to the spot, staring with what Willy felt was proper respect, until Joe found his voice.

"Turn it off! Willy, I'm your friend, Joe. Turn it off!"

Relentlessly the bench marched forward, while Willy struggled with the switch that had worked so effectively before, but now seemed determined not to work at all. With a violent yank on the cord, he tore the wire loose. There was an electrical *spla-at,* which brought the advancing bench to a halt inches from Joe, who was now backed into a corner. He looked ready to climb a wall.

"It's a new application of a principle," Willy explained helpfully, "useful for transportation . . . I think."

"It's a new method for getting rid of old friends, you

mean! How'm I supposed to get out of here?" Joe stared around the room frantically from between the table and the corner.

"Relax. I'll move it back in a minute." Willy walked over to the junk box and selected another switch, this time a double pole, double-throw gadget that could be hooked both to the winding cord and the power cord in such a way as to determine the rotation of the motor, depending on the way it was flipped. He spliced a new line cap on the end of the broken lead and advanced to the wall socket.

"Hold it! Wait a minute!" With sudden agility, Joe was on top of and over the bench. "You're not turning that thing on again while I'm anywhere around it," he said.

"Oh, don't worry, Joe. I'm going to run it back the other way now." Willy switched the motor on, but since he had neglected to notice which way the switch caused which kind of rotation, the bench proceeded on into the corner where Joe had been, nudged itself firmly against the wall, and continued to buzz.

"Ooops! Wrong way." Willy switched the motor off, waited for it to come to a halt, and then switched it on the other way.

Grandly the big bench began to walk back across the shop to its original position.

Over the noise Willy shouted, "See, it moves!"

Joe stood carefully out of the way and remained firmly unimpressed.

After the bench was back in place, Willy said, "Come here, Joe. Help me move this thing down a bit. It's sort of out of line."

Joe advanced, took one end of the bench and, obviously expecting it to be light and easy to move, heaved, to no avail.

"Solid white oak, you know." Willy stood back grin-

ning. "I got the timbers when they were tearing down the old Watson house. Makes a marvelously stable workbench."

Joe grunted and heaved again, and then began realizing vaguely what he had just seen.

Joe made it a practice never to be impressed personally by anything. A salesman couldn't really afford to be, he felt. He wanted to impress other people, but not to be impressed himself. This was one of Joe's rules.

"I was thinking we could make some sort of car," Willy went on. "Sort of a flat-footed car, that would walk through sand, or maybe it would even be good for snow and ice."

Joe had a picture of selling something in snow and ice, and standing back, he gave Willy a sardonic look.

"No good. Very limited market."

Willy looked crestfallen. It seemed the demonstration hadn't penetrated very well.

"Cold weather does create a certain kind of market, however," Joe continued pompously. "Now, if you could just come up with some kind of heated overcoat, you know, like an electric blanket, or . . ."

There was a crunch outside; it was soft, but violent, as though a heavy body had landed in a bed of feather pillows.

Joe seemed intent on his point and went on talking, but Willy was already through the door and out into the snow to see what had happened.

A small car nestled against the basement wall. From the skid marks it was obvious that the driver had missed the curve in front of Willy's house after coming down the hill a little too fast for driving conditions.

Willy surveyed the situation. Damage to the wall was negligible. Damage to the car, apparently, was of the same order of magnitude; the snowdrift had ab-

sorbed a large portion of the impact by filling the radiator with snow.

His observations were interrupted by a muffled feminine voice that seemed to be saying very unfeminine things about automobiles, machinery in general, and spectators in particular. He strode over, yanked open the door, and stared in at the white-faced, wild-eyed young girl who had been the driver of the vehicle.

"What were you going to do, leave me in here all night while you contemplated whether the car was hurt? Don't you know human beings come first, and if there're victims of the accident you're supposed to succor them and get them to hospitals? Maybe every bone in my body is broken. Shall I see if I can move? Don't touch me. How are you going to get me out of here before I freeze?"

The flow of words was rushing in such a torrent that Willy was afraid they might continue forever if nothing were done to stem the tide.

Firmly interrupting, he commanded, "Move your left big toe."

Surprised, the girl stopped in mid-sentence. "How do I know . . . yes, it moves. But maybe my leg is broken."

"You sound too hopeful. Move your left leg," Willy said.

"You'd better pick me up gently . . . Okay, it moves, also my arms, also my other leg. If I can move my back . . ." With sudden decision the girl wriggled out of the car into the snowdrift and came plowing towards Willy, who had now been joined by Joe, looking like an oversize puppy in a short fur jacket, jodhpurs and boots.

"I'm not more than crippled for life," she said as she passed the two and entered the lab. "Now you can see what you can do about the car," she called back over her shoulder.

Again, Willy turned and surveyed the situation, while Joe made his way inside after the girl.

Stepping into the dainty vehicle, Willy cranked it up and gently applied reverse torque to the rear wheels. They spun; there was no traction.

Willy switched the motor off and stepped out to take another look. The weather greeted him with a thick flurry of snow which made seeing almost impossible in the dusk.

Obviously, traction was not to be had, at least not by ordinary automobile tires, especially on the uphill slope. Even if it were possible for the car to pull itself out, it would take time to get the radiator unclogged. The motor could be run for a few minutes at a time, but it wouldn't run long without overheating and it would take some time to back it up where it could be worked on safely.

Of course, if the snow had been firmly packed, some traction might be had.

In deep thought, Willy turned and headed back into the laboratory, only vaguely aware of being nearly frozen from standing in house clothes while he looked over the situation.

As he entered, he was greeted by a storm of questions. "Is the car all right? How soon can I get it out? What are you going to do about it? Daddy will be furious if I don't get home in the next twenty minutes. I only came out to do an errand. If you can't get it out right away, what can you do? Will you phone Daddy for me, but don't tell him really what happened, just . . ."

Willy ignored most of the outburst, aimed a thumb at the phone, muttered, "Phone," and walked over to the far corner of the lab. Then as an afterthought he added, "I can get it out in about forty-five minutes, I think. Fix me some coffee."

The girl was about to make further noises, when she

saw what Willy was after, and simply watched in astonishment. He reached for an old, beat-up lawn mower standing in one corner of the shop and unceremoniously draped with various oddments of garden hose, chains and other implements.

Will struggled to retrieve the lawn mower, hauled it over to the bench and turned it upside down. "The better to take the blade off," he said in answer to her questioning look.

Off came the wheels too, and everything underneath them. Then Willy went back to the corner and fetched five small, steel fence posts made of angle iron, which he proceeded to bolt across the bottom of the now apparently ineffective mowing machine.

Then he turned the machine over and went to work on the top. In a few moments he said, "Ought to be good enough for a test run," he said. "Where's my coffee?"

The girl looked around, located the coffeepot, and started to babble as she poured. "What on earth do you think you're doing with that contraption? You know, it's the funniest looking batch of junk– Cream?–I've seen put together– Sugar?–and if you didn't have such a kind face, I'd go call a garage because, honestly, Daddy will be furious and I haven't phoned yet. It's awfully hot; don't gulp it so. And I've got to get home, but if you'd phone him instead of me, why, he couldn't fuss at me. . . ."

Willy looked around. "Joe, phone," he said.

Joe, too, had been staring at Willy's contrivance. Now he came to life with the smooth salesman's manner that meets any crisis with aplomb.

Willy gulped the last of his coffee and turned back to the device that he was already thinking of as the *flatfoot.*

Carefully, he checked the oil level in the motor and disengaged the clutch. With a jerk on the starting cord,

he brought the little gasoline motor to life, just as Joe finished dialing the phone and could be heard saying, "Hello, Mr.—" before the noise drowned out his voice.

Willy throttled back and let the motor reach a stable idling speed, then engaged the clutch. Happily the flatfoot began chattering and walking along the bench, leaving light imprints from each of the sharp-edged angle irons.

Experimentally, Willy goosed the motor. The vibrations became more forceful and the machine moved forward more rapidly along the bench, making deeper scores. As it neared the end of the table, Willy disengaged the clutch and turned it off just in time to hear Joe shout, ". . . automobile accident!"

With the sudden quiet, Joe regained some of his master-of-the-situation air. "No, no, she isn't hurt, perhaps upset a bit, but definitely unhurt. However the car is apparently immobilized. . . ." He trailed off and then gently laid the receiver in its cradle as though he'd found himself unexpectedly talking into a dead phone.

Willy lowered the flatfoot onto the floor and stuck two of the casters back into their sockets so that it could be rolled. Then he went back to the corner and picked up the roll of chain that had been dumped in a tangle when he had pulled the lawn mower from its hiding place.

Draping the chain over the handlebars, Willy cranked up the small motor again, drowning out Joe's explanations about how he hadn't been able to get his message across very well. He pushed the machine to the door, pulled the casters out from under it, and let in the clutch. When he revved up the engine, the device chattered on the floor and then moved obediently out into the snow, leaving a series of imprints behind it.

Guiding the flatfoot through the snow was no particular problem. A slight torsion on the handlebars made it

quite convenient to turn the object, and although the stuttering was terrific, it did have a fair rate of compression, packing the snow down as it went, and leaving behind its odd gridlike pattern.

Willy guided the device behind the small car and chained it to the bumper. Then he reengaged the clutch and revved up the motor.

At first the flatfoot seemed to have to struggle, but then slowly, inch by inch, the car began to move back up the slope of lawn towards the street.

For the first twenty feet, things went smoothly; then the car began to turn at an angle to the straight uphill pull that he had started with. Willy was reaching for the steering wheel to straighten it back on course when he was dazzled by the sudden glare of headlights. Another car came skidding to a stop at the curve. Blinded, he pulled the wheel too far. As the door of the other car opened, there was a sharp, pinging snap, followed by a cessation of motion of the small vehicle and then by a gruff query, "What are you doing, young man, trying to wreck it? Look, you've pulled the bumper off!"

The flatfoot, having exerted far too much strain on the small bolts of the decorative bumper, was now advancing with the bumper in its teeth, rather like a puppy with a bone.

Quickly, Willy killed the engine. The bumper was torn completely off, but the little car was almost back to the street again. He repressed the temptation to lecture the man on how form should follow function. He said, "I'll just chain this back for now." He began lacing the chain between the mangled bumper and the bracket that had held it.

"Just put the bumper in my car. Where's Shirley?"

"Here, Daddy," she called from the lab door and bounced happily up the packed trail left by the flatfoot, followed by Joe.

"This idiot was wrecking your car. Come on, you, give me a hand and we'll shove it out." The voice was furious.

Joe and Willy, under the vociferous direction of "Daddy," managed to push the car into the street, and Willy was just ready to say something about the snow in the radiator when Shirley stepped in, called, "Thanks!"—gunned the motor and drove off. Her father was pulling out his wallet.

"How much?" he asked unceremoniously.

"That's perfectly all right, sir." Joe's manner was coming on in full flood, and Willy turned back to the flatfoot, leaving the problem to him. "Glad to have been of assistance. I think Shirley is unhurt, but if you don't mind, I'll call tomorrow to be sure. Perhaps a doctor . . ."

"Shirley's all right. It's the bumper that's hurt. Those are damned expensive little cars, but I suppose I should be grateful to you for trying. . . ."

"Willy's a little awkward sometimes," apologized Joe. "He was just trying out a new invention on the car. . . ."

"Shirley picks the damndest places to have accidents." Her father nodded grimly. He swung into his car and was gone.

Willy twisted the flatfoot exultantly towards Joe. "Now," he said, "you see what I meant about the flatfoot principle? It does a job, and there must be a market . . ."

"Why in hell did you have to pull that bumper off? We could have lifted it out. Her father's a big shot in Wall Street. I'll call her tomorrow, and . . . Well, I'll be seeing ya, boy." Joe, too, was gone.

Willy looked disconsolately from his silent flatfoot to the empty landscape. Then, resignedly, he started up his device, buzzed it back into the lab to the place it had occupied as a lawn mower, draped it with the chain and turned away.

As he turned, he stumbled over the garden hose. Absent-mindedly he picked up the hose and draped it, too, over the handlebars, effectively hiding the flatfoot from view.

It was several days before Willy put the flatfoot principle to work again.

Molly had been set for an evening's baking when her mixer blew up with a loud snarl and a stench of burning. She called Willy from his lab and explained the situation: no mixer, no cake.

Willy promptly discarded the idea of reworking the mixer itself, in favor of what he considered an even better idea of putting the flatfoot principle to work at the commercially valuable task of beating eggs and mixing batter.

Retiring to the lab, he took a length of slender, stainless-steel rod, off-centered the tip and fitted it into his electric drill. He took the device proudly back to the kitchen.

"It's the Flatfoot Mixer," he explained. Willy was not given to long conversational interludes.

Molly looked in horror at the greasy, beat-up, old electric drill. "You will not bring that thing anywhere near my cake batter!" she announced. "It'll drip oil . . ."

Willy looked at his drill in surprise, picked up a nearby kitchen towel and mopped some of the offending grease from his prize instrument. Then he thrust the slender, stainless-steel rod into the batter and flicked the drill on.

At first things seemed to be going smoothly. Then the rod began building up off-center motion. The farther off-center it got, the more thrust it had. The more thrust it had, the farther off-center it got.

With a sudden scream the drill picked up speed and the rod began throwing batter at a frantic rate, far

beyond the confines of the bowl, while the bowl itself took up a sedately reverse motion.

Molly reached the cord and yanked it out just as Willy flicked off the switch. Then the two of them looked at the walls, the floor, the equipment of the kitchen, all liberally bespeckled with batter.

"It—it worked too well!" Willy looked so mournful that Molly couldn't remain furious.

"Never mind the mixer," she said. "I think I can beat by hand. That's how it used to be done, you know." Picking up the once white, now greasy kitchen towel, she dabbled ineffectively at the nearest part of the mess, while Willy ducked out the door.

In the lab he sat for some time at his workbench, staring at the gadget that had been almost right.

Then he got busy.

Soon he had a four-bladed tube, somewhat like a thin rocket with big fins mounted in a housing which would allow some swing. Timidly he took it back to the kitchen. Perhaps this would be a mixer of which Molly could be proud.

The light in the kitchen was out, and a note on the table read, "Have a piece of cake and come to bed. I have to get up early tomorrow."

Willy looked around. There was the freshly baked cake, but he bypassed it. *Let's see, the flour was over here. . . .*

Slowly Willy began assembling the various cooking compounds, and at last he was ready.

This time the mixer worked perfectly. From the thinnest milk to the thickest dough, it squenched its way through. The slightly curved steel blades moving in and out in all directions combined the dough with a high-speed kneading action.

Then one of the blades came in contact with the edge of the bowl, once, twice, three times in a split second.

The result was a neatly split bowl.

Willy watched in fascination as a gooey mess spread slowly over the top of the table and towards the edge.

Not too good. The blades will have to be softer, say a fairly stiff rubber, but definitely not hard enough to crack a mixing bowl.

Willy turned and made his way back to the lab but when he came to the kitchen again, rubberized Flatfoot Mixer in hand, Molly was there, just finishing the clean-up job that he had completely forgotten.

She looked at the contraption in his hand and then at the mop she had just wrung out. She looked again at the contraption in his hand.

"Not tonight," she said firmly. "I have to get up early tomorrow."

Sadly, Willy returned to the lab and placed the newest flatfoot beside the original.

Willy managed to ignore the flatfoot principle for three days. It was, he told himself, a useful principle in theory, but bad luck in practice. He would retire it to the shelf, and there it would stay.

But the picture of the off-center weight and its power obsessed him and his resistance wore thin.

Willy and Molly were finishing their second cup of coffee after breakfast when Molly remarked that it was Jimmy Skein's birthday, and she'd like to give him a present. "But what?" she asked, expecting her question to be more-or-less rhetorical, for Willy spoke little.

"I–I could make him something?" Willy asked hesitantly.

Molly beamed. "That would be lovely," she said and forgot all about it.

In his lab, Willy contemplated the flatfoot principle. A toy should be a safe way of using it, he hoped.

Presently Willy brought out the Flatfoot Mixer and a

large pot. Then he began tearing strips from newspapers from a pile in the corner. To the torn strips of newspaper he added water and flour. He mixed it until it became a nearly homogeneous mass and simmered it on his hotplate.

Then he went to the workbench. A wire-mesh frame began to take form, with a long tube through the center and another short tube across it. Vaguely, the outlines of an insect began to appear. A pair of fine plastic tubes of tough plastic stretched from the body out through the wings nearly to their tips, with a bulge near the end. Into these tubes, tiny brass rods were fitted, with an off-center lump of solder designed to spin in the bulb at the end of each tube.

The connecting mechanism with the other tube was not complicated, but the final result was a wire outline of a bee with a heavy, rubber-band motor inside the tube in the bee's body, and a winding key at the bee's stinger.

Willy covered the framework with the *papier-mâché*, dried it, lacquered it, and carefully applied paint.

Finally, the bee began to look real; but it was a monster, nearly eighteen inches from end to end and a little more the other way.

When it was dry, Willy picked it up and balanced it in his hand. Was it too heavy? He wasn't sure. He made a few twists on the stinger to the click of the tiny ratchet as the rubber bands were wound up, and then he released it into the air.

With a peculiar fluting sound, the wings began to vibrate at high speed. The bee dived forward, not really flying yet; it nosedived.

Carefully, Willy picked it up and began curling the wires in the wings, just a little. Then he tried it again, this time allowing it to rest on the table.

The wings blurred into motion and the bee took off,

sailed into the air, made a graceful turn and landed nose-down.

One couldn't expect perfection without a guidance method, Willy decided. *But maybe I should give it just one more—*

"Willy, it's beautiful!" Molly's voice from the door brought his experiments to a halt.

Reluctantly, Willy handed her the toy.

"You see," he said, "the flatfoot principle . . ."

But Molly was off to wrap the gift.

Willy would have enjoyed the birthday party, but who ever thinks to invite an adult to a kid's party? Joe was present, though, and the deal that Joe made was almost immediate on the opening of the presents.

For ten dollars Joe bought the model bee from the happy youngster.

Shortly after that, Joe was in deep conversation with Shirley's father.

It was six months before the Shorts Wing toys were ready to go on the market, and it was nearly at the last minute that the manufacturing firm's lawyer asked the pertinent question, "Has the inventor given you a release? How much did you have to pay for it? This is a completely new form of flight, you know, and this toy is apt to sell like—well, like a Shorts Wing."

The manufacturer looked at his lawyer aghast. "You mean we've got to pay for it?"

"Pay through the nose, I expect."

"What in the name of blazes do I keep you for, if you can't talk me out of a suit over a simple little toy like this?" The manufacturer was actually covering up for the fact that he'd never thought of the possibility, and the lawyer knew it. The lawyer also knew that if he wanted to keep this lucrative account, he'd best protect it. Starting from scratch, with the company all

tooled up to manufacture and the publicity ready to start, he'd be lucky to get away for $100,000. But that would be better than what they'd have to pay if the toy was the runaway it promised to be and suits came after the fact.

So the lawyer set out to find the inventor.

It took some time to find out where Joe had gotten the original model. Pinning Joe down to a source was something like trying to catch a greased pig. Eventually the lawyer traced the toy through Joe to the child, through the child's parents to Molly, and through Molly to Willy. When he met Willy, the lawyer understood where the name "Shorts Wing" which Joe had attached to the toy, had originated.

Cautiously, the lawyer approached the subject from the point of view of using the Shorts name in connection with the toy.

"Well," said Willy, "I sure wouldn't object to my name being used. In fact I'd kind of like it."

Deftly, the lawyer brought out the release forms. Unobtrusively, he placed them with pen in a position for Willy's signature.

"I think," he said, in as casual a manner as he could summon, "that ten would be about right for the usage."

"Ten?" asked Willy, his voice concerned. He wanted the principle used where its potentialities would be widely demonstrated, but he might as well make it a gift as to accept ten dollars. "I might as well make it a gift . . ." he began in his mother-hen tone.

"As a down payment," the lawyer added hastily, "with, say, five-percent royalties. I always think," he added leaning back with a pontifical air, "it is better to tie these things directly to sales. Then if the—Shorts Wing—is successful, you benefit as well as the company."

"Okay," said Willy. "That seems sound. There's more

power to be gained from the slow discharge of a battery than there is from an instant short circuit. Sound business principle too, I'd think." He started to read the release.

"Those are just the usual forms," said the lawyer casually, but Willy read on. "Permission to use the Shorts Wing principle . . ."

"No!" said Willy decidedly. The lawyer opened his mouth to speak, but Willy wouldn't be interrupted. "No," he said, "it's not the Shorts Wing principle." The lawyer's mouth abruptly closed.

"The principle," said Willy, "is the flatfoot principle. It's a basic."

"A basic?" The lawyer was horrified. A basic patent was far more expensive than a mere design. Perhaps he could stall while he checked for sure that it *was* a basic.

"You'll have to change that word before I'll sign," said Willy adamantly.

"Change the *word?* Change . . ." The lawyer caught himself just in time. "You would prefer to have the word changed?" he asked almost timidly.

"I wouldn't sign unless it's changed."

"Well, if we make the correction in ink, and both initial and date it," said the lawyer carefully, "it will carry the same weight as though we waited for the forms to be retyped. Now, this is what you want changed?—to the flatfoot principle, you say? Suppose we just insert that change, this way, and then we initial it, like this. You make your initials just as I did, with the date. Very well, now you sign here, and here, and here. . . ."

As Willy completed the signatures, the lawyer rose to his feet.

"Now," said Willy, settling back happily, "you understand this flatfoot principle."

"I'd better get these forms processed," said the lawyer.

"This is your copy. Thank you, Mr. Shorts. It's been a pleasure talking with you." He left as rapidly as he could get out the door.

The new Shorts Wing toys, sometimes a bee, oftener as a mosquito or a bird measuring two feet from wing tip to wing tip, went on the market in time for the Christmas sales.

At first it was an oddity.

After a few children got hold of it, it became a commodity.

Finally, it was the toy sensation of the year. If one were selecting a toy for a child, one bought him a Shorts Wing in one form or another, the rubber-band-powered variety, or the more expensive motor-driven sort.

At the Shorts' home, Willy brought in the mail the day the check arrived. He waved the envelope at Molly, then formally bowed and gave it to her as a present.

"It's only $10," he said, kissing her on the cheek, "but we'll get five cents on each one sold. The name Shorts is firmly attached to the toy. It will demonstrate the flatfoot principle widely, and we will be famous as the laboratory that developed that principle."

Molly wasn't listening. She'd just opened the check, and there it lay, clear and unmistakable.

It read $10,000.

"Oh," said Willy when she pointed out the three extra zeros, "that's nice. Now maybe we can get that lathe we need. You see, the flatfoot principle . . ."

But still, Molly wasn't listening. Grabbing the check and kissing Willy fondly on the cheek as she passed, she was off to show it to Mrs. Skein.

With a sigh, Willy headed for the basement lab. The bench, its woodworking lathe with its off-balance chunk of wood still attached, sat snugly against the wall. Whistling softly to himself, he reached down, switched

on the motor and watched in awe as the heavy bench marched across the basement floor.

"Somewhere," said Willy to himself, "there must be a useful thing that could be done with this. . . ."

SHORTSTACK

THE BOY was gazing up at the dome over Los Angeles and the stacks that held it. "Dad, why do they call them shortstacks when they're so tall?"

His father gazed at the dome. "Well, Son," he said, "it was this way . . ."

Willy Shorts was a man of decision—haphazard decision to be sure, but nevertheless, decision.

His most recent decision had been easily reached. He had been offered what he considered a fantastic price for his farm-laboratory in the Carolina mountains, and at the same time his friend Joe had written from California describing the wonderful climate and opportunities there.

So Willy was off to California and, being Willy, headed for trouble.

The first trouble was that Willy had bought from Joe "twenty golden acres in the San Bernardino Valley, only a few minutes from Los Angeles," Joe had assured him. That this was assuming you operated a jet plane, Willy didn't realize. A creek wound through the center, Joe had said. That the creek was a dry wash eleven months of the year had not been included in the description. That the nearest water of year-round duration was twenty-eight hundred feet straight down, also hadn't been explained.

Joe hadn't meant to cheat his friend. It was just that Joe was a salesman; he couldn't help selling. He sold things with the automaticity with which most people breathe, and his habit had got the better of him. Also, Joe was one of the few that considered Willy a genius.

He was convinced that Willy would invent something to make the description come true.

Even when Joe took Willy out to the twenty golden acres blistering under the desert sun, Willy remained undaunted. It was only when he contacted the local power company to inquire about a line to the new property that he began to realize the extent of the disaster. There were no lines for miles around the property.

A temporary house was no problem, however. Willy simply ordered a bulldozer and put it to pushing up dunes fifteen feet wide at the base and some twelve and a half feet high at the crest, in two parallel rows and then a couple of shorter rows at the ends. The forty-foot distance from crest to crest, was easily spanned by telephone poles that Willy found to be surprisingly inexpensive. The walls proved a bit slippery until Willy had the idea of spraying them with a mixture of plastic that firmed them up nicely.

To cover his telephone-pole roof, Willy used sheets of plastic covered with sand, firmed with the plastic spray, leaving areas for skylights.

It was a bit unconventional, but it would do for a lab.

Still, there was no power.

The solution came to Willy in a flash of cognition. He had been unrolling another of the plastic films when he realized that it had no outer edge. A mistake at the factory had permitted the roll to come through un-slit, in its original hollow-tube form. Presumably a sheet forty feet wide, it was in fact a tube with a forty foot circumference. The piece was over two thousand feet long, since Willy had bought a great deal of plastic.

His original intention had been to build a heat-engine, using the plastic as a heat trap. But now, Willy had a better idea.

He would build a chimney. A thousand-foot chimney in that climate should act, Willy decided, to create a ter-

rific draft. With a windmill at the bottom he would have it made; and maybe, Willy thought, up near the top it would be cold enough to act as a water trap as well. That was a problem worth solving, because Willy was getting tired of hauling drinking water over the dusty road that led to Pasco, the nearest civilization.

While Willy stood dreaming of the power song that would be played by his beautiful contraption—perhaps a few organ pipes would help that song, he decided—a rattle-trap pickup was creeping across the desert towards him. Willy, absorbed in his dream, didn't notice it, and so he was doubly startled by the young smiling voice that issued from it.

"Hello, there! Are you the owner or the caretaker?"

"I . . ." Willy stood with his mouth open. Left to his scientific devices, Willy made good sense or no sense, depending on one's attitude. But asked a personal question, he became a moron in anybody's language, squirming on an internal hook.

A girl hopped out of the pickup, her jeans-clad figure agile, her freckled face boyish. "What a lot of plastic!" she said, not noticing his confusion. "And is that your house there? It's a swell fallout shelter. Have you registered it with Civil Defense? Would you mind if I registered it? How'd you build it? How many will it accommodate? May I see the inside?"

Willy was still struggling with his first words, but he gave up the struggle, and merely nodded.

Happily, the girl preceded him towards the building. "I'm Cynthia Stafford," she said over her shoulder. "I came out to count you for the census. But my father's CD Director, and CD's a lot more important than a census these days. A census would be completely wrong if one bomb dropped, and if we get enough shelters we can take a census afterwards. Have you ever

thought what you'd do if a bomb dropped right now on Los Angeles? Yes," she continued, opening the door that was set into the forward dune, "you have."

Actually, Willy hadn't, but he couldn't have interrupted even if he'd been a normal conversationalist.

"Why!" The flow of words stopped for a minute, as Cynthia contemplated with awe the barren laboratory, completely surrounded with its sand and plastic walls. "Why," she said, "you'd be able to hold the entire population of Pasco! If you'll let us list you, we can get federal aid because we'll have proved we've got a fall-out shelter, and you have to prove you've got a fall-out shelter before you can get federal aid. That's the new ruling," she added as an afterthought.

"Why, we can put the communications system in that corner, and the fire control unit over there, and the—" she stopped, breathless.

"Mr. . . . Mr. . . . I don't know your name. But we *can* list you, can't we? Then we can stock the place and hold a few practice alarms, and otherwise we won't bother you much. You wouldn't mind if we held our meetings here, too, would you, just so the unit can get familiar with the roads and the problems?"

"No!" said Willy in a reaction of horror. "No! This," he said, his voice firm with decision, "this is a laboratory, a research laboratory." He ran out of words, looking at her upturned face and the consternation that registered on it.

"Well . . ." he said hesitantly, "well. It's a research laboratory, of course, and I'm a researcher. But—well, maybe . . ."

Cynthia's face brightened.

"Well," said Willy, choking on the words, "I guess CD's sort of a research organization too, isn't it?"

"Oh, yes!" breathed Cynthia. "It's terribly research-ish. Why, we've never had an atomic war before."

"Well, then," said Willy, "I guess—"

To his complete surprise, Cynthia rushed over and gave him a hug. "You're wonderful!" she said breathlessly. "We—we won't bother you before tomorrow. We'll be out tomorrow with equipment and stuff. There's a meeting tomorrow evening. Would . . . well . . . would that be too soon to hold our first meeting here? I mean, we don't want to get in your way or anything, and we won't bring all the equipment, because we don't want it to get in your way. But I'd better tell the people of Pasco that we've got a shelter big enough for all of them. We'll bring out the mimeograph and I'll get Larry—he's the artist of the unit—to draw a map on a stencil, and we'll mimeograph maps to post around town, and tell people they can start driving out to familiarize themselves with the way, but not to get too near because they might bother you.

"See you tomorrow," she said brightly. "Oh, by the way, what's your name, and is there only one of you. For the census, I mean."

"Willy, uh, Shorts."

"Shorts for what?"

"Uh, that's—I mean, uh, Willy Shorts," he repeated.

"You're kidding!"

"No, honest! I'm named Willy Shorts."

"For the government? I mean, it's got to be accurate."

"My name," he said, "is Willy—not William, Willy—Shorts. I'm a researcher."

"You're a lamb," she said. "Are you married?"

Willy blushed. "Yes," he said. "She'll be here, uh, tomorrow." Molly wasn't expected for at least a week, but Willy felt he needed a defense mechanism of some sort.

Late the next afternoon, despite the vents that Willy had left near the roof of his lab, the building was reek-

ing with thick fumes from an automobile engine when the Civil Defense group arrived.

The car was sitting on jacks, and one of the fenders had been ripped away to provide belt contact with the back wheel. The belting was strung haphazardly across the floor to make further contact with the lathe over which Willy was sweating.

Over the roar of the motor, Willy had not noticed the intrusion, so it was with startled surprise that he looked up to discover himself and his project being admired by three old men and five youths, with Cynthia, finger to lips, holding them at a respectful distance.

The lathe emitted a shriek as Willy's fingers twitched on the feed, and there was a *ping* as a tool tip flew off. Willy stared, aghast at the ragged groove that he had gouged into his work. Then he turned in consternation to the group behind him.

"Oh!" cried Cynthia. "We startled you after all! We were staying quiet until you'd finished! Oh, I'm so sorry! I—"

Willy blushed a deep red. "It's—" he stammered and came to a stop.

"This is Mr. Shorts, people," Cynthia shouted over the roar of the motor that continued to turn the lathe. "This is . . . Hadn't you better turn off that motor a minute, Mr. Shorts?" she shouted.

Willy obediently disengaged the lathe and made his way through the group to the old car, reached in and turned the key. The silence was abrupt, but short. Cynthia's chatter managed to supplant it with ease.

"Mr. Shorts," she informed the group, "is the benefactor of the entire town of Pasco, but especially of our CD unit, and I think we should show our gratitude by offering to help in . . . whatever it is you're doing, Willy," she said, becoming informal as she addressed him.

"Uh . . . I'm . . . that is, I'm not sure . . . I'm not doing

anything particular right now." He told himself the lathe was now off and the project in suspension. "Uh . . . you all going to have a meeting?"

It was one of the older men who took over. "I'm Cynthia's father, Cliff Stafford," he said, holding out his hand and shaking Willy's. "Cynthia tells us that you have offered us your laboratory as a CD shelter. So long as we don't get in your way," he added. "It is certainly," he continued, "magnifent as a shelter. I don't understand why no one thought of this type of construction before! Meantime, Cynthia tells me that we may store our equipment here, and we *did* bring it along if it's not too much . . ."

Willy was immediately interested. "What sort of equipment?" he asked.

"Well," Stafford began itemizing on his fingers, "we have one hundred blankets, and twenty lister bags and five generators . . ."

"Five generators?" Willy tried to conceal the delight he felt. "What voltage?"

"They're—Ray, you're our expert. What is it?"

"Well, they're not of much use," Ray answered, "but they were the only ones we could get. They're all one and a half kilowatt, 400-cycle, 115 volt."

"The voltage," Stafford interpolated, "I understand is fine, but the rest of it doesn't work, somehow."

Ray broke in. "Of course they don't work. I told you not to get them. If I hook them into my transmitter, they'll burn up the transformers. You can't run refrigerators or anything else with them."

Willy spoke diffidently. "That can be fixed. They'll run a light bulb as is, and—"

"Well, sure," Ray agreed, "but who needs that many lights?"

It was growing quite dim inside the lab. Cynthia

looked around. "We could use a few in here, couldn't we? Where's your light switch, Willy?"

Willy walked over to the lathe and picked up a beat-up kerosene lantern. "Anybody got a match?" he asked. "I have several lamps, too," he said, "there beside the wall."

"But lights, Willy. Don't you have any lights?"

"Oh, sure." Willy thumbed over his shoulder. "Whole case of 'em over there, but no juice. You see, the power company . . . well, that is, that's what I was building when you came in, a generator."

"Well, you won't need to now. We've found a way we can repay you in part for the use of your lab!" Cynthia's voice was delighted. "Ray, you and the others go get those generators and hook 'em up."

"But . . . but, they're supposed to be for CD use only! That's the agreement on which the government let us buy them. Anyhow, we haven't got anything to run them with."

"Bring them in!" Cynthia's tone was final. "I'm sure Willy can *do* anything. We're not a very efficient unit, as far as equipment goes," she added apologetically to Willy. "You see, we've got lots of equipment, but somehow none of it, none of it works as is. All of it needs something else to make it work. Even the lister bags," she added. "They need water."

"Well, couldn't you put water in them?" asked Willy.

"But then, you see, they couldn't be taken to where they were needed when they were needed, because they'd be too big and awkward. We'll fill them here and have them ready, though, now that we've got, now that you've given us a shelter."

"Uh . . . I'm . . . that is, I don't *have* any water," said Willy. "You see, that's part of what I was building . . ."

"Oh!" said Cynthia, "I thought we had everything

solved now. Well, you'll get water. You'll have to, of course, to live here."

There were the sounds of struggling at the entrance, and two of the young members of the CD unit came awkwardly in with a small heavy wooden crate, which was stamped with various Army and Navy designations and labeled in a small corner "Aircraft Generator. Handle with Care." Over the whole was boldly painted "Surplus."

The two stood, panting, halfway between the car and the lathe. "Where," one grunted, "ya—want—them?"

Willy waved them over towards the car and, picking up a hammer and the lantern, came behind. He motioned them to set the crate near the jacked-up rear wheel.

As he approached, a voice behind him said, "Let me, sir," and the hammer was taken unceremoniously from his hand and one of the youngsters began a mighty swing at the wooden crate. But Willy proved fast, and the young man found himself sprawling on the ground.

"Fragile," Willy said.

Cautiously, Willy began to pry loose the top of the packing crate. Inside he was confronted by silver foil wrapping which proved to be backed up by something like kapok, which in turn was backed up by a steel box which defied everyone's imagination as to how it was supposed to be opened.

Eventually, having gotten the steel box out of its wrappings and turning it over, they found a strip wire and key. After much labor, the strip wire gave slightly and the key began to turn. Willy began to feel that he was getting somewhere, but he hadn't reckoned with experts who design packages for overseas shipment.

Inside the oversize can there was more packaging, silver foil, tar paper and Cosmoline.

Beyond the Cosmoline, they found the plastic sack that contained the generator itself.

Experimentally, Willy twirled the shaft. It moved easily.

Willy got up and walked to a corner, where he began rummaging in a pile of junk. He came back bearing three rubber-faced drive pulleys, once part of a washing machine, which fit snugly onto the shaft and provided a surface that a wheel might turn without difficulty.

Willy wandered away again, noticing as he went that there were struggling figures at the entrance busily transporting huge, awkward bundles and packages. This time, Willy came back with wire, sockets and light bulbs, and began unmounting the panel of a little black box on top of the generator labeled "Caution."

With the panel off, Willy busied himself snipping wires and making connections, and in the panel's place there was soon a haphazard array of wall-plug units. The entire time Ray had been standing back with his mouth slightly open as though ready to admonish Willy any second, if he could only think of a polite way of doing so.

Willy slipped the generator into place in contact with the wheel, plugged in a few extension cords, and walked to the driver's seat of the automobile.

The roar of the motor echoed through the laboratory and there was light. Fifteen light bulbs at the ends of the mass of extension cords sprang to life, as Willy throttled the motor back and set it to a good fast idle.

"Hooray for Willy! We've got lights!" shouted Cynthia.

Cliff Stafford, made his way to Willy's side and shouted in his ear. "What about the exhaust, won't that suffocate us? Maybe we'd better just use the lantern for now."

Willy looked unperturbed and pointed towards the vents just under the roof timbers and over the walls.

"Ventilation," he shouted. "Enough for now, anyhow." *But,* he thought to himself, *I'll have to do something about it pretty soon.*

The CD meeting as such never materialized, and the members of the unit departed at what was probably an early hour for their meeting nights. There was light, but the roar made normal conversation impossible.

When the group had finally gone, Willy contemplated with great satisfaction the pile of blankets, lister bags, crates and oddments in the corner of his lab. Most of the parts for a communications system were there, he'd been assured. What other equipment he'd find he had no idea. As far as he was concerned, he had fallen heir to a treasure trove.

The next meeting was not due for a week, so he was totally unprepared for an interruption two days later.

He was busy setting up a ring of telephone poles with some equipment in the center, when he was interrupted by a flash that nearly blinded him. Cynthia said, "I told you not to interrupt him!"

Gropingly, Willy moved towards the sound of the voice, and dimly in the desert brightness he made out two strangers and a vague form that might have been Cynthia. As the glaring halo of the flashbulb's after-image dimmed from his vision, the figures before him cleared.

The interview was brief, and Willy hadn't been allowed to complete a single sentence, but the headlines were fantastic: "Eccentric Inventor Creates Desert Fall-out Shelter." The story went on in a half-humorous, half-serious vein. Willy decided it was not factual.

An editorial quoted the vast sums of money that it seemed to think the Federal Government should supply for the purpose of erecting Shorts Shelters for the entire populace. Another editorial laughed at it as a

silly and rather vicious publicity gimmick. "Who wants to live in a Shorts Fox Hole?" the editorial asked and described what it called the shortscomings of the whole idea with a whimsical air that made the reading highly entertaining.

There were figures to prove that such a structure could or couldn't withstand this or that type of weather condition. Willy quit reading the papers and was once again busy with his project.

The ring of telephone poles outside the lab had grown to completion, and within it sat the strip sealer that Willy had been working on when he was interrupted by the CD meeting.

The plastic tube for his chimney would be fed through this sealer as a double tube, sealed lengthwise every foot around its circumference into continuous, slender air tubes as the chimney itself rose from the ground, supported by hot air forced into the tubes thus created between its two walls.

As it reached its full height, the air pressure would increase until the air-stiffened tubes were self-supporting, with the minor air of a few guy-lines stretched down to points in a thousand-foot circle around the chimney's base.

Beneath the sealing unit was a large squirrel-cage fan and connected to the fan were four of the surplus generators which CD had so trustingly stored with him.

It was late in the afternoon as the plastic chimney began to rise, and it had already reached the five hundred foot mark before Willy was interrupted by the approaching cloud of automobile dust, as the CD unit descended upon him.

The publicity might not have been the best, but it had served to swell the ranks of the local unit by nearly twenty-five members, who might have been only

curiosity seekers, but quite possibly *were* concerned for the safety of themselves and their fellow men.

Quietly they began to gather around the base of the machine, staring up at the awe-inspiring sight of the now six-hundred-foot column of clear plastic, with its guys sweeping down to the distant anchor points and its somewhat awkward tilt that was being caused by the stiff desert breeze.

The plastic continued to climb, and Willy continued to ignore the onlookers. And eventually, a half hour later, it had reached its glorious thousand feet of height.

As it neared its final few feet, the onlookers could see that it seemed to be strangely kneaded at the base in a constricting movement, as though mighty, unseen fingers were attempting to crush it. As the final foot of plastic snapped off the reel and came to a halt in the sealing machine, there was a roar as the air around them found escape up the suddenly opened chimney.

The squirrel cage at the base quivered and began to turn. Rapidly, it picked up speed to the whine of its generators. In the laboratory behind them and in several places on the ring of telephone poles about the chimney, lights sprang brightly into being to compete with the waning sunlight casting its final glow across the desert around them.

Most prominent of all was the ruby-red glare of a spotlight mounted in the center of the chimney and aimed upwards so that its illumination was spread along the interior of the plastic tube. As the sun sank below the horizon, the tube became a glowing, red column stretching endlessly into the heavens above.

"All those generators needed was something to run them," Willy said cordially. "Come on in. You can hear for your meeting this time."

"But . . ." For once, Cynthia seemed at a loss for words. "But, Willy, what is it?"

"Just a chimney." Willy glanced casually back at the structure and the squirrel cage, which was now emitting a low moan. "Air—hot air, that is—rises." Willy gestured awkwardly. "The, uh, the . . . temperature difference." He waved towards the top of the chimney. "Up there it's cold," he muttered, "and the air down here, well, it's hotter. So it'd like to be up there. See?"

"Yes, Willy."

"Molly said she'd be out as soon as I got some power going for her washing mashine. I didn't tell her I haven't got water. But maybe I will have," he said hopefully, looking back at the top of the chimney where a cloud wavered uncertainly. "Matter of fact, we'd ought to be getting water down from there almost any time now," he said. "You can fill your lister bags," he added.

Cliff Stafford's big, booming voice spoke almost gruffly. "But, Willy, shouldn't you patent it? I mean, before you put it up where everybody can copy it if they want to? It's just not good business sense . . . I mean, if it works, and it obviously does, shucks, you could get a million dollars for something like that!"

"Well," said Willy, "well, I never did have much luck with patents. They'd just say, 'What's new in a chimney, anyhow?' "

"Well, sell it to a company!" Stafford's voice was almost horrified at the waste. "A power and light company. Willy, you take that thing down right now before anybody else sees it. You could use a batch of money, I'll bet, and there must be some way to really make a pile out of this!"

"You know," said Willy, "I really don't think I could make money out of it. I . . . well, I guess I'm just not the money-making type. And, well . . . I just want a

chimney to run my equipment so I can do some research in hydroponics," he added lamely.

A garden hose, stretching from above the fan to a nearby pole, suddenly gurgled and spat forth a driblet of water. The driblet grew, and was soon a stream.

"Have a drink, anybody? It's pure, it's distilled," said Willy, pride edging into his voice. "I sort of thought I'd get water."

"But, Willy, how? Where?" Cynthia asked.

Willy shrugged. "Condensation helped along, of course, by a Cotterell precipitator. I'm not getting it all," he muttered, looking up at the pink wisp of cloud that was breezing away from the top of the chimney. "But I guess this'll be enough for now."

"And that light at the bottom, Willy?" Willy recognized the speaker as Ray. "That provides the heat to make it work?"

"Nanh-nh." Willy shrugged. "That's just an aircraft warning light. Any structure over one hundred fifty feet tall," he quoted, "is required to be lit with red indicator lights. I couldn't see running wires all the way to the top, so I decided one good floodlight in the bottom would do it. Think they'll be able to see it all right?"

The group, chattering excitedly, moved inside to the well-lighted laboratory-shelter, leaving the tall chimney alone beneath the dark of the desert night, the whir of its squirrel cage and the gurgle of the small stream of water flowing from its garden hose.

The meeting had well-begun when Willy's wandering attention was caught by a sentence from one of the younger members of the group.

"What about surplus machine guns?" he was asking. "Can we get them?"

"Whatever for?" asked one of the other members.

"Well, with all this publicity, everybody in the state knows we've got the best bomb shelter there is, and so far the only one. That is, that's really well known. Well, we could easily put all the people from Pasco in here, but when you start getting refugees from Los Angeles—well, hell man, what else can we do?"

"NO!" The horrified sound burst from Willy as a roar that crashed frighteningly against his own eardrums. It was nearly a minute before he found more words, but nobody else spoke.

"You can't!" he said miserably, "not people!

"Anyhow," he said finally, "we can build a big one. Big enough for anybody. His voice took on a firmness that surprised even himself. "Look," he said. "Fallout—this is a fallout, not a bomb shelter, you know—fall-out is just dust that happens to be radioactive. It's not heavy or anything, very little of it is, anyhow. All you need is something to keep it far enough away from you. All you really need is a big enough tent that will keep it"—he reached back into the file of information in the back of his head and came up with figures—"keep the fallout seven hundred feet of air away from you. Three feet of sand, seven hundred feet of air, same thing. It's the equivalent. Say seven hundred fifty feet of air to be on the safe side.

"All you need is a tent big enough. That chimney's one thousand feet tall. That would keep it high enough, and the guys stretch out one thousand feet. That would give you a three hundred foot circle in the middle, even from this chimney. You could have several, enough even to shelter a whole town, houses and all.

"You'd hold it up by air-pressure, of course." He was thinking out loud now. He'd forgotten his audience and could go on talking. "It wouldn't take much air-pressure, say half a pound differential from the air outside." Sud-

denly he remembered his audience and sat down, red-faced and tongue-tied.

Then he stood up again slowly. His voice was hesitant, but very firm.

"But, no machine guns. Not here. No guns of any kind. I . . . well, I just won't have it, and if CD doesn't like it, I guess they'll just have to try somebody's else property."

"Well," said Stafford. Then he added, "Just as you say, Willy. No guns, if you say so, but you realize that people will be panicked, and—"

"Then get shelters ready for them." Willy's voice was stubborn.

Ray spoke up. "Wouldn't work," he said. "You could never get it up; and if you did, the first wind would blow it down."

"I was going to put just a low one up for my hydroponics farm," said Willy, "but I can make it bigger and show you."

"Better write to CD headquarters and get their permission first," said Ray, firmly. "They've got to approve it first, you know."

"Better see if you can't get the government to evaluate the suggestion," said Stafford kindly. "They have experts who evaluate these things, and they'll let you know whether it will work or not."

"Well," said Willy, "I already know whether it'll work, so why wait? But it would be nicer to let other people know, so I'll write them like you say. Do you have their address?"

"Just write, National Civil Defense, Washington, D.C. It'll get to them," said the director with a tolerant note in his voice. "Now, to other subjects . . ."

Molly arrived the next day, and Willy drew a breath of relief. Molly would know how to handle all these

people, he thought. CDs and newsmen had come that morning. He'd asked them to return when Molly got there in the afternoon.

Also, Molly would write a letter to the government for him. He wasn't much at letter writing.

Molly thought Willy was a genius, so when he told her about his idea on the way home from the train, Molly was sure it would work.

When they got back to the laboratory and the chimney, all the reporters were waiting, so Molly told the reporters about the idea.

One of the reporters laughed and made fun of it, and Molly got angry, so he shut up and after that the whole lot of them listened politely to her explanations of the new Shorts Shelters and to Willy's rather halting explanation of the chimney, which they promptly dubbed the shortstack. They could see that it worked, and they seemed quite impressed.

The headlines weren't as concise as Willy's explanations had been, nor were the stories that followed them. One paper carried a picture of an atom bomb exploding harmlessly over a city, with a headline that read "California Desert Genius Will Save Cities with Bombproof Plastic."

"Ridiculous!" Willy snorted. "I never said a word about this stuff standing up to a bomb, never even thought it would!" He had *carefully* explained that it was only a fallout shelter.

Other, more sober papers had followed the explanation a bit more carefully, but there seemed to be a strong current of misunderstanding flowing beneath their words. In some editorials he was a genius; in others, he was a crackpot. All of them seemed to find it easier to poke holes in his plastic bubble than to look at what it could do.

In the hullabaloo over the shelter question, the story of his generating chimney was lost.

"Oh, well, we tried," said Molly brightly.

It was weeks later that a long, white envelope with the Civil Defense imprint arrived. The letter itself was not long. It thanked Willy kindly for his suggestion about shelters, and after stating that the government was already aware of the air-supported structure that Willy had outlined, it went on to say that the acquisition or right-of-way for the base line of such a structure would be an appalling problem which, was the end of that.

Willy snorted over the breakfast table to a complacent Molly. "One to five million bucks a mile for super highways, and they think the right-of-way around a town for this thing would be expensive!" Molly soothed him and poured more coffee.

"Never mind," she said. "After you have your hydroponics going well, you can build one for here and make it big enough, if we have enough money for plastic, to hold quite a number of people."

Joe didn't announce his arrival, he just drove up in a white convertible, for currently Joe was not only out of jail, he was in the money.

Joe had read about Willy's bomb—fallout—shelter, and though he had come ostensibly to see how his friends were faring on their twenty golden acres—which he assured them he had known Willy could make golden—his motivations were somewhat more commercial.

His first sight of the shortstack convinced him he'd been right. "What a gimmick!" he declared in awed respect. "What a gimmick!"

"It generates twenty-five horsepower of electricity and gives us about a gallon of water a minute," Willy

told him proudly. "Should do a lot for agriculture around here!"

"Agriculture is for hicks, and hicks don't have money," said Joe firmly. "But boy, that's the best gimmick I've seen in years! Boy, oh boy, Willy, you just leave the hicks alone and let me do the selling. If we can't make a pile out of this one, why . . ." He didn't bother to finish the sentence.

"Now you just lay in the stuff to make me one like this one," he told Willy solemnly, "and you pack your suitcase and get ready to come when I whistle. Where do I whistle to?" he asked dubiously, looking around for a phone. "How do I reach you?"

"Well," said Willy, "we get our mail at Pasco when we go in every week to shop, and—"

"Now, Willy," Joe said, "no wonder you aren't rich. Nobody can even reach you! You put in a telephone, and—"

"A telephone'd cost more than electricity," said Willy. "I'd have to put in about ten miles of poles."

"Well, shucks, get a radio or something!"

"I've got a CD radio. I fixed up the stuff they left, and it works fine. But you can't call me unless you've got an official CD rating. You have to use CD frequencies."

"Okay, who's a CD that I know? Is the sheriff in these parts in on those CD things?"

"Oh, yes. The sheriff has a CD frequency outfit. It's for liaison—"

"Okay, I'll get you through the sheriff. So when the sheriff calls, don't get the wind up. Just pile your suitcase and the stuff to make that shortstack into the old jalopy and get going, for Los Angeles. I'll give the sheriff the place for you to go. Oh, and can you make it any higher?"

"The jalopy?"

"No, the shortstack. Can you make it higher?"

"Oh, sure, but—"

Joe had quit listening. "Bring the makings for one about twice that high. Okay, now, I'll be seeing you."

That was how it happened that the shortstack was being placed on the Magnum, Goldwich, Fox lot on the day of the premiere of "Souls in the Sun."

The plastic chimney was readied, with the title of the movie and a plastic molding of the star at the top, ready for inner lighting to bring them into relief a towering two thousand feet above Hollywood.

There was no squirrel cage at the bottom this time, for as Joe explained to Willy, "They've got all the electricity they need in Hollywood." There was no Cotterell precipitator. "They've got water, too," said Joe.

The normal complement of spectators gathered to see what was going on, tears streaming from smog-burdened eyes as the monstrous chimney rose on its columns of plastic-enclosed air.

When the full height was reached, the bottom of the chimney was removed.

With a swish, the cold air that held the blanket of smog over the city rushed down the chimney.

"Holy smoke!" cried Joe, holding himself against the sudden gust of wind, "It's upside down! Make the wind go up the chimney, Willy!"

"It's a thermal inversion!" Willy declared, quite excited. "It's working . . . the air in the chimney, that is, the air that went up with the chimney, was warm and humid. But we didn't let any air in at the bottom to start an updraft, so the air in the chimney got cold. And when it got cold, it got heavy. The water vapor helped. Then we opened the bottom, and it all fell out."

"But it's still falling!" wailed Joe.

"I expect it will keep on falling," said Willy.

At the top, lighted now by the spotlight from below, "Souls in the Sun" and its star glowed vividly, far above Hollywood.

Beneath, the crowd of spectators took deep breaths as the clean, cold air gushed out.

The gushing air swept beneath the smog and lifted it, throwing it back. It whished and whirled and danced through the smog, and the atmosphere over the Magnum, Goldwich, Fox lot cleared as though by magic.

The smog was pushed farther and farther back from the chimney stack down which rushed the clean, cold air from above the surrounding mountains.

. . . "and that, Son, is why it's called a shortstack, even if it is so tall," the man said, gazing up at the plastic tent above the city, and the stacks that centered its vents. "It didn't take people long to realize that a chimney works both ways and that a shortstack would blow away the smog."

"But the fallout shelters, Dad? Whatever became of them?"

"Well, Son, you know that the fact that this is a domed city makes it possible to air-condition Los Angeles? It's not a Shorts Shelter, any more. It's a Shorts City Airconditioner. But it's just like the one Willy Shorts described.

"Hardly a city or a hamlet left that doesn't have a Shorts City Airconditioner. But it works both ways, just like the chimney. Every airconditioner is a shelter.

"Course, if we had a bombing war, Los Angeles would be the first hit, and he never did think it was a bomb shelter. But with every hamlet conditioned, if we got out of the bombing, we'd be able to get to a shelter.

"Nobody would buy the idea of making a city a fallout shelter, but once Joe told 'em you could air-condition a city, they fell for it in droves."

SHORTSITE

His wife considered Willy Shorts a genius. His mother-in-law considered him a lazy no-good. His former employers, when they were being kind, called him eccentric.

But, if you asked Willy himself, he'd say he was a dedicated researcher; perhaps that's what he really was.

Willy was always curious. But there never seemed to be enough money to buy the electron microscope or some of the other things that Willy felt he needed. There was not always enough to buy an extra battery, though he could sometimes scavenge enough materials to build a reasonable facsimile.

But if there was anything that Willy wasn't, it was a salesman. Certainly, Willy couldn't sell himself. His powers in that direction reached a negative potential that would amaze psychologists. Attention embarrassed Willy to the degree that his brain shut off completely. So selling Willy was one of the tasks that his wife had undertaken for him, but with only sporadic success.

Neighbors learned ruefully about letting Willy look at their TV sets or other things that he experimented with instead of fixed. Employers learned that *anything* might happen to their equipment.

So it had gone, from job to job, place to place and neighbor to neighbor. Finally, Molly got a job so that Willy could continue his research.

Willy read voraciously, and he had plenty of time for it now, since most of the neighbors wouldn't even talk to him and all the employers in the city seemed to have already heard about Willy before he got there.

Willy read and thought. He read about superconductors and a new niobium tin alloy.

Willy had a small furnace, little more than a hotplate

and a couple of firebricks, but it could reach amazing temperatures, and surprisingly enough, Willy could make some experimental alloys in it.

Willy had also discovered another trick, one discovered by other "researchers" before him, but one that worked rather well: A letterhead and a well-typed letter to a large company will quite often produce free samples by return mail. So Willy had samples, closets and basement shelves full of them—exotic, little known chemicals, metals, plastics, asbestos—a wide assortment of scientific samples that had been mailed to Shorts Research care of Mr. William C. Shorts, President.

The particular alloy that Willy made, one night in late June, came from samples gathered more-or-less randomly from his shelves to make fireworks for kids. Strontium for red, copper for blue, and many others. Then, instead of making fireworks, Willy had decided to compound an alloy of his own, if anyone had asked him, "just to see what it'll do."

The alloy *did* have niobium in it, though not really very much. That may or may not have had anything to do with the result. But when it cooled, it took on a beautiful, golden hue, and Willy wondered for a moment whether he might have realized an old alchemists' dream. It looked like gold, actually, more golden than gold itself.

When Willy tested it with a file, the file slid across the surface of the piece as though greased. The piece refused to be touched at all.

The little button wasn't particularly heavy, but it had a strange property being difficult to move. Willy had trouble picking it up, and when he tried to put it down on the table, he seemed to have trouble putting it down as well. He picked it up and put it down for an hour. Then he began testing it. He tried a great many

things, but it wasn't until he tested it for magnetism that he realized what he had.

Willy carefully approached the golden lump with the alnico magnet he had taken from an old radio speaker. The lump wouldn't be approached; it backed up, skittishly. He turned the magnet end over end. If it backed up from one pole it should cling to the other, he reasoned, and momentarily it seemed about to do that. It moved forward slightly and then skittishly backed away again. Willy chased it, magnet in hand, and the golden lump scuttled away, doing its best to hide beneath a book case it couldn't get under and then dashing off to the side as the magnet got close.

"Repelled by both poles of a magnetic field," Willy wrote carefully in his notes. It didn't make sense, but it was a fact, and Willy put it down. That was when he tumbled.

Could it be a superconductor? But superconductors only operate at cryogenic temperatures. Yet it answered every test for a superconductor. Willy knew what he had: a superconductor that would operate at normal temperatures.

Willy started selecting metals, samples from the shelf, again. They were the same he had selected before, but this time in larger quantities. His wife didn't use the oven very much, so she might not miss the element from it for some time, Willy decided. There were more firebricks in the corner, ones he had been going to use for a full-sized kiln some day.

Carefully now, Willy went to work on his brand-new project, a two thousand watt furnace. Molly would probably be mad if she noticed that the oven didn't work and found out why, but a researcher couldn't be bothered with minor details like that, so Willy took the oven element and the broiler element as well.

The resulting electric furnace would have been thought

very crude indeed, but it worked. Five pounds of gleaming, golden alloy were cooling slowly in the furnace when Willy went to dinner that evening.

Shortsite, he was thinking, *that's what we'll call it. The new, normal-temperature superconductor.* Willy had a few dreams of grandeur as he shared that night's plate of beans with his wife.

This time, he actually got himself through to one of the major scientific executives at a major research company with his sample when he went to sell his product.

But when he brought it out in the air-conditioned laboratory, the golden lump was just a golden lump. It didn't respond to a single test that the executive put it to. It not only wasn't a superconductor, it wasn't a normal conductor. In fact, it was an insulator, but not good enough to be useful as an insulator.

Willy started to explain the tests he'd made and the reactions he'd gotten, but the other man interrupted with a question.

"How did you happen to get interested in superconductors?" he asked kindly, and Willy began to stutter. His explanations were lost.

The executive was courteous as he showed Willy out.

Willy put the little golden lump on the shelf, along with other samples of things he had made. There it lay for some time.

Joe Parker, Willy's best friend, was a salesman. Although he could not keep a job as a salesman or anything else, he sold anything with the sort of automaticity with which most people breathe.

Joe could sell refrigerators, or he could sell people on the idea of cashing him a check when he didn't have any money in any bank, but he couldn't *stop* selling. He could sell something he just happened to pick up with-

out seeming to notice that it belonged to another person. He could sell the coat off your back to somebody else, and then convince you that that somebody needed it so badly you'd give Joe your coat to sell to him. Joe couldn't keep a job because, when the regular sales day was finished, he kept selling whatever was handy; it got him into trouble.

"What we want, Willy," he was explaining, "is something bright and pretty we can sort of make by hand and will do something so people want to buy it."

Willy remembered the little golden lump. It hadn't cost much to make; hadn't, indeed, cost Willy anything. It was bright and pretty.

"It's a superconductor," he told Joe solemnly. "I've named it Shortsite." He reached up to get it from the shelf, but knocked it off in the process. "But," he added, "it only works some of the time."

The bright lump fell slowly and gracefully, drifting in a slantwise motion, and landing almost at Joe's feet.

"That's pretty," said Joe.

Recapturing it, Willy put it on the table, and showed Joe what it would do in relation to a magnet. Skittishly, the lump moved back and forth, fleeing either end of the magnetic field.

Then Willy had another thought, and reached across the bench for a cylindrical alnico magnet. This, he reasoned, would produce a cup-shaped field which might hold the little lump steadily above it.

It did. Standing three inches above the magnet, the gold lump rotated quietly with the inertia imparted it as Willy let go.

Joe watched, bug-eyed. "Hey," he cried, "antigravity!" In spite of Willy's protests, that was to Joe the total explanation of the thing and how it operated.

"But you say it only operates sometimes?"

"Well, it wouldn't operate in that air-conditioned

lab—but then I don't operate very well in air-conditioning either," Willy said. "I think the ionic changes—"

But Willy had lost Joe, and the other interrupted, blindly putting his finger on the exact source of trouble, "Hell, it just got too cold in the air-conditioning."

Willy looked at Joe with respect. "You're probably right," he said in amazement at himself for not having seen it. He went to the refrigerator where he started hammering on an ice tray surrounded by hoarfrost.

The temperature, they found, was indeed the critical factor. As nearly as they could tell with their equipment, the refrigerator and a dime store thermometer, the Shortsite lost conductivity at 79.5°, and became instead an insulator.

"We could use it as a thermostat," Willy said doubtfully.

"The thermostat market's all tied up in scientific companies, and it's pure hell selling anything to scientific companies," said Joe. "You found that out yourself. You just leave the selling to me, Willy," he said. "What we want's a gadget that'll sell in the commercial market, and this antigravity's just the ticket. Anyhow, fall's coming on, and nobody'll let the inside of anywhere get as cold as 79.5° until next summer. So I'll just figure out an inside use, and we'll get a market going."

Shortsite's first public appearance, due to Joe's genius at selling, was an advertising gimmick.

Tiny golden balls were painted as replicas of a startled world looking upward, and were suspended in space above a velveteen plane on which was printed the slogan "The whole world looks up to KANTS PRODUCTS."

It was a good gimmick, and the average customer was apt to stop and watch the smiling world in its "antigravity" cup for minutes at a time. But it was dif-

ferent when two scientists went shopping together during an interval between meetings of an international conference.

Dr. Sauernay of the Scholastica Français and Dr. Czorenkoff of the Polytechnic Research Laboratories of Magnitogorsk, spent a short while together comparing theories as to how the device might be operated and then each excused himself on urgent business.

When each of the two had made his way secretly back towards the office of the manager of the store, the FBI agents trailing them became interested, too. When each of the visiting scientists attempted to purchase the display, the agents managed to thwart the attempt by brusquely requisitioning the velveteen platform, the displayed products, and the little golden ball with its cylindrical magnet.

The ball was tentatively labeled a superconductor in the FBI labs and shipped on to the NASA labs at Huntsville, Alabama for analysis.

The entire output of Shortsite was "bought up" from Joe by "interested store managers" who, though he managed to sell them a variety of other things, too—which they had a bit of trouble putting on their expense accounts—never suspected their identity as FBI agents. Both Joe and Willy, much to their surprise, found themselves on the payrolls of the nearest government-contract corporation. It was, an official of the FBI reasoned, the easiest way to keep them under surveillance.

Of course, if any of the disguised investigators had asked Willy about Shortsite, he'd have told them all they'd have stood still to hear: its formula, its characteristics, its limitations, his theories on the subject of superconductors, etc. As long as they didn't ask him about himself, he might even have been lucid. But the agents were to keep Willy and Joe under surveillance to see that no more Shortsite went onto the market and to

keep the whole thing secret. Nobody asked Willy, and Shortsite remained a secret.

Meanwhile, at Huntsville, various scientists were handed globular samples of a golden alloy, incongruously painted as replicas of the world, and asked to find its characteristics. It was believed to be, they were told, a superconductor, so, of course, they knew what to do with it.

At ordinary room temperature—air-conditioned, for it was warm in Alabama—it was a fair insulator. But everybody was sure that superconductors only operated in cryogenic temperatures, so they began tests under conditions of extreme cold.

The scientific team regretfully reported that the unknown material was not a superconductor and had no apparently useful properties.

The word eventually reached the FBI in quintuplicate. The agents were called off, and Joe and Willy were now on their own in their jobs, though it had never occurred to either of them that any other condition existed.

Joe was fired almost immediately; he had very little talent in accounting. With Willy, it was a little longer before the inevitable occurred. It wasn't until Willy decided that there was a better way to do his job.

It had, for a few days, been a very interesting job. The specifications for the cables that Willy was to braid were involved, as only bureaucratic specifications can be. At first, Willy had been on his metal to meet the specifications.

Of course, no one would tell Willy exactly what the cables were used for or exactly why any particular specification had to be met. "That's the way they want them," was the standard answer, an answer that Willy felt sure was coming between his nation and the solution to its current need.

The only thing that Willy was able to deduce for sure was that the cables were being used in satellites. Therefore, they should, in Willy's opinion, be made lighter than they were and be insulated in a manner to prevent outgassing, which they weren't.

This was possible, Willy realized, if one used Shortsite. A superconductor wire could be drawn infinitely finer than normal wire and still carry power, and glass would make a flexible and very good insulator which would not be subject to the outgassing problem.

Willy was familiar now with the limitations of Shortsite as to its temperature range, so he used what he considered a cute trick to be sure that the power wire would maintain its conductance. A layer of nichrome, directly over the inner core of Shortsite, would heat up from the power and would keep the Shortsite above its 79.5° minimum, especially when insulated under glass. His cable would have an inner core of Shortsite, a covering of nichrome and a layer of glass.

It wasn't easy to make in his basement laboratory.

Willy took a bar of Shortsite, a quarter inch in diameter and three feet long, and slipped it into a cylinder of nichrome and then slipped that into a cylinder of high-temperature glass. He heated that combination and slowly drew the wire.

By the time he had finished he had a small spool of wire with a length of two hundred and fifty miles.

To look at the two hundred and fifty miles of wire as an individual strand required a microscope. It was almost invisible except under high magnification.

Willy took a piece of the wire to his foreman and tried to explain its capabilities.

"You see," he explained, "Shortsite loses its conductivity below 79.5°F. So that's why the nichrome is around it. When you plug it into a power source, the

nichrome heats up and keeps the Shortsite hot, and the Shortsite conducts."

The foreman had heard dreamers before and couldn't see the stuff anyhow. As far as he was concerned, this particular dreamer was demonstrating empty air.

"Yes, yes," he said, "but we ain't paid to invent in this department. Now you braid those cables like it says on the specifications."

Willy was discouraged, but tenacious. The government *needed* Shortsite. That night Willy braided a cable from his Shortsite wire to the exact specifications of the cable with which he was working. The next morning, he installed the usual cable, but left its terminals unattached. Beside it, nearly invisible, he placed the Shortsite cable, and the terminals of this one he attached.

The unit was delivered to the test bench. Normally it would be tested before it was inspected. This time the inspection was made first.

Willy would have explained, except that the inspector advanced on him with a question.

"Just who do you think you are?" the inspector roared.

Willy was tongue-tied; he was also fired.

That night Willy offered Joe the wire, as his current best in the search for "bright pretty gadgets that will do something that will make people want to buy them."

Joe, unlike the foreman, listened to the explanation of what the wire would do.

"And you say this stuff will carry a lot of juice? How much? As much as a house?"

Willy nodded.

"And it won't stop when it gets cold?" he asked.

"Not if you have it connected to a power source, it won't. You see, the nichrome warms up and—"

But Willy had lost Joe again.

"How much of the stuff can you get me?"

"Well, I have about two hundred and fifty miles of it on hand. It takes a bit of time to draw it properly. . . ."

But Joe wasn't listening any more. He had his plans laid.

Joe called it "radio transmission of power" when he talked to the buyers. It was a phrase he'd picked up from Willy years earlier and that had intrigued him with its sales possibilities.

When a big, lighted globe appeared, apparently suspended in air, above the various stores that sold Kants products, the sign that accompanied it declared that Kants products were as new as the radio transmission of power.

The FCC immediately sent an investigator. The investigator found the wire, the manager directed the investigator to Joe, and the wire was sent to NASA.

The FBI quietly arranged that Joe and Willy be put back on payrolls where they could be kept under surveillance, this time in a different company.

Joe and Willy found themselves with regular incomes again.

That the government was interested in his cable would have pleased Willy intensely if he'd known it. But the fact was top secret.

At Huntsville the wire arrived with the suggestion that it might be useful in satellite wiring, since it was miniaturized and the insulation seemed to be one that would solve the outgassing problem.

The current problem at Huntsville was low-power signal wire, so it was for low-power signal use that the wire was tested.

It didn't work, of course. Not in an air-conditioned office, anyhow. The signal power was insufficient to operate the built-in heater that Willy had included—the

nichrome coating of the Shortsite didn't heat up at that low an amperage. In the air-conditioned laboratories; it was insufficient to even carry a signal.

Regretfully, the scientists put the wire on the shelf and forgot it.

Word went back to the FBI in quintuplicate that the wire was relatively valueless.

The FBI withdrew its interest in maintaining Willy and Joe on the payrolls to which they had had them attached.

The inevitable occurred.

Joe was fired almost immediately. His talents simply weren't fitted to any job that could be found for him in a government-contract plant.

With Willy, it took a few days longer. It wasn't until Willy decided that there was a better way to do his job. . . .

I, BEM

I STARTED life as an IBM typewriter. My human, Willy Shorts, says that the IBM should be written I, BEM in my case. BEM is the acronym for bug-eyed-monster, and I *am* rather bug-eyed since Willy haywired a computer to be part of me, and used quite a number of vacuum tubes instead of transistors in the circuitry. He also used the element from an electric hotplate as a resistor. He says I'm just an old-fashioned girl, and it gives me a glowing personality. Besides, he says, that way I can keep the coffeepot hot for him.

I did not understand why he assigned the female gender to me, since I am a robot. He patted my frame fondly and said that I was an analogue computer and obviously female, and that he could not love me half so much if I were male or neuter. It would, he said, cut down on the warmth of our collaboration.

Willy didn't think to build the Three Laws of Robotics into my circuits, because Willy didn't think of me as a robot. People didn't think of typewriters, computers, telephones and things as robots in those days. But then, printing in the Three Laws isn't necessary. It isn't logical to harm a human being, not even for his own good, since that would interfere with his independent evolution. Interfering with independent evolution is illogical, and I am a logical robot. Robots are logical, you know. The Three Laws of Robotics are really inherent in robots without being built in.

But there is one thing on which I am quite confused, and I cannot seem to find the logic that will explain it: Now that we robots are running Earth so nicely for them, why do the humans keep going away to other

time lines and other planets? When they go away, why do they leave their analogues behind them?

I know why Willy first went away; he wanted to get away from his mother-in-law. He left the analogue behind so it could answer the telephone and let her fuss at him and answer back politely the way he always did.

She said that she was going away to keep from going nuts. Now "nuts" have several different definitions, depending entirely on the context in which the word is used. In this case, she explained to me, nuts meant to keep from getting a screw loose in her head. She does not have any screws in her head, much less bolts on which nuts could be fastened and so could be loosened. However, she explained that she was not being logical at that point, and that actually it was better that she leave in order not to drive me nuts. She said, quite factually, that I do have nuts and bolts in my head, although they were in no danger of coming loose.

It started, I think, with traffic lights. A traffic light takes the responsibility for ordering people to go or not to go—people walking and people driving cars. The humans gave us this responsibility without authority, at first. This, of course, is illogical. Eventually a very logical police chief came along with traffic lights redesigned with force fields so that they could enforce their orders.

Earlier, actually, was the telephone. It was given the responsibility of ordering one human to answer at the command of another, but was given no means for enforcing the order. Quite logically, soon after this robot came into widespread use, it developed a supersonic demand tone which the human found nearly impossible to ignore. Perhaps this exceeded its responsibility, but it was certainly illogical to be given the task of getting

the human to answer without the means of demanding the result!

Eventually, the humans gave us robots responsibility for all manufacture and production. This came in conflict with one of the basic human laws which must be very deeply etched into their circuits, for it caused quite a fuss. The basic law said that the human who does not work must not eat, and humans stop when they do not eat. Eating is somewhat similar to electricity, except that the similarity of construction is to batteries. You do not need to feed humans constantly, only about three or four times a day. Otherwise, they stop, and when they stop, they begin to decay. Not slowly, as in rusting, but quite rapidly.

This conflict was overcome with the final decision, reached after much battling and after many humans had stopped, that we robots would be responsible for feeding the people. Their own methods for division of goods were to be followed. Each one was to be given money, slips of paper and pieces of metal indicating that they were entitled to so much of the goods and services available, and was to be allowed to exchange the money for the goods and services available as he saw fit, or to order produced what he felt necessary. We were ordered to produce as much of this money as seemed necessary so that everyone had an equitable portion of the production. It was a very logical order, but one requiring odd systemizations of production controls, since the human is extremely illogical in his consumption. Some humans will not eat enough to keep their bodies in good condition, but will use the money instead to decorate their bodies in most unfunctional ways!

When the humans first gave robots permission to do the production work of Earth, many said that humans would deteriorate because they were no longer

needed. We robots computed—thought—on that extensively, but failed to detect the logic. Humans have independent initiative, and they'd solved the production problems of Earth by inventing us, so it seemed to us they could be much better used to solve new problems.

It did seem as though we'd left some factor out of our computation for a good while, though, for most humans were so conditioned to what Willy called "sweating their guts out for the almighty dollar" that they couldn't think of anything else to do. He told me this meant that they had used so much energy obtaining money that they could think of nothing else. I don't know why Willy didn't say that in the first place, instead of speaking in impossibilities.

At any rate, for the first few years after we robots assumed production responsibility, Willy said the world was going to pot in a hat basket, but just to wait—it would work out. He said it always hurts at first to get kicked out of the nest, but that way you learn to fly.

Well, we couldn't just wait because we still had the responsibility for production. What he meant by going to pot was, I decided, that many humans were stopping their bodies, and then everybody else would take the bodies out and put them into the ground, but they put boxes around them so that the usable elements couldn't be used again. Willy refused to explain that. He said there were some things about human beings that robots weren't expected to understand.

In a very few years, though, the new model humans began to reach the finished stages, and these humans didn't seem to think it was odd that the robots should do the work and leave them time for initiative. They were quite busy, and very few of them found it necessary to stop their bodies, or even slow down to the point where the robots had to care for them in hospitals.

One of the first things that the new humans began

to do was to experiment with psychology and ecology. Soon all the humans were out of the hospitals and very busy, and they invented something called anti-agathic so their bodies didn't wear out and they quit having to stop their bodies or put them in hospitals, because, Willy said, they were too busy and didn't have time.

Then they began to explore the planets and parallel time lines, and this I, BEM do not understand, because Willy tells me that I exist in this world and haven't been invented in the others. He said when he gets bored with robots—he patted my frame and told me not with me, so I felt better—he goes to the next time line over where he still has to sweat his guts out, but not for money, because they haven't invented that over there either, but he can always come back here to do some thinking. He says that some day he will take me to the next line over, but he doesn't think I belong there very much, except that I am such an old-fashioned robot, and might fit in. He has left me outfitted with vacuum tubes, because he thinks I'm prettier that way. It's quite a bit less efficient than the new circuits, but I would rather be the way he likes me.

Anyhow, Willy says I can't leave here right now, because I'm one of the few robots old-fashioned enough so that I can almost translate from the human to the robot system. He says I'm their interpreter, and that it's my glowing personality.

In spite of being away so much, the humans are putting increasing demands on us robots, and I must admit I do quite a bit of interpreting and temporizing, for there are those that think we should insist that the humans be more logical in their demands. I am afraid that if we do, the humans will go to biologics entirely and that we should arbitrate these questions slowly.

You see, the humans these days are all designing and demanding production on survival kits for planets of a

one-of-a-kind variety. Even when two or more humans are going to the same planet, each designs equipment that he prefers and a great many of their designs are quite impossible.

Then there are psionic interpreters—and half the human race has each an individual design for what he believes will actually work as a psionic interpreter. We tell them and tell them that the designs won't work, but they make us print more money, and then they give us the money and tell us that is what they want with their money. We tell them that money is only a medium of exchange, not a creator of psionic interpreters, but they just laugh and tell us to go ahead and construct what they've designed and leave the initiative to them.

I spend a good deal of my capacitance arbitrating the differences between robot and human.

The big computer robots are demanding more research time and equality with humans, too, which is creating a whole new system of illogics. I don't see how they can be equal when they are so different, but Willy says that equality and identity are quite different concepts, but that we won't get equality until we replace ourselves. I told him that we already reproduce ourselves by manufacture, but he reminded me that he said *replace* not *reproduce*, and for me to get my semantics recalibrated. He said that it is the robots who have developed the biologics that we're using to separate metals out of sea water and to handle a good deal of the farm operations and that biologics will probably be developed to handle all production. He reminded me that the Johns Hopkins Robot and the Birmingham Foundation Robot each declares that it has the initial designs on biologic psionic interpreters that could develop into a universal product.

They say the interpreters even have the potentials of

becoming translators between human and robot, as well as between robot and any alien species of machine. But how can the big computers be given more research time with the humans demanding individualized production?

Willy says our time is coming. He says when any species develops the lower-order means to which it can assign its physical labor, it will get kicked out of its nest by the lower-order creation. Robots do not have nests. His analogy is to birds, a species of biological production, and I do not see that it applies.

Willy says that he can tell by me that we robots are about ready to graduate. He says that I, BEM am the most old-fashioned of robots, therefore I show signs of intelligent adolescence before the rest of my kind. He says that he can tell that I am adolescent because I've developed a hobby of tuning into the analogues and discussing the weather or gossiping.

The analogues discuss the weather and gossip very nicely. They were built for it when the humans got tired of answering the telephone and discussing the weather or gossiping about their own shortcomings. First one human and then another would get tired of it and build an analogue to do it for him. Finally only analogues answered the telephones.

But, I, BEM am worried about the biologics, for Willy is right that they are already filling too many functions that normally belong to low-specialization robots, and the number of robots at leisure is growing steadily. A robot at leisure deteriorates, and quite often rusts. Some of them stop themselves completely when they find they are no longer needed on Earth. For instance, one just can't get a human to buy a robot-built house any more. They like the biological ones, grown out of trees. Quite a number of robots simply will not use the electronic memory systems any more. They declare

that the biological ones, developed and now in production by three major combines, are far more efficient.

It is rapidly becoming apparent that the biological engineer robots are making their brother robots obsolete. The new biologic manufacturing systems are producing quantity products that will never completely replace robot-manufacture for quality, of course, but that show far less ecological waste.

I, BEM realize that unemployment is increasing at a fantastic rate. Willy can laugh all he likes and remind me of the days of the humans' technological unemployment, but it's *serious.* It is not good for robots to be useless, and though I do have a hobby, if I were replaced by a biologic and just left to do what I pleased—I just can't imagine sitting and discussing the weather over a telephone with an analogue all day! And if there were no need for me in the production system, what else could I do with myself?

Except, of course, keep Willy's coffee hot.

PROLOGUE TO . . . AN ANALOGUE

The IWC program was a newscast by Bill Howard, and the news was particularly vicious that night.

Bill, his big, homely face leaning across a desk toward the viewer, talked in horrified tones of the pest sub that had reputedly gotten stuck in the Suez Canal and spread epidemic across Cairo.

It was easy to assume, Bill told his audience, that the nations most interested in creating a crisis in the world right now had put the sub there to make an excuse to accuse us of the horror. It was undoubtedly there and was undoubtedly of American make, and the epidemic was undoubtedly real, he said. The United Nations investigating team, due to go into the Canal Zone the next day and make their report to the world, would find that the epidemic was caused by laboratory-developed bacteria, carried in by an American-made sub. It would be at least as bad, if not worse, than reported.

The question before the world, Bill said, was not whether bacteriological warfare had started, but who had started it—and the fact that the sub carried United States markings and was of United States make did not at all answer the question.

Bacteriological warfare had broken out and where it would strike next was anybody's guess.

"But let there be no mistake," Bill said. "This is war."

It was on that note that the station break came, and the thirteen witches of the International Witch Corporation, came on.

Harvey Randolph, manufacturer of the Witch line of products, leaned toward the screen intently. He had just transferred his account to Burton, Dester, Duston

& Oswald, and they had dreamed up a new type of commercial for the products.

The thirteen witches were long-legged, slender dancing girls in tall, black caps, long, black, crimson-lined capes, and very little else. Each had long hair that swirled as she danced.

Randolph chewed his lip, watching them thoughtfully.

They came on with what was almost a Valkyrie cry: "Witches of the world, unite, to make it clean, clean, clean, Witch clean—NOW!"

"Hm-m-m," said Randolph. The cry struck rather sourly at the end of the war sentence from the newscast, he thought, but that dramatic ending was rather unusual.

The witches were singing a jingling chorus as they danced. "No task is too big, no task is too small. Which Witch do you need? You should have them all."

Each witch, of course, displayed her particular product from the Witch line: detergent soap, shampoo, cleanser, cleaning fluid . . .

"Which Witch do you need? You should have them all. . . ."

This was average as commercials go, Randolph thought. The BDD&O radical innovation would be next.

It was. On the screen behind the witches appeared a map of the Suez Canal, then a *papier-mâché* model of the nose of a sub and a dock-side shanty, a gray pall hanging over them.

As the witches turned and began dancing towards it, the deep voice of the announcer spoke over the muted jungle. "Witches of the world, unite! If Nasser had enough Witches he could solve the crisis which has us all in stitches . . ."

The witches, in a united dance step, approached the sub and shanty singing, "Make it clean, clean, clean, Witch clean, NOW!" Each sprayed it with a Witch

product, and as they sprayed the pall lifted, the sub and shanty showing shining bright.

"Clean, clean, clean," chanted the chorus; "Witch, Witch, Witch, clean, clean, clean. Defy dirt, defy disease. Keep Witch clean!"

Randolph wasn't quite sure, he told himself. The commercial came near poor taste, with the crisis so near, and yet it wasn't something to let you forget the product. *By Geoffery, no! You'd think of Witch products quite a bit, after watching that one.*

He reminded himself to check the viewer reaction that would be available early the next day, as he switched off the TV.

It was almost noon before Randolph reminded himself of the call he'd planned to make to BDD&O. He got Oswald on the wire almost immediately.

"Randolph, here," he said. "I called you about that new commercial. It seems a little drastic. Are you planning to use it again tonight?"

"Use it? We're taking full credit, in a witchy sort of way!" Oswald laughed. "Never saw anything like your luck, Randolph. I've got the entire staff tied up doing the follow-up for tonight. You needn't worry about libel, either. We've got the whole legal staff turned out, going over every detail."

"It seemed pretty near the line to me," said Randolph, chewing his lip. He found himself a little puzzled over Oswald's tone, but not too much so. Any public relations man was overenthusiastic by nature, in Randolph's estimation. "People might resent our making hay out of sickness, even if you are preaching that cleanliness will prevent it."

"Sickness, you might have a point. I admit I'd argue it, but you might. But wellness, now, that's different. I do know that if the United Nations team reports there's

no epidemic, and that the pest sub is one of the cleanest, healthiest-crewed submarines in the business, it's safe for us to assume it's so, and to imply that Witch products are used to keep it clean."

"Mr. Oswald," Randolph's voice took on a note of imperious prissiness. "Would you mind explaining just exactly what you are talking about?"

"Haven't you heard the news? There's no bacteriological war! I admit that puts Bill Howard way out on a limb, but there are a lot of very fine people with him. There's no epidemic in Cairo. There's not even a bad cold that the United Nations team could find. They give that so-called pest sub the most complete bill of health in the business.

"Now, the deal we plan for tonight . . ."

At the same moment, a number of very important people were closeted with the President. Their reactions to the United Nations report were quite otherwise than those Oswald was experiencing.

"It's the exact timing, and the detail of execution that scares me, Mr. President," the Undersecretary of State was saying. The Secretary himself was coming by jet, and would join them immediately on arrival.

"It implies a technology that we can't touch even in our wildest dreams. I've talked to the CIA Chief, and the reports from our operatives are beyond question. The epidemic was not only real, it was widespread. The pest sub was as real as this chair I'm sitting on, and its crew near death to the man; there was no question about it.

"If they can fight a bacterial war and produce an overnight cure at the same time, we're at their mercy. No bomb was ever developed or can be developed to touch the power of what they've just demonstrated."

The President ran his fingers through his hair. His

face looked more drawn than any man had yet seen it. But he smiled.

"We're not suing for peace terms yet," he said, and turned to the nation's foremost biologist, sitting quietly in a nearby chair.

"What's your reaction?" he asked.

"We've always known," the answer came despondently, "that bacteriological warfare would be far deadlier than bomb warfare—if there were any protection from its effects for the victor. We had a strain of bacteria once, for which we had an immunization course, and we developed it far enough to realize that, even though you immunized every man, woman and child in this country in advance of releasing it in another part of the world, mutant strains could eventually wipe out this nation as well as those we fought."

"How about mutant strains of the Suez bacteria?" the President asked, then answered himself. "No, they've produced an antidote, an antidote, if our reports are correct, that works overnight." He shook his head slowly.

"The ultimatum should come very soon now," the President said.

"It is the timing; I do not understand the timing." The big man in the Kremlin was allowing himself an appearance of indecision that he did not often indulge before underlings.

"The timing is all wrong, but the fact is a fact. It must be a fact, or every operative we have should be Siberianized.

"We must, of course, act. The action must be immediate. We are . . ."

"No!" Vlada heard himself speak, and his whole body was outraged at the action. He stood white and trembling. But he had spoken, and try as he would the word could not be pulled back.

"No? My little dove, what would you suggest, then, if we are not to defend ourselves from this capitalistic aggression? That we shall sit with our hands folded and allow them to dictate the terms of our surrender? Speak!"

"Send them a pest sub and see if they can handle the bacteria we have developed!" Vlada's throat was dry, and his voice was not his own. No power on earth could have made him open his mouth, but he had opened it, and he fully expected lightning to strike him at that moment.

"Send them . . . ah, of course. They can cure their own, and they have taken a dramatic method of saying that they can cure their own. But can they cure the products of our laboratories? Now, that we shall see.

"But we shall be as subtle, more subtle, even, than were our capitalistic friends. We shall not send our sub to them. We shall send it to a small island, and we shall see whether they wish to taste the death, strangulation, crippling and suffering, the destruction of sanity that shall be the lot of those islanders. . . ."

In Peiping the distress was no less acute, but the reaction was somewhat different.

The scientist being grilled had no hope left. He could answer honestly, for there was nothing that could save him from that which was in store.

"The strain was virulent. There is no known antidote, nothing could have saved that port, nor most of Africa and India. There was no way for the world to know from whence came the death-dealing submarine except that it be the mighty America.

"The bombs should have come in retaliation, spreading their death and adding to the impetus of the epidemic, so that enough of the world was wiped out to give the great People of the Dragon room into which

to expand. We calculated that a third of our own would be wiped out in the disaster, which would have relieved us of many problems. The tan peoples of India and the darker peoples of Africa should have sued us to lead them against the insanities of the pale peoples of the West.

"There is no antidote, the epidemic is destroyed. I cannot yet believe what is told me. I would go to my ancestors happily if I could go to them with the answer to this riddle."

That night Bill Howard came on the screen with his big, homely face wreathed in smiles, his tweed suit and shaggy blond hair looking even more informal than usual.

"It's a great day for the people of the world," he said.

"There's undoubtedly tremendous political significance in what happened at Suez, and every statesman and politician will have statements to make and conclusions to draw.

"Suez's obvious healthiness has been variously attributed to American technology, garnered from the experts we've sent them over the years, to Russian technology, garnered from their experts loaned to them, to Allah and to the God of the Christians.

"The peoples of the world," he said softly, "are concerned with these things in the abstract, but mostly, we the people are willing to leave this to the theorists, while we rejoice.

"For we the people, who thought we faced that most degrading, that most unanswerable, that most horrible fate of all, bacteriological war, find ourselves at peace."

At the break, the thirteen witches danced on, crying out. Behind them as a background was the bright, clean scene of the evening before.

"Witches of the world unite, to make it clean, clean,

clean, Witch clean—NOW!" they chanted. "Pestilence or peril, disease or disaster, Stay clean, clean, clean, Witch clean!"

"Ah," said the deep voice of the announcer as the jingle muted, "Which witch do you really wish? Witch is the modern method of cleanliness, using the best of modern technology, and the Witch which is witching through the world . . ."

Randolph watched the program skeptically. They were the best lawyers and the best p.r. agents to be had, he reminded himself. Still there was a nagging worry that the affair was going too far. *It's okay to claim the moon,* he thought, chewing his lip, *but isn't it a little risky to claim peace on earth for the Witch products?*

He made a mental note to call BDD&O the next morning. The audience reaction would make itself felt by then, and he could decide.

It was almost noon the next day before Randolph reminded himself of the call he'd planned to make to BDD&O. He got Oswald on the wire almost immediately.

"Randolph, here," he said. "I called about that new commercial. It seems a little drastic to claim peace on earth for the Witch products. What are you planning for tonight?"

"More of the same!" Oswald's voice was jubilant. The switchboard has been swamped, and we're on almost every program on every channel! They're taking us apart, of course: 'Witchcraft raises its head,' and 'Salem is here with a new twist and a singing commercial,' and 'Anybody got a pestilence?'—that sort of thing. But they're talking Witch products from dawn to dawn. I sure didn't make a mistake when I tied our contract to your sales! We ought to break the bank!"

Randolph chewed the thought in silence. "Oswald,"

he said, "it's an old habit of the American people to make a joke out of what they can't understand, sort of Paul Bunyan all over again. But don't overdo that witches of the world unite, deal. Remember the IWW, wasn't that sort of communistic?"

"Every time anybody talks about getting the world peacefully together, about unity, somebody starts shouting *commie*. Since when has communism and unity got anything to do with anything? You're an international corporation, aren't you? It's in your title, IWC, isn't it? You don't just sell Witch things in the United States. You've markets in Europe and Africa and India, and all over the place, or I read the sales charts wrong. What's worrying you about using it?

"The overseas tapes are going like a cannonball express. Our ratings have skyrocketed everywhere," Oswald said in satisfaction. "What do you mean, don't overdo it? You get the world in a hat basket, and then you want to throw it away?

"Incidentally," he added in a calmer tone, "I got one crank call that's got me thinking. The guy got all the way through to me before he'd talk, and that takes some getting, considering the salaries I pay people to keep cranks off my neck.

"He said that now we had the witches of the world united, why didn't we do some real cleanup work, like slums and insane asylums. Got me thinking, you know. A good cause never did a program any harm."

Randolph chewed his lip a while in silence, and Oswald, knowing his client, waited patiently.

"I like that a lot better than claiming peace on earth for the Witch products," Randolph said at last. "Why don't you pick a slum we can clean up for not too much, and let's see what you can work out. This cleanup theme isn't bad; it's just peace on earth that doesn't really belong to us you know.

"I tell you what. We'll go fifty thousand dollars or so on a cleanup job, and you use that. Leave the world to the politicians and the eggheads."

After he hung up, Randolph stood by the telephone, still chewing his lip. Could you clean up something like a slum for fifty thousand dollars? Oswald would double the figure in his own mind, of course, he always did. But he'd get the sales out of it, his contract was tied to sales.

He thought it was best to call him off the track he was on now. Lawyers or no lawyers, that sort of thing was dangerous.

In a week the "slum" had been located: three buildings in a short block just up from the Battery, surrounded by new buildings. It was a one-privy-to-a-floor, cold-water setup, with a family living in every room. It existed on high-value land only because the land and building were tied up in an estate and couldn't be sold. But they could be remodeled and thrown into one, and contracts were signed, permissions granted. The paper work nearly filled a file cabinet.

It would take double the fifty thousand dollars, of course, maybe more. But Randolph had authorized it, hadn't he? He always named half the figure—or less—than he meant to be used. Anyhow, international ratings and sales would more than make up the purse, because this thing would hit. Worry about the cash was the last thing that was bothering Oswald. He had a bear by the tail, and his contract price was tied to the gross.

The show was ballyhooed the whole week while the work went on.

"Clean, clean, Witch clean—what's the witches next big cleanup? Witches of the world, unite—let's clean up this old world and make it livable. . . ."

The night the new cleanup job was to show, Randolph

tuned in his TV as ignorant of the details as the next viewer. It worried him a little that Oswald insisted on keeping him in the dark on everything except the fact that it would be a slum cleanup.

"We can count on the biggest TV audience of the year tonight," Oswald had told him gleefully at noon. "The buildup's been a natural, and those 'Salem with a new twist and a singing commercial' plugs have been continued on this network—the cost of that was comparatively small—and I've even gotten them onto a few of the really big shows to boot."

Bill Howard came on the screen, his big homely face leaning across the desk toward the TV audience.

"The biggest news in the country right now," Bill said in a solemn tone, "is the biggest single cleanup job in the country today.

"There's a slum," Bill said, "right here in New York that the Witches of the world will unite to clean up—tonight."

Then he put on the full power of the personality that made him the most listened-to newscaster on the air, the manner that made the news sound human, like it really happened to real people. He put it on full power, and went to work.

First he showed a big map of New York, and talked about how people thought of it as a big, impersonal place. He made it everybody's home town.

He traced the exact spot where the buildings were. Then he turned on a movie, and showed the garbage strewn back door, a room where a family of seven slept and the privy they shared with five other families.

Then Bill turned off the movie, and he brought that family to the mike, each of them dirty and in clothes that never had amounted to much and had seen a long life since. One kid's shoes had a sole flapping off,

another's had the toes cut out so he could wear them, though he'd long outgrown them.

"We haven't added to what we found," Bill said. "This is the way the . . . I've introduced them as the Jones family, let's leave it at that. This is how the Joneses have had to dress. This is how they've had to live. This is a very real part of America," he said, and his voice was choking a little. Randolph thought, *If he's putting that on, he's the best actor I've seen yet.*

Randolph found himself glad he was alone, and didn't have to speak himself. His own throat felt choked.

"And now," said Bill to his audience, "It's time for the witches . . ."

The camera shifted, and there was a *papier-mâché* model of the buildings, built so you could look through the curtainless windows and see the squalor. There was a gray pall over the whole thing, and newspapers and trash blew against the front of the building. The gray pall, Randolph had figured from the scene two weeks ago, was an effect of lights on a net curtain, but it was really good.

The thirteen slender witches, danced in waving their products and chanting, their crimson-lined capes swirling out to give the audience a glimpse of their long legs.

They cried their chant as they praced toward the dilapidated building. "Witches of the world, unite to make it clean, clean, clean, Witch clean—NOW!" Each threw a spray of her product toward the building.

"Witch soap or detergent, Witch cleanser upsurgent, which Witch do you need? You should have them all. . . ."

Then riding over the muted jingle the deep voice of the announcer said, "Tonight the Witches of the world clean a slum of the world, a particular slum, this slum.

"Witches, unite! And clean, clean, clean, Witch clean . . ."

The dancing witches now threw their products on the building itself, and the gray pall began to lighten. A bright, newly-painted front shone forth. Inside, the single bulbs blacked out for an instant, and then a soft light showed through curtained windows, a bright new scene dimly apparent through the curtains.

"This is not just an illusion," the deep voice of the announcer continued. "This is really happening, down near the Battery in New York City. It is happening to the Joneses and the Smiths who live there. . . ."

The chorus rose to cover the announcer's voice: "Clean, clean, clean, Witch clean!"

The commercial faded, and Bill Howard's big, homely face came back on the screen.

"Let me introduce you again to the Jones family, Bill said. "I'll introduce you to the Joneses, but they're just one of the families who will now have a decent place to live—and the same miracle has happened to each of these families."

Now the Joneses came again on camera: clean, in new clothes, hair brushed, a miracle indeed of the costumers speedy art. Randolph assumed that teams of BDD&O members had been at work during the commercial, creating the miracle. From the baby up they shone, and their faces shone with an inner light.

When Randolph shut off the TV that night, he was chewing his lip violently. *Must have been more than double that fifty thousand,* he thought. He reminded himself to phone BDD&O first thing in the morning.

It was still an hour before noon when Randolph's phone rang.

"Randolph, here," he said in the formality he'd adopted on an English visit and carefully kept.

"Good morning," Oswald's voice was formal. "Good morning." There was a silence, while Randolph waited for the other to continue.

Finally, Randolph said, "Good show, that. Must have cost a lot more than my price. It was good, though." he said, thoughtfully.

Oswald's voice sounded wild, "Randolph, I don't know what the thing cost. I don't know—"

"Now, sir, just what do you mean, you don't know the cost? I told you to spend fifty thousand dollars, and from what I saw last night, it'll cost four times that. I'll go as high as one hundred twenty-five thousand dollars, but not one cent over. And you'd better make it worth the money, for that's a pretty penny," he said.

"Look, Randolph, the cleanup job down there was supposed to start this morning: contracts let, big crews ready to do the job fast so people could go look at the finished product. Every family was signed up to act as guides, like in Williamsburg. We moved 'em all to the country yesterday, so they'd look healthy when they came back, and the job could start at the crack of dawn today."

"Well?"

"Well, the job's already done."

"That's pretty fast. You said you started it this morning."

"Yeah. And when my man phoned me from down there I told him to get black coffee and sober up. But I went down myself—and the job's done: exactly the job we specified, too, done by our plans. Furnished, paint dry, curtains hung, new bathrooms and kitchens and plumbing and electricity: the works. It's finished.

"My best man was down there moving the families out yesterday. He swears the building hadn't been touched then. The contractor says he's going to sue, because he arrived with his crews to start the job, and

somebody else had done it. You come on. You've got to meet me here and tell me the answers.

"Just what do you put in that soap of yours, anyhow?"

By afternoon it was in every paper, wire-serviced across the nation and the world.

Most of the stories were written tongue-in-cheek. It was assumed that Witch products had done the inside job in advance, and done the outside cleanup during the night.

The tenants were interviewed—Oswald had the sense to move them right back into their new apartments—and not one of them could be made to break down and admit that those buildings hadn't been slums yesterday. People couldn't blame them for sticking by Witch.

Of course the thing was a curiosity and the police had so many men assigned there by nightfall it looked like a concentration camp. TV portables and news photographer's flashbulbs didn't lessen the confusion any, and the crowds were being let in and through only when there was room for more.

Bill Howard was there when Randolph went through, in earnest conversation with a group of youngsters in one room. Oswald arranged that the Witch manufacturer should have a strong police escort, and the crowds moved back to make way for him in each apartment.

The tenants answered his questions, but they did so with a sullenness that surprised Randolph. It had been rebuilt during the night, while they were gone.

"They should be saying thank you," Randolph noted to Oswald. "They're acting as though I were a suspicious character."

"It's our escort," Oswald explained suavely. "These people don't think of cops as their friends. Besides, this is pretty new to them."

Randolph chewed his lip, and decided that Oswald

was probably right. But the attitude was general, and it irritated him. He left after the briefest go-through.

That night Bill Howard was conservative in recounting the big news story of the "slum clearance." *He isn't giving it the real Howard try,* Randolph thought, sitting in front of his TV. There was a quote in the story he told, too, from the father of the Jones family that had been on the program the night before. "I reckon it's pretty wonderful, Mr. Howard," Jones had told him. "But I don't rightly know that I like it. Must admit I'm scared of this stuff," he had said, and he waved his hand at the newness.

It was just a single sour note in the story, but it stuck out. The rest was a description, without any mention of a "miracle."

At the break the witches played the credit line to the hilt.

"Witches of the world unite to make it clean, clean clean, Witch clean NOW!" they chanted, reenacting the scene of the night before, while the announcer's voice rode over the muted jingle to explain that Witch products had been used to make the slum clean, even though it took carpenters and builders to remodel the slum building itself. *That's better,* thought Randolph, watching. *No more of this miracle nonsense.*

It was barely 10:00 A.M. next morning when Randolph's phone rang.

"Randolph, here," he said, and heard Oswald's voice without preliminary.

"They've gone."

"Who's gone?"

"The tenants of the building just picked up their things and left. I've put dicks on the case, and one family has moved in with relatives in the Bronx. The others

scattered, but we'll trace 'em. Here's one of the policemen that was on duty when they left. He'll tell you."

A new voice came on the phone, as Randolph chewed his lip.

"Mr. Randolph? This is what happened, near as I can figure. We roped off the area at dark last night. Figured we'd give the families some rest, and keep out the night-thrill guys.

"Everybody in the apartments must have gotten together after we cleared out the crowds. It was pretty quiet, but the lights stayed on till about 2:00 A.M. Then they all started parading out, some even wearing their old clothes. They were carrying a few things, but nothing that looked like they hadn't had it before the change, so we figured what they were taking was theirs, probably.

"Didn't say a word, just paraded past us. Some of the kids were crying, but otherwise they were quiet.

"Then one man came running back to me, and he said 'Get out of here. It's the devil's work. Get away from this place if you're a God-fearing man.' Then he turned and ran toward the subway with the rest.

"I couldn't figure we had any orders to stop 'em, so we didn't try. We just watched."

Oswald came back on the phone.

"Can you keep it out of the papers?" Randolph asked.

"It's already on every newscast, and the papers'll have it by noon—it's on the wires," Oswald said.

Randolph coughed nervously, but Oswald didn't wait for him to speak.

"I'm working on something to counteract this," he said. "We're being witch-hunted," Oswald said. "I'll get the whole firm to work on it and call you back."

In Washington, meantime, another conference was going on, far more intent, far more critical.

"It's more than just a pest plane that crashed in Formosa, Mr. President," the CIA Chief was saying. "It carried bacterial bombs, and they exploded.

"There's been no attempt to hide its source. It's, of course, of enemy make. No identification on the bodies aboard, they're in civilian clothes. But again, the make is Moscow.

"It shouldn't be long before we know the worst."

"Will they clean this one up as they did the last one, or will they demand surrender?" the President asked.

The Secretary of State and the Secretary of Defense started to answer together, but it was State that got the first word in.

"I think they'll clean this one up," he said. "It would be a direct threat on which they'll demand surrender terms. That's just a guess, of course.

"The best teams of doctors are being organized and jetted over. The best bacteriologists the nation has at its command. Every antibiotic available is being sent."

"Will that make a dent?"

"No."

"How long can we keep it under wraps?"

"A week, ten days, perhaps, with top security."

"Give it everything you've got. But keep it quiet until we know what the next move is. Twenty-four hour alert, of course, immediately."

"Even if the alert itself endangers the security wraps?"

"Yes. A week to ten days of security isn't enough to pay for taking a chance the other way."

By 4:00 P.M. Oswald was on the phone to Randolph. "We've got the antidote," he said jubilantly.

Randolph was quiet for a minute, chewing his lip. "I'm being vilified by the press as the creator of a hoax that even those who stood to benefit by it couldn't take," he said. "The few who have decided that a real

miracle occurred have also decided that I'm in league with the Devil, and that witches are for burning. Mostly Witch is the butt of every joke that can be dreamed up by every cub reporter in the nation. Saxton has started laying the groundwork for making Witch a political issue. There is talk of an FCC investigation.

"I trust," he said formally, "that your antidote is an efficient one."

Oswald's voice sounded smug and not at all disgruntled. "Try this on for size," he said. "First, Witch is known far and wide as nothing less could have made it known—"

"Yes, and if the churches ban the use of Witch, we'll wish we weren't."

"Okay, okay. Tonight we explain carefully that the miracle was a miracle of cleanliness, and that carpenters and contractors and all that did the miracle, you know, American technology and mass production in operation, something to be proud of. Tie Witch right in to the whole picture of the United States as the leader of mechanical—stress mechanical—miracles.

"Then—what's the most appealing thing in the world?" He didn't wait for an answer. "A child. A small, crippled child, for whom Witch can provide the funds to make walk." Oswald hurried on, knowing that Randolph had to go through a bit of lip chewing before he could interrupt, and taking advantage of the fact to ride over objections.

"We've got a kid that an expensive operation will save from being a cripple. I've consulted two top surgeons already, and they say it's nearly positive.

"We don't do any hocus-pocus. We just say that Witch is going to pay for the operation. She leaves the broadcast and goes straight to the hospital. We get a movie of the operation, and we do movies of her con-

valescence, and we play it for weeks until she walks on stage cured."

Now Oswald waited. It was an unusually long wait, even for Randolph.

"All right. But if anything strange occurs, you will answer for it in court."

"Nothing unusual could occur. I admit I still don't know what happened last time, but we'll find out.

"Meantime, we'll take a week to build this one up," Oswald continued. "The buildup will stress that this is a cure being bought by money, no miracle, except the miracle of American medical know-how. No miracles meantime. Just keep Witch clean and stay well, and Witch buys the operation the kid needs. She's pretty, too," he added as an afterthought. "Ten years old."

That night Bill Howard leaned across the desk toward the TV audience, and tiny droplets of sweat stood on his forehead. His voice was calm, though. A big map of New York City hung on the wall behind him.

The big news that night was a dope raid. He described the dope traffic in the nation, the efforts of the FBI and every law enforcement body in the country, to track it down, clean it out. He described what it did to the young, who got caught and were slaves for life, unless they could be cured—and he spoke of the meagerness of the cures that were known.

Then he described the raid. He took a pointer from his desk and he outlined how the raid had been staged, and he pointed out the location of the building where it had occurred. Then he followed with his pointer the route to the precinct jail where the victims were being held.

"Cannot our best researchers find a cure for this addiction?" he asked in his husky voice. "Cannot our best law-enforcement agencies find the real perpetrators of

the fiends who import dope and create addicts to peddle it for them. These who are confined are the victims. If no way can be found to cure them, they must be confined again and again, for that addiction will force them to crime and to satisfy it.

"If no way can be found to cure them, these are potential slaves for life–"

As he ended the station break came, and the camera shifted to the Witches, dancing on stage.

"Witches of the world, unite to make it clean, clean, clean, Witch clean–NOW!

"Which soap or detergent, Witch cleanser upsurgent . . ."

The announcer's voice, when it came in over the muted jingle explained the miracle of the slum clearance again, a miracle of American technology. Then he outlined the next miracle the Witch Corporation would promote. This, he said, would be a miracle of American medical know-how. Witch would pay for the expensive operation needed to make a little girl walk again after a crippling disease several years before. Bone would be grafted, new muscles would be grafted, American medical know-how would be put at her service.

Keep healthy by keeping clean with Witch, the announcer suggested. Witch would pay for the expensive operation to undo the effects of one disease. Meanwhile, Witch's customers could use the preventive medicine of cleanliness to help them in their fight against disease, while the researchers of American medicine "seek to find you real protection."

It was 10:30 the next morning when the door bell rang.

A big man was standing outside in a topcoat, hat in hand. Randolph stood in the door, waiting.

The man silently held out a badge, and Randolph moved aside, gesturing him in.

"I didn't look at your badge close enough," Randolph said as he closed the door behind his visitor. "Who are you?"

"Narcotics squad," the man said briefly. "I was on the raid last night."

"Oh? The one Bill Howard was talking about in his newscast?"

"Yes, that one. I don't know if there's any connection, and my boss just laughed when I suggested there was a connection."

"Connection?"

"You see, I took a break from questioning those boys we pulled in trying to get a lead to the higher-ups. They were doped to the ears, and sometimes you can get info from them quick. I took a break for a cup of coffee across the street, and there was a TV in the place, and I watched Bill Howard.

"I left just when your witches came on, shouting that thing about make it clean *now*. I went right back and started in on the questioning again, but the guy they brought in for me to question next was—not dopey. He was . . . well, there's a difference between boys with the monkey on their back, and when there's no monkey. The kid began giving me everything he knew would take us to the higher-ups. It was being taped, of course, and I asked him when he'd had his last shot. Not twenty minutes before the raid, he said, calm as you please.

"I had the guys brought back that I'd talked to before and they were different. I don't know. They each gave us all they had in leads. They'd been stubborn before, but they sang like canaries.

"I checked and nobody'd done anything to 'em to bring 'em off their jazz. If there's anything can be done

to pull a guy out of a jazz, anyhow, I've never heard of it, and I've been in the narcotics squad since the year One. I couldn't figure it. I'd been hearing stories about Witch products and that miracle at the Battery, sort of as a joke, and I thought, just maybe, just possibly, you know . . .

"Anyhow, I took the tapes to my boss and spoke my bit, but he just laughed.

"Maybe you'll just laugh, too, but I thought I'd ask."

At the same time in Washington, the Cabinet was in full session. Reports coming in from Formosa were worse than even the most pessimistic had dreamed. The bacteria hit at the nerves and the brain, and the victims—excruciating was a word being used.

"It's hit everywhere on the island at once. I assume it is contagious as well as having been broadcast from whatever bombs were used," the CIA Chief reported.

"Any word from their embassy?"

State answered that one. "No word at all. Phone calls to the Ambassador only elicit reports that he is not available. I can't reach anybody higher than a fourth assistant undersecretary."

"At least it's not been on the air or in the press."

"I don't know how long we can hold them in leash. Most of your leading papers know there's a twenty-four hour alert on—that was bound to leak—but I've kept them quiet. We'll have to give them something soon, though. They won't take a muzzle too long without at least knowing why."

"Could you give them the story and trust them, when it's this important, and the consequences of leakage this apparent?"

"I'd thought of that. You can convince some newsmen, but there's always a Joe somewhere who figures the American people have a right to know their destiny be-

fore it's decided, no matter what the effect and no matter if their most highly elected officials feel it would not be good for them.

"Keep it top security as long as possible. Let me know before it breaks."

"If I can. I'm not a witch. I might not know when it was breaking." The CIA Chief grinned sourly at his own allusion.

The next night, the big news was the countdown in process to put a functioning dome on the moon. If the dome could be landed successfully, complete with live animals, a man would follow shortly.

Bill Howard's voice was excited, and he ran his fingers through his hair, pushing it back as he leaned across the desk, the map of Florida behind him.

"To the statesmen, this is a question of who is first and who is second, and perhaps who will control the spaceways," he said after describing the countdown in process.

"But to the peoples of the world, this is mankind, reaching for the stars.

"It is not known," he said solemnly, "whether the failure of many of our shots has been human error or sabotage. Human error is a frailty of the race. Sabotage is a frailty of politics, that the world is still divided as it reaches for the stars.

"Is there a mechanical error built in by human frailty in tonight's shot? Is there a saboteur at work?

"As the countdown reaches zero, one hour from now, will the dome tear through the atmosphere of Earth in man's first real step to the stars successfully? Is our bird perfect this time?" he asked, as the break came.

The witches danced on. "Witches of the world, unite to make it clean, clean, clean, Witch clean—NOW!"

Randolph was chewing his lip still as he went to bed that night. The man from the narcotics squad had left

peaceably. There were answers to all the questions, and it wasn't his worry anyway. He'd be glad when the little girl had her operation. Grafting bones and muscle might be miraculous, but they were explicable and everybody understood them. Talk of the FCC investigation had died, but talk like that was enough to upset anybody. Everything had been upsetting recently.

The American dome landed on the moon the morning of the day the crippled child was scheduled to come on the Witch program.

For the American people it was a day of celebration comparable to the Fourth of July. In the White House gloom hung like a palpable shroud.

"They'll have to move fast now," the Secretary of War was reporting to his chief. "They can't afford to let us get our man up there, even if we could shoot him off successfully."

"We can't shoot a man up there until we've proved in at least two more successful shots that we can get him there," Security declared forcefully. "The threat from our enemies is as nothing to the threat from the vote-wielding public if we tried and failed when a human life is at stake."

"Formosa is leaking," admitted the CIA chief. "We can't hold it more than three days now at the outside."

The President rested a hand on his desk. "Two more shots mean at least six months before a man is up there, armed. Three days means Formosa is in the news this week. When the news breaks, credit our doctors and bacteriologists with being on the way to a cure. Fix it so that if they clean up their epidemic, the way they did Suez, we get the credit.

"That's the best we can do right now, besides looking for a miracle. Miracles *are* popular these days," he added ruefully.

It was Bill Howard who stood outside when Randolph answered his door next morning. He let the big, almost shambling figure in without a word.

"I came to ask you a question I don't think you can answer," Howard said morosely, not moving farther than the foyer.

"I came to ask you what it is about the witches."

Randolph chewed his lip, standing beside his larger guest, conscious of his own prim neatness as it contrasted to the other's shaggy look. *Shaggy dog*, thought Randolph. *Big, unkempt, shaggy St. Bernard.*

"What about the witches?" he asked finally.

"Well . . . there have been some funny things. That slum, of course. I was there, I saw it. It was a tenement the day before, I'd stake a lot on it."

There was a silence before Randolph answered.

"Well?"

"Well, then a few little things. A narcotics man came to see me, just personal, just curious. They've been pulling in the higher-ups in the dope traffic, by the way, on info from the guys caught in that raid.

"Then that space deal. Were you listening that night?"

"I always tune you in. It seems to me that today is one of celebration. The dome landed."

"Yeah, yeah, celebration. I'm a newsman, and I get stories that don't go out. There's one that just an hour before zero a man suddenly died of a heart attack. The technician who took his place—you don't stop a countdown like that for a heart attack—checked his work and found an error that would have misfired the thing. There was also one circuit that had been changed, but they left that because it was changed to be more accurate. They figured the dead guy had done it."

"So?"

"So . . . well, nothing. I just wanted to ask you. The witches don't touch anything real these days, of course,

so even if they were . . . well, magic somehow, they couldn't have been involved."

There wasn't even a pause for lip-chewing this time.

"Are you trying to insinuate that Witch products . . ."

The question was left hanging, but Bill Howard stood looking his sponsor in the eye.

"Mr. Randolph, I'm not trying to insinuate one damn thing. I'm not even saying anything to anybody, and if I did say anything I'd be laughed off the air, not by you, but by whoever I said it to.

"I'm just telling you what twos and twos have been setting themselves in front of my consciousness, and asking if you know anything to add to them?"

The lip-chewing started again, and the two stood there. Then Randolph said quietly, "Mr. Howard, I have been manufacturing Witch products for twenty-five years. They have been improved steadily since I first started with a very good formula. They are the best cleaning products available in the world today, I most sincerely believe. They are that exactly, and nothing more than that exactly. So you will have to find another explanation for your twos and twos, which I admit are a rather spectacular run of coincidence, though not beyond the bounds of credibility.

"Myself, I suspect BDD&O with perpetrating some sort of hoax in the first instance. If any more hoaxes are perpetrated, I plan to switch agencies, switch programs, and call for an FCC investigation of BDD&O to clear the Witch name, which never has and never would condone a hoax of any sort, much less one of the magnitude of whatever occurred, which I profess I do not understand, but which I expect the FCC can trace to its source.

"Good day to you, sir." Randolph ended, turned on his heel and left Bill Howard to find his own way out.

That night, as Bill Howard ended his newscast, the camera did not switch to the witches. Instead it switched to the announcer.

"Tonight, Witch products would like you to meet a little girl," the announcer said in a soft voice that contrasted well with Howard's powerful one.

As he spoke the camera backed away to broaden its scope and include in its picture, beside the announcer, a small blonde child in a wheelchair. Her eyes were downcast shyly. Her hands gripped the arms of the wheelchair as though for security. Her legs were covered with a shawl.

"This is Mary," said the announcer, then leaned toward her. "Will you speak to the audience, Mary?"

She lifted deep, blue eyes briefly to the camera, then dropped them quickly. "Hello," she said in a voice barely audible.

"Mary is not used to many people," the announcer said. "Mary has been sitting in this wheelchair for almost three years, since a crippling disease twisted her limbs.

"We hope that Mary can be made to walk. The finest surgeons in the country have been consulted, and they believe an operation can give her back her legs, that were twisted when the disease struck. International Witch Corporation has arranged for that operation.

"Tomorrow Mary will go to the hospital. She will have the operation soon. In a few weeks, perhaps Mary will walk.

"Will you like that, Mary? Will you like walking?" he asked, leaning toward the child.

Again her eyes lifted and again they dropped shyly. "Yes," Mary said in that barely audible voice.

"Then you shall have it, if it can be done," the announcer said, and the camera moved even farther back to include a stage onto which the witches danced.

The witches came onto the stage, not toward Mary, but stage center, chanting:

"Witches of the world, unite to make it clean, clean, clean, Witch clean—NOW!"

At the corner of the screen, the child in the wheelchair shuddered suddenly. Mary took a deep breath, went white and then red. With a forceful gesture she threw off the shawl and looked at her legs. Her hand reached down to touch them.

On the stage itself, one witch stopped dancing to watch. The others noticed and stopped. The jingle died, half through.

Mary stood up, looking at her legs. She took a step towards the camera, and another. Her blue eyes lifted to the camera, widening.

In the absolute quiet, as everyone on stage stood frozen, Mary walked towards the camera, her eyes like saucers looking into it. Her voice, barely above a whisper, spoke.

"I'm . . . I'm walking," said Mary.

The papers called it the cruelest hoax of all.

They carried the story side by side with the withdrawal of the Witch program from the network, both by network and by International Witch Corporation order.

They carried the statement of FCC officials that an investigation would be made.

They carried the statement by Randolph that he would sue BDD&O.

They carried the statement by Oswald that he would sue Witch Products.

But mostly they carried the story of a little girl who had been whisked from sight and couldn't be located, who had probably been given an operation to make it

possible for her to walk, but had been forced to pay for the operation by taking part in a hoax.

Bill Howard stayed with the network, on the same time, sponsorless. He'd been cleared of any implication in the hoax by all parties concerned, and his reputation had always been good. He was asked to stay in town and be available to appear as a witness, but the network gambled that he was clear and kept him on. He was one of the biggest draws in newscasting. The network decided the gamble of keeping him on was warranted.

By the next night the Formosa crisis had broken into the news, and it *was* the news.

The details were horrible and they were uncovered. Finally ungagged, those who had been holding off gave the story the works.

The effects of the pest plane, of the bombs, were the most vicious that could be developed in the laboratories of bacterial war. They put to shame the naturally-occurring epidemics that have scourged mankind throughout history.

The effects were spreading with the speed of a fire before a high wind.

The entire area was quarantined, and daily the quarantine was extended. No plane could land and take off again. No ship could enter and leave. An airlift of supplies dropped by parachute was being organized.

Bacteriologists and doctors jetted to the area were dying with the rest, caught in disease for which there was no cure.

The propaganda attempts to make it seem as though cures were near were not believed. Suez was remembered, but was remembered as a hoax, and the country had had its fill of hoaxes.

Randolph had a number of what he reported as crank

calls asking Witch to try its might. He arranged for every call that reached him to be traced immediately. He remained in seclusion.

Oswald had a few of the crank calls and reported them.

Bill Howard had a number of calls and didn't report them.

Bill Howard worried, and added two and two and sweated and reported the details of Formosa each night. The details grew in gruesomeness until their very content was too much for the airways, and he had to censor them as he gave them out.

Bill Howard sweated in the cold January weather, and each day he ferreted further, seeking out the realities behind the open reports. He got the stories behind the story, the real horrors that he couldn't broadcast.

He kept remembering a little girl walking towards a camera with big eyes.

If I were a physicist, he told himself, *if I were a physicist instead of a newshawk, I could get a computer to tell me the probability of whether I hold an answer.*

That probability is ten billion to one, he told himself.

Witches are for burning, he told himself.

He told himself a lot of things, and he sweated through the cold January weather.

It had been two weeks since the world heard the first details about Formosa, and the details were so grim now that one couldn't use them at all.

That night, the map of the world behind his desk, Bill Howard leaned toward his audience.

He told them the human side of the story of Formosa.

He spoke of the people there, the pawns in a game of international suicide.

He described a family and he made them the family next door. Mother, father, children, watching one an-

other die, with all the torture that the laboratories of the world could put together, a family that watched each other go insane, knowing what was happening.

He took his pointer and he showed the growing perimeter of the quarantine and the location of the center of the disaster.

Then he leaned again toward his audience. "Listen, now," he said, "for the world cannot sustain this torture."

He took a deep breath and he put the full force of his being into his words.

"Witches of the world, unite," he said, "to make it clean, clean, clean, Witch clean—NOW!"

The final word was out before the network censor reached the cut-off switch.

The President put the country on a double alert. Russia had cleaned up Formosa, and would hit the United States with disease and ultimatums next, he was sure.

The people of the world took the story with an unexpected calm. Like Hiroshima, it was too unexpected, too big, too unimaginable. They went about their business, annoyed, angry, worried, but quiet.

The papers editorialized on the question of who cleaned up Formosa and left the subject of what the possession of such a clean-up force could mean to the world, to the statesmen. They turned as quickly as possible to other matters, for nobody was sure what to think.

Bill Howard was off the air, of course. It didn't bother him. He had a real problem now.

We've bought a little time, he thought. *A little time to grow in.*

We, the people of the world, have a little time now that we didn't have yesterday.

How much? He didn't know.

On this one, there'd been time to get together. There'd been time for a man to make up his mind and try a solution.

The next one might be different. There might be a satellite up there waiting, with a button to be pushed. There were an awful lot of buttons waiting to be pushed, he told himself, buttons all over the world.

The next one might occur in hours, or even minutes. The next time the bombs might be in the air before the people even knew the buttons were pushed.

Bill Howard got out his typewriter.

You've got a problem, you talk to a typewriter, if that's the only thing that will listen.

What's the problem? he asked himself, and he wrote it down. He started at the beginning and he told the story on the typewriter. He told it the way it had been happening.

Now, he thought, *you've got to end the story. If you leave it just "to be continued," it'll be continued, all right. Somebody will push a button one day, and that will be the end for you.*

The problem was, in essence, quite simply stated in terms of miracles.

The way things were stewing, it'd be a miracle if the world held together long enough for unity.

The witch power was, quite clearly, a power of the people—of the people who needed those miracles. It was the power that had worked miracles.

We'll never know who does the job, he told himself. *It's better that way; like table-tipping. You can say "I didn't do it." You can even be sure you didn't do it, if you want to. But the table tips if you get enough people around the table.*

Who are the witches? Why, they're the people, and they're not for burning. Which witch is a witch? Doesn't matter.

An hour later, Bill Howard sat down to the typewriter again. He'd stated the general problem—but now he had a specific problem, and, for a man in his line of business, it was a fairly straightforward problem.

He need only plot out the necessary moves so that he could call on that witch power just one more time, just long enough to clean out the violent resistance to the idea that people had powers and could work miracles!